Dearest Protector

J.S. SCOTT

Writing as Lane Parker

Dearest Protector

Copyright © 2023 by J.S. Scott

All rights reserved. No part of this document may be reproduced or transmitted in any form or by any means, electronic, mechanical, photocopying, recording, or otherwise, without prior written permission.

ISBN: 979-8-399956-26-8 (Print)
ISBN: 978-1-959932-05-5 (E-Book)

Contents

Prologue 1
Prologue #2 6
Chapter 1 9
Chapter 2 24
Chapter 3 34
Chapter 4 42
Chapter 5 51
Chapter 6 59
Chapter 7 68
Chapter 8 78
Chapter 9 89
Chapter 10 97
Chapter 11 106
Chapter 12 112
Chapter 13 118
Chapter 14 126
Chapter 15 136
Chapter 16 144
Chapter 17 151
Chapter 18 158

Chapter 19 166
Chapter 20 175
Chapter 21 184
Chapter 22 192
Chapter 23 198
Chapter 24 206
Chapter 25 212
Chapter 26 219
Chapter 27 226
Chapter 28 233
Chapter 29 240
Chapter 30 247
Chapter 31 254
Epilogue 263

Prologue

Ariel

New York City
Ten Months Earlier...

I was exhausted but still running on pure adrenaline as I hurried down a familiar New York City street toward my destination. I didn't slow down to admire the beauty of the big city lights at night.

I didn't look at all of the people around me who were rushing to their own locations.

I never did.

I was working, and nothing else interfered with my focus when my attention was on advancing in my career.

My fixation on being the best ballet dancer I could be was the only thing that had gotten me this far.

"Dammit! I'm late! But I'm nearly there," I grumbled unhappily under my breath as I stopped at the corner, waiting impatiently until it was safe to cross the street.

I looked across the busy thoroughfare, relieved to see my final destination ahead of me.

I lived and breathed on a very rigid schedule with zero flexibility, so running behind probably upset me more than most people. My daily planner notebook kept me on track, but this particular late-night afterparty hadn't exactly been planned way in advance, unlike all my usual work-related activities.

An unplanned event like this one had thrown me off balance, and I was completely wired when all I wanted to do was to wind down.

Really, all I'd wanted to do after my very first performance as a principal dancer in Tchaikovsky's Swan Lake was to go home, ice my feet, and then sink into a warm bath.

Unfortunately, that idea was a no-go since I'd been invited to a small gathering at a swanky club that was being hosted by one of the ballet's largest donors. It was mandatory that I attend since it was a very large donor hosting the party, and he'd specifically asked for me to be present since I was a principal dancer.

To say I *wasn't* a party girl was an understatement. Maybe I was young, but I felt like I'd been born an adult. In fact, I couldn't *ever* remember being a carefree child.

I'd started studying ballet at four years old.

I'd never really had much of a choice back then since my mother had been a ballet dancer here in New York, too, and she'd wanted the same for me. She'd been insistent that I'd needed to start as early as possible.

I'd joined my dance studio's professional company at the age of eleven, and after that, all I could remember doing was dancing and making sure my grades stayed up in school.

The day I'd been offered a scholarship to attend one of the most prestigious ballet schools in the country had made it worth all of my hard work over the years. I'd packed my stuff and moved to New York from Florida right after my graduation from high school.

I'd grinded hard since I'd made that move years ago, but I'd finally become a principal dancer.

I just did something tonight that I've dreamed about my entire life.

Dearest Protector

I let out a sigh of pure joy. My heart was soaring, even though my mind and body were completely wasted.

I tapped my foot as I peered at my watch, my euphoria fading just a little as I started to stress over being fifteen minutes off schedule. *Maybe I'll catch a break and be able to slip into the club without anyone noticing.*

It wasn't that I minded being nice to donors, but dancing the principal and dual role of Odette and Odile this evening had been mentally and physically draining.

Maybe I was still flying high because dancing that particular role had been a dream of mine for a very long time. Really, wasn't that nearly *every* young ballerina's dream?

Out of the corner of my eye, I caught the forward movement of someone else who was waiting to cross the street.

As freaked out as I was about lagging behind, that small motion was all it took to send me on a mad dash to get across the street and into the club so I wasn't any later than I was already.

I didn't hesitate.

I didn't notice that the person moving forward suddenly stopped.

In fact, I never noticed my mistake at all.

I never had time.

Almost instantly, I was slammed by some massive force that sent me flying up into the air.

Pain ripped through my entire body as I finally crash-landed hard on the cement.

I felt one more agonizing sensation tearing across my foot, and then for a moment, it felt like the whole world just...stopped.

I couldn't breathe.

I couldn't move.

I couldn't speak.

I was held immobile and insensible by the most agonizing pain I'd ever experienced.

Breathe, Ariel. Breathe.

Trying to focus, I sucked air into my oxygen-deprived lungs and then let it out. I kept taking those excruciating breaths because I knew I had to, but every single one was more torturous than the one before it.

Why can't I see anything?

I panicked because my vision was blurry. I kept blinking, but the ugly cloud over my eyesight didn't clear.

What in the hell just happened to me?

I fought the rising darkness, something I probably should have welcomed because it would take the pain away. But I refused to give in to the temptation to take that escape route.

I needed to stay conscious.

I was confused, but I knew I was lying in the street.

I was vulnerable.

Oh, God, why am I in so much pain, and why is my brain not working right?

"Jesus, lady, I'm sorry. I never saw you," a male voice shouted. "I'm calling an ambulance right now."

Ambulance?

My muddled brain still couldn't figure out what was going on.

I have to get up off the pavement!

I tried to move, wanting to rise, but I couldn't move a muscle before the searing agony of my injuries curtailed that plan.

I'm hurt. Maybe I do need an ambulance.

Fear and a sense of helplessness washed over me, which was highly unusual for a woman who was used to doing everything on her own.

Terror and trepidation seized my entire being as it suddenly dawned on me that I'd obviously been hit by a vehicle as I was crossing the street.

When a suffocating sense of impending doom washed over me, I wasn't quite sure if I was going to live through whatever had happened to me.

I couldn't breathe, and I was so damn scared.

I kept sucking in painful breaths, determined that I wasn't going to die on this damn pavement.

Darkness might be beckoning, but I sure as hell didn't have to answer.

The ambulance was coming, right? Hadn't some guy just said exactly that?

I'd be okay.

I'd live through this.

All I had to do was keep breathing until the paramedics arrived.

Prologue #2

Ben

Ten Months Later...
Fort Myers, Florida

I stood in the shadows of my mother's patio, my fists clenched, every muscle in my body tense as I saw an older man snatch the young woman's wrist and yank her onto the pavement.

She'd been trying to hide in the bushes, but her hiding spot had obviously been discovered by her predator.

She winced and stumbled a little, then tried to pull away, but the hold the asshole had on her was obviously relentless, not to mention painful judging by the look on her beautiful face.

A haze of red clouded my vision, and it took everything I had not to completely lose my shit.

It was *her*.

Ariel Prescott.

The woman who had haunted my dreams for months now.

A female who had been untouchable for me when we'd first met.

It was possible that she didn't remember *me*, but I sure as fuck remembered *her*.

I'd been looking forward to seeing her ever since I'd discovered that Ariel Prescott was my stepsister Katie's best friend, and that she was *no longer* untouchable.

Hell, I'd been astonished that Ariel was here in Fort Myers. That she was actually closely connected to Katie.

What were the chances of *that*?

I wanted to kill the bastard who dared to treat this woman with anything other than reverence.

Judging by something that Ariel had just said, it sounded like this guy was her *boss*.

What the fuck?

What boss treated an employee like this?

What kind of asshole manhandled *any* female?

I shook myself as the heated blood in my body pounded in my ears, surprised that I could barely contain my fury.

I wasn't usually a guy who lost my mind over a woman. *Ever.*

I was careful, even-tempered, and steady. I calculated every move I made, in business and in my personal life.

I was the guy who picked up the pieces when bad shit happened and tried to smooth things over until everything was back to normal again.

I *liked* everything calm and sensible.

I wasn't like my older brother, Ian, who had silently stalked our stepsister, Katie, *for years* just to make sure that she was safe because he'd been completely obsessed with her.

Yeah, Ian had eventually ended up with the woman of his dreams, but he'd nearly lost his mind in the process.

That wasn't *me*.

I *wasn't* that kind of guy.

What in the fuck was wrong with me right now?

Okay. So I had some idea why I felt this way.

Ariel was the one woman who was almost impossible to forget.

I wanted to eviscerate the piece of shit who was abusing Ariel, regardless of the fact that there was a special birthday ball for my mother taking place inside this home right now.

That's right, idiot. There is a special event for your mother happening within a stone's throw of this incident. Pull your shit together, Blackwood! Much as you'd like to kill this son of a bitch right now, you can't!

"Let go of me," Ariel said angrily.

I could hear the fear in her voice, which almost made me forget that I couldn't make a scene on my mother's patio right at the moment.

The bastard scoffed, "You're a tramp. An out of work ballet dancer. Who would invite you here?"

Oh, hell no! Birthday ball or not, I couldn't stand in the shadows for another second.

My protective instincts toward Ariel overruled any other thoughts in my head as I stepped into the dim light.

"My family invited her," I growled. "And if you don't let go of her and back off, I'll put your head into the cement so hard that nobody will recognize your face again."

Every gut impulse I had insisted I act on those words.

Right. Fucking. Now.

Chapter 1

Ariel

The Present...
Fort Myers, Florida

I was in very big trouble, and I knew it.
I just didn't know exactly what I was going to do about it.
After stepping out of the shower with a heavy sigh, I grabbed my towel and dried myself off hastily, trying to breathe slowly through my panic.

What in the hell am I going to do? How am I going to survive without a job?

All night, I'd laid awake in my bed, looking for a solution to my dilemma, but I'd failed miserably at producing any answers.

Puddles of moisture flooded my eyes. The large tears that dropped onto my cheeks were a result of the pain and stress I'd been through over the last ten months.

I swiped the droplets from my face immediately.

I didn't have time to cry just because I was exhausted from a sleepless night and scared shitless.

I've avoided homelessness for ten months. I'll think of something. Eventually.

I'd lost my job the night before, and it wasn't going to be easy to find another one quickly.

Everything…absolutely everything…had been a nightmare since the accident that had ended my ballet career.

I'd moved back home to Fort Myers, hoping it would be easier to find a job and survive in a place with a lower cost of living than New York City.

I'd quickly discovered that finding a job *anywhere* without the skills to do anything other than dance was almost impossible.

Now I'd lost the one job I'd been able to secure here in Florida.

My landlord had already slapped an eviction notice on my door days before the mortifying event last night that had left me jobless.

I probably could have paid my rent in time to avoid eviction—had I not lost my job the night before.

Teaching yoga to a small class of beginners once a week was not going to pay my bills.

My small fridge in this crappy studio apartment was empty, but really, eating was the *last* of my worries. I'd gone hungry for so long I was almost used to being continually in that state.

I yanked on an oversized T-shirt, a pair of leggings, and then pulled on the socks I never went without anymore.

I'd sustained a severe injury to my foot that had ended my dancing career, and it wasn't pretty. I rarely bared my nasty looking foot. It was scarred from the initial injuries and from the multiple surgeries that had been necessary to get me walking on that foot again.

I let out a nervous breath as I got to my feet, avoiding the mirror like I usually did because I didn't want to see the desperate woman I'd become.

I'd really *wanted* to fit into the swanky birthday ball so badly last night, and I'd done everything I could to make that happen, despite the fact that I *knew* I hadn't belonged there.

For the first time since my accident, I'd worn a dress with heels, even though it had been somewhat painful on my foot. The occasion

Dearest Protector

had called for a cocktail dress, so I'd torn an old dress apart and restyled it myself. The matching pumps had been low compared to the heels I'd worn before the accident. I'd donned thicker, black tights to hide my unsightly foot from the influential guests at the party. Still, it had been a bold move on my part considering that I never went *anywhere* without a pair of thick socks on my feet anymore.

My best friend, Katie, had a new boyfriend, someone really important to her, and I'd wanted to be dressed appropriately to meet him and his family for the first time.

God, if only I hadn't gone to that damn birthday ball in the first place!

Last night is over. Forget about it.

Unfortunately, that was easier said than done considering all that had happened at that exclusive event.

I *especially* didn't want to tell my best friend about the scene on the patio last night.

Okay, so I had finally gotten the chance to meet Ian Blackwood and his mom, but the rest of the night had gone downhill fast after that.

Stop procrastinating, Ariel. Katie is here. Tell her everything. She'll understand.

Katie had arrived at my apartment unannounced, and I was still so mortified about last night's events that I hadn't known what to say to her.

I'd simply let my best friend in earlier, and then given her my laptop so she could finally look at the photos I'd taken in New York. Since she'd been badgering me for months about seeing my pictures of New York, Katie had snatched the laptop immediately. Once she'd started looking at the pictures, I'd retreated to the bathroom with the sad excuse of needing a morning shower.

Actually, what I'd *really* needed was a quick escape and to pull myself together after a sleepless night.

I had no idea what she knew about the incident the night before, but I was so tired of feeling like a total loser.

Most likely, Katie had shown up early this morning to ask more questions about the bruises she'd seen on my arms the night before.

I'd blown her off and made another excuse, just like I always did.

What woman wanted to tell her best friend that she was allowing herself to be bruised in order to keep her job?

Ian's younger brother, Ben Blackwood, had been there on the patio. Had he told her about what had occurred?

God, I really hope not. I'd rather tell her myself. I'll try to make it sound like it's no big deal.

Katie's life had been an even bigger tragedy than mine. She was finally happy, and I'd do almost anything to make sure she stayed that way.

She'd come back home to Florida after college, not long after I had returned home from New York due to the abrupt end of my dancing career.

Luckily, Katie's misfortune hadn't lasted long. She'd managed to find her dream job here with Blackwood Technologies, and her dream man in one of the two owners of the mammoth tech corporation.

Maybe Ian Blackwood's courtship had been more than a little weird, but the end results had made my best friend happier than she'd ever been in her entire life.

The last thing she needed was to worry about *me* right now.

I took a deep breath and opened the bathroom door.

No more stalling. No more making excuses. I have to tell Katie the truth.

Because I lived in a tiny studio that wasn't much bigger than many people's bedrooms, I didn't have to take a single step to see that Katie was still gazing at my photos, her eyes glued to the screen of my laptop.

"Ariel," she said absently because she was still focused on the computer. "These other portfolios of yours are amazing. How in the hell do you create this kind of work?"

One glance told me that she'd gotten through the regular photos I'd taken of New York City and was now perusing my hobby files.

Digitally altering my own photos of wildlife, flowers, and objects was something I'd done to alleviate the stress of my dancing career, and I'd gotten plenty of practice at it over the years.

It was my *only* hobby, and the one other thing I could focus on when I wasn't dancing.

I had thousands of those unique images in many different portfolios, but in my opinion, they really weren't worth studying so carefully.

Yeah, I shared them on a few anonymous social media accounts, mostly to get feedback, but they were far from extraordinary artwork.

"They're nothing, Katie. It's just a hobby," I told her dismissively as I took a few steps into the kitchen to make some coffee, grateful that I still had some to brew.

I was out of almost everything else *except* coffee.

"They're fabulous," she contradicted. "The colors are so bold and the creativity and emotion is all there in every image you create from your pictures. I love these, Ariel. Obviously, your huge social media following loves them, too. Sorry, but you didn't close the window to your social media accounts where you post these."

I rolled my eyes. I knew that Katie wasn't all *that* sorry. She was a computer nerd, a programmer and a software designer. She was curious about anything that involved technology. Obviously, she'd trolled around a little in my portfolios while I was showering.

Honestly, I didn't mind.

We'd been really close friends since grade school. There was very little we didn't share with each other. Okay, maybe I didn't want to reveal the fact that I'd screwed up again, or that I was in dire straits because Katie had just come out of a tight financial spot herself. But I knew I *could* tell her anything and she'd never judge.

I hadn't really been *hiding* my photography hobby. We'd been physically separated for years except for occasional visits, and we were still catching up. It just hadn't seemed all that important to mention a useless hobby.

"It's more than just a hobby, Ariel," Katie admonished, finally raising her head to look at me. "Why aren't you monetizing your success with this? You obviously love creating these pieces, and you must put your heart and soul into them. You have a huge following on social media that seems to be clamoring for more. You could easily make this into a business. Sell this work."

I shook my head. "I was a ballet dancer, Katie. I was trained in dance from the age of four. I have no formal education or training in photography or art. That's never going to happen."

"It doesn't matter. You have a gift. This work is part photography and a lot of creativity that you use to make these into works of art. And who says you have to formally study photography to be good at it? You've obviously done self-study, and you've been taking pictures since we were kids."

She was right. I had studied photography on my own whenever I had any downtime. Other than dancing, my only additional passion was my hobby. I'd never had the time for anything else.

I posted my work on social media simply as "Ariel." The only thing I posted on those accounts was my digital art. No personal pictures. No personal posts. It was something I'd always kept separate from my real identity. No one knew who I really was on those social media pages, and I liked it that way.

Honestly, I was surprised that I'd amassed such a huge following over the years, but it was probably more about curiosity than admiration.

"I think you should make *this* a business," Katie said adamantly. "You've been killing yourself working as an assistant for the boss from hell. He expects you to be at his beck and call day and night, seven days a week. I also don't buy that the bruises I've seen on your wrists and arms lately are from some careless accidents. Talk to me, Ariel. I had to come here as soon as possible after I saw those bruises last night. I don't believe the excuses you've been giving me. We've been friends for a long time. Is something weird going on with your boss? I know you aren't seeing anyone. You disappeared after I introduced you to Marilyn and Ian last night. We never got a chance to really talk about those bruises on your wrist. What happened? Why did you leave? Was your foot bothering you? Is that why you left without saying goodbye last night?"

Crap! That's a lot of questions I need to answer!

I'd met Ian and his mother right before I'd stepped onto the patio to try to avoid my boss, Leland Brock, who had shown up at the ball unexpectedly.

I'd left right after the incident on the patio, too embarrassed to face my best friend or anyone else after it had happened.

I stalled, taking a moment to hand her a mug of coffee, and then grabbed my own mug and sat on the other end of the couch.

She's going to have to know at some point that I no longer have that job with the boss from hell. I might as well start there.

Quite honestly, I was surprised that Ian's brother hadn't already shared what had happened on his mother's patio the night before. The entire event was for his mother. *He* most definitely hadn't left early. Ben had probably had many opportunities to tell people after I'd gone.

God, I *really* wanted to talk to Katie. Keeping anything from her was difficult. She was my only close friend, and I had no immediate family anymore.

I just didn't want to burden her with my bullshit when she'd just gotten to a time in her life when she was finally happy.

I'd tried to explain away bruises from Leland's manhandling several times because I'd known that she'd be upset if she knew the truth. She would have wanted me to resign immediately, which would have been the sensible thing to do, but I hadn't been able to stop working for Leland because I had to survive.

"I no longer work for Leland Brock," I confessed. "He showed up at the ball last night. I know he didn't have an invitation of his own. He must have talked someone into letting him be their plus one. He was pissed because I'd been invited and he wasn't. We got into an argument on the patio. Ben came to my rescue. I was embarrassed. I left right after that incident. I'm sorry I didn't stop to say goodbye."

Ben Blackwood had been furious when he'd seen Leland humiliating me on the patio.

I'd been mortifyingly embarrassed.

What other idiot female would allow a boss to abuse her that way?

The only reason I'd endured it for so many months was the fact that I hadn't been able to find another job, and I needed to eat and pay my rent.

A year ago, I would have sworn that I'd never put up with a boss touching me that way, but it's surprising what a woman will do just to survive when she's desperate.

It wasn't that I hadn't appreciated the fact that Ben had been willing to stand up for me, but it was, nevertheless, humiliating that I'd ever needed someone to stand up to Leland in the first place.

Ben and Ian Blackwood, the two CEOs of Blackwood Technologies, were billionaires, and they came from a wealthy family.

What woman would want a ridiculously gorgeous billionaire to see her being physically and mentally abused by her lowlife boss?

How in the hell could either of the Blackwood brothers possibly understand my hopeless circumstances or what motivated me to keep my head above water, no matter how much abuse Leland had handed out?

I couldn't just…give up, even though I'd been tempted to do exactly that many times over the last ten months.

I'd fervently hoped that I'd get another job and nobody would ever have to know what Leland was doing.

Unfortunately, things hadn't worked out that way.

Katie shot me an expectant look, so I continued, "Ben booted Leland from the property because he was being an abusive jerk to me and informed him that I was never coming back to work for him again. Before Ben and I parted ways, he gave me his business card and told me to call him today so he could find a place for me at Blackwood. I was so flustered by what had happened that I left soon after that. Because he terminated my employment with Leland, I guess Ben felt like he *had* to find me a new job, which he doesn't. I knew I had to quit, Katie. You're right. Leland was out of control. I'm pretty sure he hates me, but I've never figured out why. I gave him everything I had as an assistant, but it was never good enough. I am really sorry that Leland showed up and acted like that, but I don't think anyone knew except Ben."

Dearest Protector

"Please stop apologizing for something that wasn't your fault. I've never met Leland Brock in person," Katie said angrily. "But I already know he's a major asshole. And I think he hates women in general, not just you. He had you running days, nights, and weekends for him, and he paid you next to nothing. I'm glad that Ben booted him out of Marilyn's birthday ball. I'm also happy that you no longer work for him. My stepbrother just became my hero for removing Leland from the ball. Are you upset with Ben? Obviously, you haven't called him yet."

Technically, both Ian and Ben *were* Katie's stepbrothers, but they'd never met until they were all adults. After Ben and Ian's father had died years ago, Marilyn had married Katie's loser father, probably because she'd been horrifically lonely after losing her beloved husband.

No doubt if Katie's father hadn't died of a heart attack, Marilyn would have divorced him by now.

I took a sip of my coffee and swallowed it before I answered. "Ben Blackwood is a billionaire, Katie. He has better things to do than to help an unemployed nobody to find a job."

Not to mention the fact that I'd want to crawl under a rock if I ever saw Ben again.

The more I thought about our encounter, the more I hoped I'd never run into him again.

The entire scene on the patio had been brief, but it was a short period of time I really wanted to forget.

Ben Blackwood was perfect. Gorgeous. Educated. Classy. Confident. Everything I…wasn't.

It was horrifying to me that he'd needed to come to my rescue because my boss was manhandling me like I was his property.

Most intelligent women would have dumped the job I'd hated a long time ago, and I was doubtful they would have put up with Leland's crap for more than a day or two.

Hopefully, I'd have my shit more together if Ben Blackwood and I ever met again.

And honestly, we *would* probably bump into each other in the future.

My best friend was in love with Ben's older brother, and judging by the way Ian and Katie looked at each other, that relationship wasn't going to end anytime soon.

The two of them were already exclusive and living together in Ian's waterfront mansion on Sanibel Island.

Ian and Katie had *lifelong commitment* written all over their faces, which meant that Ben and I would *definitely* meet again in the future.

Katie snorted. "If Ben asked you to call, then he's expecting your call. Do you really think he's just going to forget what happened? He's not like that, Ariel. He could have blown me off. I was a stepsister he'd never met, but he treated me like a real sister almost immediately. He has an overactive sense of responsibility. He won't just forget what happened last night just because he's ridiculously busy."

Hell, I hoped she was wrong.

The fact that Ben apparently *hadn't* told Ian or Katie about the incident yet was actually encouraging to me. I was more optimistic now about him possibly forgetting everything, despite what Katie had just said.

"He's not going to forget, so you need to give up on that idea. The man has the memory of an elephant sometimes," Katie said like she had just read my mind. "Let him help you, Ariel. Please. Or let me help you. I know how hard it was to lose your ballet career. You can do so much better than that awful job with Leland Brock. You deserve so much better than that. You're also never going to be happy in an office job, even if you find one that pays more. You're gifted creatively, Ariel. You need a new career that you can put your soul into."

I wasn't so sure that I hadn't lost my soul months ago, after I was told by my doctor that I could no longer dance. Suddenly, everything I'd lived for my entire life was just…gone. I wasn't even sure who I was anymore. My whole identity had revolved around dancing. Honestly, I felt worthless and lost without it.

Dearest Protector

"Right now," I said bluntly. "I just need *anything* that will pay my rent."

"I'll pay your rent," she insisted. "And for anything else you need until you're back on your feet again. I'm making a damn good salary at Blackwood now, and I'm living with a billionaire who has more money than God. Ian never lets me pay for anything. Look, I know you always tell me that you're doing okay, but I don't think you are. This apartment is in one of the worst neighborhoods in Fort Myers. It's really not safe, but I assume it's all you can afford. You're also getting ridiculously skinny. I'd love to give you some of my extra pounds right now. I know you watched your diet religiously and stayed slender to dance, but you're beyond what's healthy at the moment."

I averted my gaze from her pleading eyes.

I had no idea what to tell my best friend, and her comment about her *extra pounds* was completely ridiculous.

Katie had always been critical about her own physical appearance. She was gorgeous, dark-haired, and she had amazing chocolate-brown eyes. She was more toward the curvy side, but everything about her physical appearance seemed to suit Ian Blackwood just fine.

And yes, she was making good money *now*, but we both knew what it meant to be incredibly poor.

She'd just gotten back on her feet financially.

Katie needed to put her paycheck away, not loan it to me.

"I'm tight, and things have been a struggle," I admitted truthfully. "I do skimp on healthy food sometimes, but I'll find a job, Katie. I'm not taking your money. It's not necessary."

I had to learn to stand on my own two feet *without* my dancing career.

I'd done nothing but scramble financially since my accident.

I appreciated the fact that Katie would always be there for me emotionally, but neither of us had ever relied on each other to survive monetarily.

I needed a *permanent* solution to my financial state.

I was so damn tired of living hand to mouth because I had no job skills that meant anything in the real world.

"God, you're so stubborn sometimes. If you won't let me help you, then talk to *Ben*," she urged. "You could get something temporary at Blackwood until you figure out what you really want. Even a temporary position at Blackwood would pay more than your idiot boss paid you for being at his beck and call twenty-four seven. Ben would never offer if he couldn't or didn't want to deliver. I'm not surprised that he offered to help. He's a sweetheart, even though he tries to hide it underneath that businesslike, calm façade of his."

After my experience with Ben Blackwood on the patio of his mother's house, I very much doubted that there was anything the gorgeous billionaire *couldn't* arrange.

However, I wouldn't exactly say that Benjamin Blackwood was a *sweetheart*.

He was large and in charge, and there was an intensity about him that was downright intimidating.

For some reason I couldn't really explain, he really didn't frighten *me*, but I did find the man incredibly intriguing, which was almost as dangerous as fearing him.

The way I'd met Ben for the first time wasn't exactly the way I'd wanted to meet one of the important individuals in Katie's life. The circumstances had been far from ideal, and I hated myself for being so attracted to him. But I couldn't help it. I might be damaged and pathetic, but I wasn't dead. What single female wouldn't react the same way to Ben Blackwood?

Except…Ben *hadn't* felt like a stranger to me.

There had been something about his overpowering presence and gruff voice that had been…almost comforting, which was kind of ridiculous.

I'd decided that I felt that way because I saw pictures and interviews with him in the media. Florida journalists seemed to love to feature him almost anywhere. Ben was the face of Blackwood Technologies, and the regional media seemed to love hosting or boasting about one of the most eligible bachelors in the world. It was natural that I'd feel some sense of recognition, right?

Dearest Protector

No matter what the cause, there *was* something about Ben that was familiar to me, but I couldn't put a finger on exactly why I'd felt that way.

And…for just an instant, I'd gotten the feeling that he might find me attractive, too, which had been a moment of temporary insanity, not to mention stupidity, on my part.

I'd *definitely* misinterpreted a few of the things he'd said last night. It wasn't even remotely possible that he was attracted to me. Maybe I had done creative work, but I was also a realist.

After thinking about what had happened, I'd come to the conclusion that a few of his comments had probably meant that he really wanted no relationship with me at all in the future.

And I could hardly blame him for that.

"So what did you think of Ben in person?" Katie asked curiously. "You told me before the two of you met that you thought he was hot."

I nearly spit out the coffee I had in my mouth. I swallowed, and then coughed, before I answered wistfully, "He's even more ridiculously gorgeous than his pictures in the media."

Katie grinned. "So you're attracted to him?"

"Yes. No. Oh hell, what single woman *wouldn't* be attracted to him, Katie?" I asked.

She shrugged. "*I'm* not, but I've already got the most amazing guy on the planet. It's hard to believe that I actually thought Ben might be my stalker at one time or that I had a very short infatuation with him. But that was before I met Ian. However, I do still think Ben is the second most amazing guy in the world, and you two would make a great couple."

I snorted. "I said I found *him* attractive. There's no chance in hell that Ben Blackwood would ever look at me the first time, much less a second. Let's get real here. I have absolutely nothing going for me professionally anymore. He's a handsome billionaire. I'm a woman who can't pay her rent and has no other job skills except for ballet dancing, which I can't even do anymore. I'm a physical and emotional mess right now. Even before my accident, I was only passably attractive. Ben Blackwood could have his pick of any supermodel or any gorgeous and successful woman he wanted. Why would you ever think he'd look at someone like me?"

Katie surveyed me carefully. "Is that really what you think? That someone like Ben would never be attracted to you? Ben's had his chances to date any number of beautiful, successful women, and he hasn't acted on those opportunities. Don't underestimate him, Ariel. I think he's looking for far more than a gorgeous face and a perfect body with big breasts. Furthermore, you've always been beautiful, inside and out. Why didn't I know that your confidence had fallen this low? So low that you can't see yourself realistically anymore?"

I wanted to tell her that I tried not to look at myself at all anymore because I knew I wouldn't like the female I saw in the mirror right now.

Instead, I simply shook my head and told her honestly, "I don't think it's just my confidence level that's fallen. My entire being was reflected in my dancing. I feel…lost. I'm not sure who I am without ballet."

Hell, I didn't know how to explain how I felt, which was probably why I'd never really discussed it with my best friend.

Since I was in preschool, almost every moment that I wasn't in school had been consumed by dancing.

Ballet had been my entire life.

My purpose.

My passion.

My reason for living.

"You're a hell of a lot more than just a ballet dancer," Katie said fiercely. "And I'm here to help you find out who you are again. You're the only person who kept me sane while I was going through my father's death and the whole stalker thing with Ian. Maybe you didn't feel like you could talk to me because I was going through so much drama myself, and I'm so sorry for that, but I'm here *now*, Ariel. I have my head on straight, and I'm deliriously happy. I'd like to see you the same way. Let's discuss this over breakfast. If you won't let me help you, at least let me buy you a meal and try to convince you that losing your dancing career didn't destroy the amazing woman that you are."

Dearest Protector

She moved across the sofa and wrapped her arms around me as she added, "Everything will be okay, Ariel. I know it doesn't feel that way right now, but it will. You're barely recovered physically from the accident. Be patient with yourself. You're a stronger woman than I am because I'm not sure I could have survived what you have. You have more strength than any woman I've ever known."

God, I wished I believed that, but I didn't.

Maybe I'd survived my accident, but I was barely making it emotionally and financially, and I definitely wasn't thriving like she was at the moment.

I felt totally and completely...empty.

I held onto her, and for just a moment, I didn't feel quite so...alone.

"Let's go eat and really talk, okay?" she asked softly, sounding a little teary-eyed and remorseful. "You let me lean on you when I needed you, but I'm fine now. In fact, I'm better than I've ever been in my entire life. You can tell me everything. We'll come up with some solutions together."

I nodded as I finally let her go.

I'd never wanted to hide things from my best friend, and I was starving. *Literally.* It was an offer that I didn't want to and couldn't turn down.

Chapter 2

Ariel

It was afternoon by the time I got home from breakfast, and my heart was slightly lighter after Katie and I had engaged in a real heart-to-heart conversation about my accident and all that had happened afterward.

She was right. There was a lot I hadn't told her to keep her from being burdened when she was brokenhearted and financially strapped herself.

I'd held nothing back this morning, and she'd been there to support me emotionally.

After we'd taken up space in the restaurant for a couple of hours, Katie had mentioned that she needed some groceries. We'd hit the grocery store together since it was right next door to the breakfast place. She had loaded up a second cart for me, whether I wanted those supplies or not.

It was obvious that she wasn't taking no for an answer, and for once, I'd gratefully let her pay for my food.

I was, in fact, destitute.

I had to be sensible.

If I was going to find a job, I needed to eat.

Someday, I'd pay Katie back for helping me out, whether she wanted the money back or not.

The fact that she was more like a sister to me than a best friend meant more than the money, which is why I could never take advantage of her kindness.

She'd departed for Sanibel after we'd finished at the grocery store, and I'd spent the last forty minutes or so trying to find a place for all the items she'd bought.

My little efficiency kitchen wasn't exactly conducive to stocking up on supplies, but for some reason, it felt so damn good to see my refrigerator full and my cupboards overflowing with food.

I'd never thought such a small thing could be such a mood booster but it was.

I felt a little safer and more secure, even though I knew it was only a temporary illusion.

Well fed, and with my cupboards stocked for the first time since I'd lived in this tiny apartment, I tried to be positive about my job prospects.

It wasn't like my landlord could just boot me out of the apartment tomorrow for being a little late.

I'd catch up on the rent as soon as I found decent employment.

I had to have faith that some kind of job would come through for me.

The beginner's yoga class I was teaching would be ending next week, but it wasn't like I'd made much money from that class anyway. I'd taken on the responsibility because I enjoyed it, but it had never really been profitable.

I had a gazillion applications out there around the city and nearby areas for something full-time, and I'd keep on putting in for any job I could possibly do.

I'd just finished putting the empty grocery bags away when someone knocked at the door.

Katie?

It wasn't like there was anyone else who would be coming to visit on a Sunday afternoon.

I looked around to see if she'd forgotten anything as I went to answer the door.

I inhaled sharply as I saw exactly who was standing on the other side.

Crap!

My visitor *definitely* wasn't Katie.

"Hello, Ariel," Ben Blackwood said in a deep, fuck-me baritone as he looked me up and down, his attractive, hazel-eyed gaze finally landing and lingering on my face.

A sense of dread snaked down my spine as I stood there without saying a word.

Oh, God. Not *him*. Why couldn't it be anyone *except* him?

I wasn't ready to see Ben.

Not this soon.

Maybe not...ever.

I swallowed hard and tried to pull my head together. I was still exhausted from my lack of sleep the night before.

Okay, maybe my sleepless night was just an excuse. How could any female be ready to see a guy like *him* or to hear that damn sexy voice of his?

He might as well have said "take off all of your clothes and get ready for me to rock your world."

His voice was just that low, predatory, and sensual. *Anything* he said in that mesmerizing voice sounded highly...sexual, even though I knew damn well it wasn't meant to be.

Ben was no longer in a tuxedo like he had been the night before, but he was just as smoking hot in a lightweight, forest green, cashmere sweater that brought out the green in his hazel eyes and a pair of dark jeans.

Seriously? How could the man possibly be even more attractive than he had been last night in formalwear?

Did he always look immaculately put together, no matter what he's wearing?

There wasn't a single lock of his dark brown hair that was out of place.

The only thing that made him look a little more approachable was a hint of a five o'clock shadow on his jawline, but unfortunately for me, *that* was also kind of provocative.

Dearest Protector

He was tall with a very muscular, bulky physique that would make most single women drool or weep, or possibly both.

The guy was so stunningly handsome and had such an overwhelming presence in general that I was momentarily speechless.

I nearly squirmed as I remembered that I was dressed in a ratty pair of yoga pants and an oversized T-shirt that bore the logo of my old ballet company.

I hadn't bothered to slap on any makeup, and I'd done absolutely nothing with my hair after my shower. The curly mass of light blonde locks on my head was probably a hot mess.

It doesn't matter. It's not like he's here to take me out on a date for God's sake! Pull it together, Ariel.

In fact, whatever the reason for his visit to my crappy neighborhood, he appeared to be deadly serious and all business.

I had to wonder if the guy *ever* smiled. I certainly hadn't seen those gorgeous lips of his curve upward the night before, either.

"Ben?" I said, hating the fact that I sounded breathless. "What are you doing here?"

This definitely wasn't his part of town. Overall, Fort Myers was a decent place to live, but I resided in one of the pockets outside of the downtown that wasn't exactly a desirable address. But I couldn't afford to be picky when I needed an affordable rental.

"You left last night before I had another chance to talk to you," he said, his expression displeased. "And you didn't call me. I just spoke to Katie and she gave me your address. Should I assume you had no intention of following up with me?"

Well, yeah, that would probably be a safe assumption.

Did he honestly think I would call him after what had happened? And if so…why? We were essentially strangers.

I had to force myself to breathe.

God, for all of his obvious kindness, this guy was intense.

And large.

And…overpowering.

I felt like a tiny mouse trying to scurry away from a predatory big cat.

"I'll figure it out," I told him, trying to sound nonchalant. "I already knew that I needed to find a new job. Things with Leland were getting out of hand. I've been…looking."

Okay, that was true. I'd put in close to a hundred job applications over the last several months, but there wasn't a lot of positions available for prima ballerinas who were no longer able to dance.

Honestly, I'd actually been surprised when Leland had offered me a job as his assistant. My office skills were minimal, and I had no prior experience with clerical work at all.

He lifted a brow. "I did tell you that I'd find a job for you."

"You did," I conceded. "And I appreciate it, but you're a very busy guy. I really don't think you need to add finding me employment to your to-do list. It's not like we're friends. You hardly know me. And you already helped me out by intervening when Leland started to get grabby last night. I'm not sure I could have handled that myself without screaming at the top of my lungs for help."

Ben glanced at the bruises on my wrist and frowned as he corrected, "He was *assaulting* you, Ariel, and you were his employee. You should have screamed for help. He was probably counting on the fact that you didn't want to make a scene. No one ever has a right to treat someone who works for them that way. Who does that to a person who is dependent on them for their living? He took advantage because he knew you were vulnerable. He knew you needed that position. I'm here to make sure that never happens again. Can I come in so we can discuss this?"

The last thing I wanted was for Ben to see the small space I inhabited. My crappy, secondhand furniture and the rest of my sad furnishings were threadbare, but I opened the door to let him enter.

How could I not?

He *was* trying to help me, and he'd obviously gone way out of his way to accomplish that task.

I also needed time to convince the tenacious man that I didn't expect him to do any more for me than he had already.

I released a long breath while I waited for him to enter.

Dearest Protector

Katie was right. Obviously, when Ben Blackwood made a promise, he took it *very* seriously.

His statement about helping me had obviously been more than a casual comment, and for some damn reason, I couldn't help but admire the fact that he was a man who seemed hell-bent on keeping his word.

In my experience, a promise was something easily broken most of the time.

My studio apartment was extremely compact, and having someone like Ben inside it seemed to suck all of the oxygen from the small space.

As I closed the door behind him, I realized just how odd it was to see Ben in my surroundings.

The two just didn't mesh.

The sophisticated billionaire and the rundown apartment were so incongruent that I would have laughed if the situation wasn't so utterly depressing.

I waved toward the sofa that was also my bed when it was folded out. "Can I get you anything? Coffee? Water?"

He shook his head and lowered his massive body onto the couch. "No, thanks."

I sat on the other end of the sofa. No doubt my discomfort with the whole situation was written all over my face, but I couldn't help it.

I'd never been in a situation even remotely similar to this one.

Generally, I liked people, and I'd learned how to mix with all kinds of them while I'd been dancing in New York.

However, Ben Blackwood and all of his gorgeous intensity was outside of my comfort zone.

I also wasn't the same Ariel Prescott I had been as a dancer. I wasn't that woman anymore. My confidence was shot to hell. I spent most of my time just trying to survive now, and I felt like a failure.

It sucked to feel this way, but maybe it was normal considering that my entire life had been turned upside down.

I took a deep breath and dived in. "I really appreciate the fact that you offered to help, but my circumstances are not your problem,

Ben. I'm sure I'll find a job. My choices are a little limited since my entire life was dedicated to my career as a dancer up until ten months ago."

He nodded. "You were doing the lead role in Swan Lake at one of the most prestigious dance companies in New York City. From what I've heard from Katie, dancing isn't in the cards for you now or in the future. Are you even completely healed from the accident? You got mowed down by a taxi. Katie said your injuries were severe."

I couldn't hide my astonishment. Maybe I shouldn't be surprised that Ben had gotten this information from Katie, but it still took me off-guard.

I'd told him last night that I couldn't dance anymore, but I hadn't really gone into the details.

I shrugged. "I'm as good as I'm ever going to be. Katie's right. I'll never dance professionally again. The taxi rolled over my foot after I hit the pavement. The doctors were able to put it back together again well enough for me to walk and function without a limp, but my foot can't take the stress of ballet dancing. Not now or in the future. The other injuries are healed."

God, why was it still so hard to admit the naked truth about my future?

"What were your other injuries?" Ben asked gruffly.

It was a personal question, but I saw no reason not to tell him. "A punctured lung, a ruptured spleen, fractured ribs, some internal bleeding, and a concussion. My foot was the worst. It took several surgeries to get me walking again."

He folded his arms over his broad chest. "So really, no other serious injuries *except* for your foot?" he asked drily.

I shot him a small smile because I couldn't help myself. I did tend to blow off the other stuff that had healed and hyper focused on my foot. His sarcasm wasn't the least bit condescending. It was almost like he was...empathizing with me.

I nodded. "Yep. No big deal."

In reality, I'd nearly died, and I was pretty sure he knew that for some reason. He seemed to know a lot about me.

Dearest Protector

"Are you following up on any healthcare that you need?" he asked brusquely. "The accident didn't happen that long ago."

Because he genuinely seemed concerned, I answered, "I'm fine, Ben. Really. My other injuries healed, and I had physical therapy in New York for my foot. I'm not running any races, but I'm pretty active. There's nothing more anyone can do. I'm not as fit as I used to be when I was dancing every day, but I'm alive and I'm walking."

His eyes narrowed like he wasn't completely happy with my answer. "You're way too thin."

Okay, *that* was blunt, but I sensed that he hadn't meant it in a derogatory way.

It sounded more like…concern.

"I've had to be lean my entire life to do ballet," I hedged.

"Not *this* lean," he grumbled. "You're obviously not eating very much. Be honest with me, Ariel. I'm not here to judge you for fuck's sake. Things have obviously been rough for you since the accident, both physically and financially. I want to help you."

I let out a sigh. He apparently wasn't going to be satisfied until he dragged every bit of misery I'd suffered out of me. "I went through all of my savings after the accident. Luckily, I had health insurance, but I lost it after I had to officially quit the ballet company. Yes, money has been tight. Really tight. But like you said, it hasn't been long since the accident. Things will improve with time."

Hell, at least I *hoped* they would.

"I have an offer for you that will help if you decide to accept it," he said. "Katie mentioned that you're an artist with your photography. I'd like to see your work if you don't mind."

Crap! Katie worked fast. She must have had a chat with Ben on her way back to Sanibel Island.

"I-I'm not. Not really. It's just a hobby," I sputtered.

"I'd still like to see your work," he said persistently. "I'm also prepared to offer you another job as a personal assistant since that's where your experience lies. I guarantee that your boss won't try to maul you this time."

~ *31* ~

I shook my head immediately. "Ben, I'm not that experienced. I was basically Leland's go-to woman for personal errands and tasks. I did almost nothing in his office. My office skills aren't suited for a company like Blackwood Technologies."

His company only employed the best of the best. Katie had mentioned that the programming exam just to get an entry level tech position was incredibly difficult at Blackwood.

Anyone who wanted to work in the offices there, even in a clerical capacity, had to have top-notch skills and plenty of experience.

"It's an unusual position," Ben explained. "Part go-to woman and part helping the boss in whatever way you can, including a lot of personal jobs. Said boss can be an asshole sometimes, but he likes to think he's fair."

My heart started to race as he went on to mention the salary, the benefits, and the perks of the job.

The pay was ridiculously high for someone with my experience, or should I say *lack* of experience.

Still, I wanted the position more than I'd wanted anything since my accident.

A fair boss?

A salary and benefits that slightly exceeded the money and benefits I was making as a ballet dancer?

God, I was more than willing to work my ass off to please whoever was my superior.

I was a fast learner.

I could handle an asshole boss if that person just treated me like I was a human being and not worthless property.

"Are you interested?" Ben asked once he was finished explaining.

"I'm still not sure I'm qualified," I said hesitantly. "But I'm willing to do anything and learn the skills I don't have."

"You understand that the duties will be outside of the office? This is a real personal assistant type of position that will require a huge variety of tasks and errands," he stated matter-of-factly.

I nodded eagerly. "I'd be happy to cook, clean, wash dishes, clothing, grocery shop—"

Dearest Protector

Ben smirked as he held up a hand. "I get it. You're willing to do whatever's necessary."

"Yes. I want to apply," I said hastily. "But you know that Leland isn't about to give me a reference of any kind."

"It doesn't matter," Ben said firmly. "I know he's a total asshole. And if you want this job, it's yours. *I'm* making the final decision."

My eyes widened. "Don't you want me to meet my boss first? What if he or she doesn't like me?"

"He," Ben clarified. "And he already likes you. The individual who needs a personal assistant is...me."

Chapter 3

Ben

If my self-esteem was at all lacking, the deflated look on Ariel's face probably would have gutted me.

Luckily, I wasn't the least bit daunted.

I'd come here to get Ariel Prescott into a decent job, and to help her put her life back together. And that was exactly what I was going to do.

She'd left my mother's ball the night before like her gorgeous ass was on fire, and I hadn't had another chance to speak with her.

Today, I was going to get exactly what I wanted.

Just the thought of her being in the vulnerable position she'd been in the night before had kept me up all fucking night.

I needed to teach her some self-defense moves, but even if I knew that she could protect herself, that probably wouldn't help, either. Not enough to make me forget what had happened on that patio.

"No, Ben," she insisted. "You need someone a lot more experienced. You're the CEO of the company for God's sake. One of the largest corporations on the planet I might add. This is just crazy. I can't work for you. My skills would suck in comparison to what you need as the CEO."

She had no idea what I really needed, and I planned to keep it that way for now.

My main objective right now was to make sure that Ariel was safe and that she took the job I was offering.

"I have a technical personal assistant at Blackwood, Ariel, and an executive secretary," I explained. "My assistant at Blackwood is dedicated office staff, and his responsibilities in the offices keep him very busy. This would be something of a more…personal nature."

The hopeful look was back in her beautiful blue eyes, and it nearly gutted me as she queried, "You don't have someone who already does personal things for you? You're obviously a very busy guy."

My older brother, Ian, was finally back at the helm of Blackwood Technologies physically with me after a very long recovery process from the same car accident that had killed my father, but I'd run the office at headquarters myself for years.

Yeah, Ian had been there mentally, pushing like hell to make Blackwood what it was today, but there had been only so much he could do from home.

I'd been the boots on the ground for every meeting, every problem, and every other task that had needed the attention of a CEO in person.

Ian hadn't set foot in the executive offices for years.

He'd been much more obsessed with the robotics program.

As a result, my personal life *had* suffered, and that side of my life was a little…disorganized.

Granted, I hadn't planned on hiring a personal assistant to help me get caught up.

This was a position that I'd have to custom design for Ariel.

According to Katie, Ariel was an artist, and I was very interested in helping her achieve whatever life goals she had.

However, she needed a source of income right now, and this was the perfect solution for the time being.

We could work on her future goals after she got settled as my assistant.

If Ariel wasn't even willing to accept financial help from her best friend, I knew I'd fail at convincing her to just let me give her whatever she needed.

This *had* to be legitimate work for her.

"You wouldn't exactly be working for Blackwood," I said carefully. "You'd be working exclusively for me. And there are...conditions."

"What?" she asked, her attention laser focused on me.

I ran a frustrated hand through my hair, knowing I was making up all of this shit as I went along. "You'll need to live closer to me in Fort Myers Beach. The position will come with a small condo not far from my place. It belongs to me, and it's currently empty. You can call it home for as long as you need it."

That much was true. I kept the place for visitors and employees who were relocating until they found a home of their own. It was a small space, but it was a hell of a lot better than the shithole she was living in right now. This area wasn't exactly safe, and I'd *never* get any sleep if she stayed here.

There were a few areas in Fort Myers where a single woman probably shouldn't live alone.

Ariel lived in one of them.

And I planned on resolving that issue as quickly as possible.

Her brows lifted as she looked at me in astonishment. "Ben, the rent in Fort Myers Beach is—"

"*That* condition is not negotiable. You offered to be a go-to assistant, and to do that, you need to be close to my home. Are you still interested or not?"

I could get her an entry position at the Blackwood headquarters if she was that opposed to working for me directly, but it wouldn't pay as well, nor would it be as suited to my plans of helping Ariel get her life back.

Katie had told me that Ariel had invested her entire life into dancing, and now that she couldn't dance anymore, she'd supposedly lost her whole identity.

Dearest Protector

Fuck that! If Ariel Prescott was lost, I'd help her find herself again. All she needed was a break to pull things together.

She'd been chasing her tail financially for months because of her accident, and once that stopped, she would have the chance to assess her other options.

She sighed as she ran her fingers through her blonde curls nervously. "This position sounds too good to be true. Honestly, I'd prefer something with a wide range of duties that wouldn't put me in an office all day. But…why me? There are a ton of people who'd love to have a job like this one."

I couldn't exactly tell her that I'd been obsessed with her well-being for months now, long before she'd moved back to Florida.

It was clear to me now that she didn't even remember me.

Truthfully, her lack of memory probably gave me an advantage right now.

Christ! I knew it was crazy for me to think about a woman I never talked to, but I had. *Every. Damn. Day.*

I'd wanted to know how she was doing in New York. How things had turned out for her.

I'd realized not long ago that there had been so many misunderstandings on my part involving Ariel, and I regretted every single one of them.

To be honest, I hated myself.

However, fate had tossed me a second chance to make things right with Ariel, and I was a guy who rarely screwed things up the first time. I sure as hell wasn't doing it a second time.

I needed her to take this job.

I wanted to help her get her life back together.

Not a single thing that had happened to her was *her* fault.

"This is a job where I'd have to trust someone with keys to my home and with private information. You're my stepsister's best friend. You've known her since childhood, and you've been a good friend to her when she needed you the most, Ariel. That's a good enough recommendation for me."

~ 37 ~

She nodded slowly. "I guess a guy like you would need someone he could trust. I'm so glad that Katie's finally happy. She has a fantastic job with Blackwood, which was her dream company to work for, and she's crazy about Ian."

I was as thrilled about that as Ariel was for many reasons.

Selfishly, I wanted my older brother to be happy after everything he'd been through, but I'd come to care about Katie like a younger sister, too.

I wanted both of them to be happy.

The fact that they'd fallen in love and were ecstatic *together* was the best possible outcome for the two of them in my opinion.

I lifted a brow. "Then I guess it's your turn to find your own happiness, right?"

Fuck knew she deserved it after everything she'd been through.

She definitely didn't need to worry about her best friend anymore.

My brother would die before he let Katie know another moment of heartache.

Ariel shook her head, her expression thoughtful. "Katie busted her ass for a college education. My situation is a lot different. I may have worked hard for my ballet career, but there was no backup plan for me. I never imagined I'd lose my ability to dance at this age."

"You're done with *that* career, Ariel. But that doesn't mean that you can't do something else. There's more to you than just a dancer."

She shrugged. "If there is, I don't know that woman. I ate, breathed, and slept dancing. There was nothing else for me. Right now, I'm just trying to survive. I'm a little nervous that I won't be able to make you happy in this position. I honestly don't have much more than some computer skills."

"I think we can figure things out as we go along." I decided to be as truthful as I could when I added, "Most of my time for the last several years has been spent at the Blackwood headquarters. Without Ian around physically as my co-CEO, I was overwhelmed the majority of the time. I tried to do everything alone in the executive offices, hoping he'd recover and start being my partner. The company has thrived because Ian and I brainstormed together, and because he's come so far with the robotics, but my personal life is highly disorganized because being at Blackwood took up most of my time. I built my waterfront home a few years ago because the right property came up for sale. It's furnished, but since I spend very little time there except to sleep, it doesn't exactly feel like home. Someone comes in to clean once a week, but that's about as far as I've gotten. It just hasn't been a priority for me."

Her eyes brightened. "I'm definitely an organizer. I always had my schedule planned down to the minute, but I got everything done. I can help with whatever you need to make the place your home. I can run any errands you need, too."

"You don't mind that this is basically a domestic position for now?" I asked, knowing Ariel deserved better, but not sure what else I could do at this point.

I was a fixer.

I'd fix this situation, eventually.

Ariel would find herself and her self-worth, no matter what it took to get her there.

She snorted adorably. "You know what I did before this job and who my boss was in that position. I'm desperate for any job right now. Do you really think I can afford to be picky? Honestly, it sounds amazing to me, Ben. I'll be able to save money, maybe take some classes to educate myself if I have time."

"I'd really like to help you monetize your art and photography, Ariel," I reminded her. "If it's as good as Katie says, you might want to think about making that your next career."

Ariel fidgeted as she answered, "It really is just a hobby, Ben. Don't get me wrong, I love creating those images. It's the only thing I've been passionate about except for dancing, and I've been taking pictures almost as long. But how does a person make a living off taking pictures and digitally manipulating them into something else?"

She'd be surprised by how many people with actual talent did exactly that. "You wouldn't have the following you do on your work if it wasn't something special. Let me help, Ariel. I do have the business skills."

She laughed nervously. "You own and manage Blackwood Technologies. I can't exactly ask for a business consult from a man like you."

Fuck! She obviously didn't realize that she could ask me for *anything,* and I'd make it happen for her.

Apparently, she'd all but forgotten the comments I'd made the night before when I became frustrated about her situation.

There were positives and negatives about the fact that she'd disregarded some of the things I'd said when I was still pissed off about the way Leland Brock had treated her.

I'd all but told her that I was attracted to her, but she'd obviously ignored those not-so-subtle hints.

Hell, maybe it was an advantage that we could start all over again now that I'd pulled my shit together.

"You don't have to ask. I'm offering to help," I said firmly. "And I'm not taking no for an answer. I'd like to see your portfolios as soon as possible."

I totally trusted my stepsister's judgment. If Katie said Ariel's work was phenomenal, it was. Truthfully, maybe all I wanted was the chance to see it for myself. Maybe I was curious to see what I could discover about Ariel through her artwork. She certainly wasn't very forthcoming about herself.

"Work first," she insisted. "Ben, this position will make a huge difference for me. My job is to make my boss happy."

Hell, I was already ecstatic that she'd agreed to take the position, but I was going to have to tread carefully. I *had* to put a lid on my own needs and focus solely on what Ariel needed from me right now. That meant no more losing control like I had last night. *Ever.* I'd barely resisted slamming Leland Brock's head into the cement for every single bad thing he'd ever done to Ariel before I'd had him removed from the property. "I'll help you move to your new place. It's Sunday. I'm not planning on going into the office. If you get packed, I'll help you move everything over this afternoon."

The sooner I got her out of this place the better.

Dearest Protector

"No," she said emphatically. "I'm supposed to be making *your* life easier, Ben. You don't need to help me move."

I dug into the pocket of my jeans, and held out the key to the condo. "This will help. The address is on the keychain."

I wasn't about to let her lug all of her things to her new condo alone, but we'd talk about that...later. After she got her stuff packed up.

She shot me a dubious look as she took the key. "You carry the key to that condo around with you?"

I grinned. "Let's just say I was hopeful that you'd accept the position. I could use the help."

"I don't even know how to thank you, except to do a good job and to help you out as much as possible," Ariel said breathlessly.

Hell, she was already helping me out.

I'd know exactly where she was and what she was doing most of the time, and I'd be reassured that she was safe, healthy, and not being abused by an asshole.

Maybe if I was able to help her, the thoughts of how we'd last met wouldn't haunted my fucking dreams anymore.

Maybe I wouldn't want to beat myself in the head because I'd been so damn stupid after that.

Maybe, for the first time in a long time, my guilt wouldn't eat me alive every time I thought about her.

"You don't have to thank me, Ariel," I said huskily.

I wanted more from Ariel than to just be her boss and her protector.

Nevertheless, *her* needs came first, and what she needed right now was a friend, a confidant, and someone who gave a shit about her well-being.

Since I was willing and able to be all of those things to her, I'd have to settle for whatever I could get and just be damn grateful that she was willing to let me into her life.

Chapter 4

Ariel

Two weeks later, I still couldn't figure out why Ben Blackwood had hired me.

Not that I was complaining.

I had an amazing job that kept me busy and active without being overwhelmed.

I also had a fantastic boss who treated me like a human and appreciated everything I did for him.

Ben's faith in me was slowly starting to change the way I felt about myself.

I felt useful.

I felt like I had some skills other than dancing.

I felt creative again, even if it was a different sort of creativity than my dancing had been.

I wasn't terrified about where my next meal would come from or if I was going to be homeless the next day.

I was also living in a very nice condo near the beach, a place that would have been unreachable for me under any other circumstances.

In a very short period of time, my life had improved so much that the dark cloud over my head and the anxiety that had plagued me for months was slowly dissipating.

Ben hadn't been lying when he'd confessed to being disorganized at home and in his personal life. His beachfront home was spectacular, but it was apparent that he did little else but sleep in the place.

We'd had some disagreements in the beginning, mostly about how much domestic work should be included in the position.

He'd wanted me to hire someone to select art and wall hangings and put them up, and to do some of the tasks around the house, which was ridiculous. If I did that, I'd have very little to do. He already had a cleaning service that did the basic cleaning once a week.

I let out a long sigh of satisfaction as I straightened the gorgeous seascape painting I'd just finished hanging on his living room wall.

"Perfect," I whispered aloud, even though I was alone in Ben's house.

I'd found most of the wall hangings and accessories for the house from local artists, and this one was pretty fabulous. I usually texted Ben with photos of anything I was buying for his place so he could have the final say on whether or not it was his style.

He hadn't nixed any of my choices, and surprisingly, he'd asked for some of *my* digital artwork in print form to adorn various walls in his home.

When it came to my hobby, Ben was my biggest supporter, and with so much inspiration around me now, I worked a lot on that particular passion.

With Ben and Katie constantly nagging me about trying to make a business out of my hobby, and with their constant encouragement, I was beginning to believe I might be able to produce an income from it.

I spent my days working for Ben, the evenings after work taking photos, and my nights in my condo working on new pieces.

I'd gotten a ton of advice from Ben, and Katie was helping me design a new website.

I wasn't counting on making a fortune, but I was going to work my hardest to make my new business fly.

Hell, I had *Ben Blackwood* doling out business advice for free. If I was going to be successful building a business from my work, I'd never have a better opportunity than I had right now.

"That looks even nicer than it did in the photo," a deep voice said from behind me.

I startled. I'd been so lost in thought that I hadn't even heard Ben come in.

My heart skipped a beat as I turned to look at him, just like it did every single time I saw him.

Dammit! Why couldn't I stop that ridiculous reaction.

Yeah, he looked ungodly gorgeous in the navy custom suit he'd worn to the office today, but he was *my boss*. I'd had two weeks to get used to being around him, and he never treated me like I was anything other than a valued employee.

He'd never given me an iota of encouragement that kept me reacting this way to him.

He was friendly.

He was courteous.

He was kind.

But he *did not* look at me like he wanted to undress me with his eyes.

Unfortunately, I couldn't say the same for myself.

I ogled his gorgeous face and amazing body every time I saw him, and it was a habit I couldn't seem to break.

I nodded as I mentally slapped myself for salivating over my boss. "It does, right? It's perfect in this living room."

"This whole house looks different already," Ben commented. "It doesn't have that unfinished, half-moved-in look anymore."

"If that was your preferred décor, it's definitely starting to disappear," I joked. "It's beginning to look like someone actually lives here now."

"You're doing an amazing job, Ariel," Ben replied in a sincere tone.

My heart squeezed inside my chest.

Dearest Protector

How long had it been since I'd gotten any kind of approval on the jobs I'd done at work?

Leland had been so cruel and so critical about everything I'd done for him.

It felt really good to hear that Ben was happy with my progress.

"I'll start organizing and filing the paperwork in your office tomorrow," I promised.

Ben's home office was a complete disaster, and I knew it wasn't because he was generally a messy guy.

He'd just never really had the energy or time to organize it since he'd worked in the Blackwood headquarters and in his home every single day for years without a break.

He smirked. "No big hurry on that. It's been that way since I transferred some of my stuff from my office so I could do some late nights from home. I don't expect you to fix something in a few weeks that it took years to accumulate. Relax, Ariel. It was never my intention to make you work this quickly."

I swallowed hard as I watched him yank at the knot in his tie.

Not only was Ben Blackwood drop-dead gorgeous, but inherently thoughtful as well.

Maybe that was one of the reasons he was so damned intriguing.

After our initial meetings in the beginning, I'd discover that he *did* smile on occasion, and the result of seeing those appealing grins was absolutely devastating on my psyche.

I was weirdly drawn to Ben Blackwood, and I hated it, but I couldn't seem to be completely at ease whenever he was around.

It was very hard *not* to like him because he was a likeable guy, but I didn't really understand him any more than I had two weeks ago.

The tension in the air that seemed to spark whenever he was around was…unexplainable.

Well, I felt that tension.

Ben, maybe not so much.

It was absolutely stupid for me to feel this inexplicable pull toward him, but I'd tried everything to make it go away, and it wasn't happening.

Snapping myself out of my silly, lust-filled daze, I said, "I made dinner. There's lasagna on warm in the oven and a salad in the fridge."

I glanced at the clock before I added, "I should get going."

How long could I stare at him like a lovesick teenager before he'd realize that I was ridiculously attracted to him?

I picked up the items I'd used to hang the picture and scrambled toward the kitchen.

Ben followed me. "I told you not to bother with cooking."

I shrugged as I put the tools away. "It's not a bother," I said honestly. "I like to cook, and you know you would have ordered takeout if I hadn't."

For a man as physically fit as he was, his eating habits were terrible.

One of my first priorities had been to clean out his fridge. The guy never cooked or ate healthy. All of the old takeout food he'd stored in the refrigerator had been my first clue about his eating habits when I'd tossed it all out.

I grocery shopped every week, trying to make sure he ate healthier than he had in the past.

Ben spent so much time worrying about others that he rarely took care of himself as well as he took care of other people and his business.

I'd made it my goal to make sure that he was more comfortable in his own home, and that included having something other than takeout to eat.

He might complain that I didn't need to cook, but he usually ate everything I prepared, which had been my incentive to keep on making him healthier food to eat.

Ben appreciated what I did for him, and that was enough for me.

"It smells fantastic," he admitted. "I'm starving. I had an important meeting, and I forgot to eat lunch today."

I frowned. I had no doubt that happened fairly often.

He didn't really eat breakfast, either.

Ben left for work before I arrived in the morning, but I saw the empty glass in the sink and the container of protein powder on the counter every morning.

Dearest Protector

I suspected that he worked out hard every morning in his home gym before work, but he didn't have time to eat something more substantial? Obviously, his idea of a decent breakfast was a protein shake before he left for work.

What kind of nutrition was that for a guy who hit the ground running the moment he arrived at the Blackwood offices?

I'd studied nutrition extensively as a dancer.

Yes, I'd had to watch what I ate, but I knew the importance of fueling up for a busy day.

Now that I wasn't short of money, I'd started to take care of myself again, and it bothered me that my boss, who was paying my paycheck, still wasn't eating as well as I did.

"You should have called me," I admonished. "I could have brought something to your office for you. I *am* your personal assistant. That's my job, Ben, and it's not like I'm overloaded with work. Next time, please call me."

He shook his head. "I guess I just didn't think about it. I'm not used to anyone helping me out with personal stuff."

I rolled my eyes as I checked on the food in the oven.

Hello? Wasn't that what he paid *me* for?

I turned and folded my arms across my chest. People probably thought he was invincible, but I...didn't. A person could only run on empty for so long without paying the price physically. "Get used to it," I advised. "That's what I'm here to do. If you need something, I'm your go-to woman. I'd like to think that I'm earning my money and the fantastic benefits."

He grinned and my heart completely melted.

God, why did he have to be so damn magnetic and gorgeous, even after working all damn day with no food?

"Just that dinner smells like it's worth every penny I pay you," he teased as he finished pulling off his tie and jacket and then draped them over the chair at the breakfast bar.

"Eventually, the work you're giving me isn't going to fill an eight-hour day, Ben," I said, blowing off the compliment. "Tomorrow, call me if you need some lunch. You shouldn't go all day without eating."

Yeah, right now I was busy doing catchup work in his home, but I'd someday run out of extra tasks to do. He was going to have to start relying on me to do other things for him.

My breath caught as Ben did a thorough scrutiny of my body from head to toe before our gazes locked.

"How are *you* doing, Ariel?" he asked huskily. "How's the condo? Your business? What are you doing for fun? Talk to me and tell me about something other than what you're doing for me."

I was stunned into silence.

Ben and I didn't talk about much else *except* my business tasks.

Yeah, he helped me with business advice when I needed it, but we didn't ever really get personal.

For me, it was easier that way.

If I let myself get close to him personally, I'd be screwed.

Right now, I could blow off my attraction to him as superficial because he was irresistibly handsome with a big, muscular, hard body that *no woman* could ignore.

What female could lock eyes with this gorgeous man without a few palpitations, right?

If I let myself get attached to him on a personal basis, I knew the way that I wanted him would be even worse.

I already lust after him. He's an incredible boss. I just absolutely cannot get to know him as a person and like him that way, too.

The problem was, I was *already* starting to like him as a person, even though we didn't really know each other very well.

"Everything is great," I said a little too brightly. "I couldn't ask for a better job, a better boss, or a nicer place to live. I really should be going so you can get some dinner."

"Stay," he said hoarsely. "Have dinner with me. You have to eat and I know you made enough food for several people. You always do."

What?

No!

My first knee-jerk reaction was to escape from here as quickly as my bad foot would take me.

Dearest Protector

But…there was a spark of something in his gaze that I couldn't quite comprehend that made me pause.

Loneliness?

A deep craving of some kind that couldn't be spoken out loud?

It wasn't obvious, but I *sensed* there was more to his invitation than politeness.

Was it possible that Ben Blackwood was as lonely as I was?

Ridiculous, yes, but there was *something* else there in his eyes, and whatever it was completely broke me.

For some unknown reason, he *wanted* me to stay.

Something inside my belly somersaulted at the thought of having an intimate dinner with the hottest guy on the planet.

I knew he was probably just being courteous. That it was probably my imagination that made me think it was anything more.

Ben wasn't and never would be interested in me as anything other than an assistant.

Still, I was so damn tempted.

I'd been alone for so long that I'd forgotten what it was like to have company for dinner, or anything else for that matter.

Katie and I were and would always remain close, but she had Ian now, and he was her priority, as it should be. But that had changed our dynamic, and it wasn't like we could just get together on a whim or chat forever on the phone every night.

Ben's expression was intense, and his eyes were beckoning as they stayed locked on mine.

Do it, Ariel. There's really no reason why you can't be friends with this man.

Maybe Ben didn't want to get naked with me, but would it really hurt to not be alone for one evening?

Honestly, I craved some kind of human connection, and there was no one I wanted to get to know more than I wanted to know Ben Blackwood.

Okay, so maybe I *did* want to get *him* naked, but my curiosity and my desire to get closer to him in other ways was stronger than my sexual attraction right now.

I also couldn't shake the feeling that he genuinely *wanted* me to stay.

I finally shrugged off my apprehension. "You don't mind company?" I asked, trying to make sure he wasn't just being polite because I'd end up eating dinner alone at my condo.

"There's nothing I'd like more than to spend the evening with you," he answered gruffly. "Stay and have dinner with me."

Breathless from his extended, persuasive gaze, I finally nodded.

Maybe it was strange that someone like Ben Blackwood would value my company, but I had to wonder if part of him didn't need some kind of real human connection, too.

Chapter 5

Ariel

About an hour later, I'd almost completely forgotten about my nervousness and my misgivings about hanging out with Ben.

Did that mean I no longer wanted to get him naked?

No. No, it didn't.

But as I got more comfortable with him, it was easier to curb my carnal instincts and just enjoy his companionship.

Sure, I still imagined what he looked like in the raw, but more importantly, I could appreciate him as a person and not a possible sex god.

My second glass of the excellent Cabernet wine that Ben had selected for dinner had probably helped disperse my anxiousness, but he was also an extremely charming companion.

Ben had shared that he was more a whiskey drinker, so he'd made a drink for himself, and had left the entire bottle of wine for me.

At his suggestion, we'd let go of all business while we were eating dinner.

Even though we were actually from two different worlds, we had some things in common.

Like me, Ben had always been a workaholic who had a limited personal life, and the two us were able to commiserate with each other in that respect.

While he enjoyed seeing a movie or getting out on the water whenever he could, he didn't have time to do those things on a regular basis.

He'd destroyed my preconceived ideas about how someone like him lived his life.

He had all the money in the world.

I'd assumed his life was more…glamorous.

It wasn't.

For the most part, Ben worked, and he worked harder than the average person.

That left very little time for him to live a billionaire lifestyle.

"Seriously?" I asked, looking at him skeptically. "You haven't had a date in over a year?"

That was hard to believe. The guy had to have women throwing themselves at him all the time.

He was a billionaire for God's sake, and he was so sinfully attractive that it was ridiculous.

He was also genuinely a nice guy, which was rare, even without all of his other assets.

Ben had changed out of his work attire and was wearing a pair of dark jeans and a Henley shirt, which, I might add, did nothing to lessen his appeal.

In fact, his casual clothing made him more approachable. It had made me more comfortable, too, since I was still wearing the pair of nice jeans and a long-sleeved red shirt I'd put on for work that morning.

"I swear," Ben said firmly as he dropped his fork onto his empty plate. "It's true. I haven't had the best luck with relationships."

"Why?" I asked curiously.

Because Ben was my boss, I knew I shouldn't get too personal, but the question had popped out of my mouth before I could stop it.

Dearest Protector

He shrugged. "Most of them have been more interested in my bank account than they are in me. Maybe I was just choosing the wrong women. Finding a good relationship hasn't really been my priority, so it's probably my fault."

I sighed before I took another sip of my wine.

Most likely, the billionaire persona and Ben's gorgeous form took priority for some women, but he had a lot more going for him than just those superficial things.

He was wickedly intelligent.

He had a dry but appealing sense of humor.

He was loyal to his family and the people he cared about.

Maybe he was obsessed with Blackwood Technologies, but I sensed that the good things that his company was doing with technology was more important to him than making more money.

"I can't say that I've been any luckier in relationships," I confessed. "My dancing career always came first. That didn't leave much time for dating."

His eyes searched my face as he questioned, "And now that you're not dancing anymore?"

I practically squirmed in my chair. Everything about Ben was intense, even casual questions. He eyed me like my responses were actually important to him. No guy had ever really seen me and not my dancing persona, so Ben's genuine interest was almost uncomfortable. I wasn't used to someone giving a damn about how I felt. I took a deep breath and answered honestly. "All I've thought about was survival since my accident. This is probably the first time I've been able to breathe since it happened, and my confidence is completely shot. It's going to take a while. I'm more interested in making sure I can keep eating and paying my bills than I am in dating. I don't think I can have a healthy relationship when I'm so screwed up and unsure of who I am."

"I know you still don't completely believe that your photography can be your next career, but it will be, Ariel," he answered, his tone reassuring and confident. "Your work is unique. Your following is extremely large, and now that I'm familiar with your work, I can understand why. Have faith in your talent and all of your other valuable assets. Dancing was just one facet of your personality, it isn't who you really are. It never defined you."

I blinked back the tears that started to form in my eyes.

How could I explain to him that I'd never had faith in *anything* except my ability to dance? It *had* defined me. It had been everything to me, and I'd lost that ability in seconds.

"Thank you," I said in a voice that was barely audible. "I want to believe that, but I think it's going to take a while. Recovering from my accident was challenging, losing my career was a huge blow, and working for Leland and putting up with his abuse nearly broke me. It's almost like I'm just waiting for the next shoe to drop. For the next horrible thing to happen."

God, I hated to sound like I was whining, but it felt good to be completely honest with Ben because I knew he wouldn't judge.

"Nothing bad is going to happen, Ariel. I'd like to kill Leland Brock," he grumbled. "The last thing you needed while you were recovering was an asshole for a boss who kept on undermining your skills and your confidence. And I don't even want to talk about him laying his fucking hands on you."

Strangely, his fierceness didn't worry me because I knew that he was pissed off *for me* and not *at me*.

Ben had no idea what it felt like to me to have a protector, someone who was looking out for my welfare.

It was something I'd never experienced, not even as a child.

I shook my head. "I'm the one who stayed and put up with it because I needed the money. I knew I had to leave—"

"He took advantage of the fact that you needed a paycheck," Ben interrupted, his tone angry. "He's scum."

"And now I have an amazing job," I reminded him. "My experience with Leland makes me appreciate what I have right now."

"I wish you had been with me from the start," he rumbled, his expressive eyes showing his regret. "You were vulnerable after your accident, Ariel, which is completely understandable."

"Don't, Ben," I pleaded. "I'm going to be fine."

He lifted a brow. "I'll make damn sure that you are fine from now on," he warned.

My heart warmed as I saw the sincerity in his gaze. "I'm not sure why you care, but I'm grateful that you do."

"You deserved a hell of a lot better," he commented as he pushed his empty plate away and took a gulp of his whiskey.

"I got a hell of a lot better," I said softly. "I got...you."

My pulse raced as Ben's long, fixed stare stayed focused on me. He seemed to be trying to convince himself that I was really going to be okay.

He cared about me.

I couldn't explain that, and I couldn't figure out how I just knew that my well-being meant something to him, but it was there in his eyes.

Unfortunately, I didn't know how to handle all that concern because no one in my life had cared this much about me except for Katie.

Even in New York, I'd essentially been alone, even though I was surrounded by other dancers and people in my profession.

"You should have someone in your life who cares," Ben rumbled and finally broke eye contact.

I shuddered as I felt the same familiarity I'd experienced several times before with Ben.

I barely knew him, yet I sensed a connection between the two of us that I couldn't explain.

What in the hell was it about Ben that made me feel like we'd met before, when I knew damn well that we never had.

The deep timbre of his voice soothed me for some reason.

His protectiveness and his constant reassurance was a balm to my soul.

The sensual attraction was...different, but the way he calmed me felt...so damn familiar.

I shook off the freakish inkling, knowing it was ridiculous.

Ben and I were almost strangers, and if we'd met before, I'd certainly remember *that*.

"You okay?" Ben questioned. "You look like you're lost in your own world."

I popped out of my own weird thoughts as I answered, "I'm good. Thank you for asking me to stay, and for this fantastic wine. Maybe I'm a little tipsy. I don't usually drink this much. I guess I'm a lightweight."

He suddenly grinned, and that smile turned my entire world upside down.

"I was going to work on your business plan with you after dinner," he commented with amusement. "Probably not a good idea if the wine has gotten to your head."

I pushed the wine glass away. "I'm not *that* impaired. I'll take all of the advice I can get whenever I can get it."

Hell, if Ben Blackwood wanted to talk about a business plan, I'd always be ready to listen.

Truth was, I really *wanted* to believe that I could make my own business fly someday.

Ben made that fantasy seem like a real possibility.

Maybe...I could.

Maybe...I could still do something meaningful and creative, even though I'd never dance again.

Part of me was afraid to hope because I wasn't sure if I could take the disappointment of failing after all that had happened with my dancing career.

But who was I kidding?

Yeah, I wanted to be successful, even though the ballet career I'd worked for since I was child was no longer achievable.

It wasn't like I didn't appreciate this job with Ben, and I felt useful for the first time in a long time, but it wasn't exactly a lifelong career goal.

Once I'd organized Ben's home, what would be left outside of running errands for him and doing some tasks around the house? I'd never be able to justify this cushy position he'd given me.

Besides, someday I wanted...more.

Katie was right.

Dearest Protector

I'd never be totally happy working in an office somewhere.

My drive to create would always leave me restless if I couldn't express it in some way.

"All you'll ever need to do is ask if you need anything, Ariel," Ben said in a more serious tone. "I'd like to think we're becoming... friends. I'd be disappointed if you didn't want that, too."

My eyes shot to his face.

Oh God, could I really be a friend to this Adonis who made every female hormone in my body stand up and take notice?

Ben Blackwood was every woman's fantasy, yet he was *human*, too.

Quite honestly, he could probably use a friend who wanted nothing but his health and happiness.

Someone with no ulterior motives.

Especially since his older brother had been personally unreachable for years. Katie had come along and pulled Ian out of his isolation, but who had Ben had to talk to before that?

Ben was close to his mom, but I could tell from a few of his phone calls to her that he was careful about not telling her anything that would upset her.

Honestly, I yearned to be closer to this enigmatic man who had stepped in to help me reclaim my life without a second thought.

I just wasn't sure if I could offer *him* as much as he was giving *me*.

I was still pretty broken, but Ben Blackwood made me want to try to be that person who really knew him and cared about him.

"Is that what you want? To be friends?" I asked hesitantly. "I'd kind of a messed up friend to you right now, Ben. I don't have my own shit together."

He lifted a brow. "I doubt we'd need friends if we had our shit straight all the time. You're helping me out right now, Ariel."

I shook my head. "You're paying me very well for that."

He shrugged. "Not for all of the thoughtful things you've done. Come on, Ariel. Everyone can use another friend who cares that they can really trust. I want you to feel like you can come to me when you need something, and vice-versa. Talk to me."

Talk to me. Talk to me. Talk to me, Ariel.

~ 57 ~

I blinked hard as those words rolled through my mind like I'd heard Ben saying them before.

Probably because he was so damn persuasive.

Oh, holy hell. Maybe Ben and I were *meant* to be closer, to be friends.

Maybe if we were *friends,* it would help me forget how much I wanted him to kiss me.

Since I wanted to get over this stupid attraction I had to him, I was willing to try almost anything.

"Okay, friends it is. What else do you want to know?" I asked tentatively.

"Everything," he answered succinctly. "Tell me about your accident, and about your career in New York before it happened. Your childhood. Your likes and dislikes. Whatever is on your mind. I'd really like to know."

"Only if you're ready to share, too," I said cautiously. "This friendship can't be one-sided."

"Agreed," he said firmly.

I called him on his proposition to be friends. "Then you go first. You know enough about me from Katie. I still know almost nothing about you."

Surprisingly, he started talking without a single hesitation. He began by telling me about the accident that had killed his father years ago and had left Ian in pain and isolated for so long.

My heart ached as he explained, and he made himself so vulnerable as he recalled those painful memories that I knew our relationship would never be the same again.

Chapter 6

Ben

"Are you sure you know what you're doing, Ben?" Ian questioned as we ate the lunch Ariel had just brought to my office at Blackwood Technologies headquarters. "It's not like I mind that we get something substantial for lunch all the time now, but do you really know what you're doing with *Ariel*?"

I hadn't asked Ariel to drop off food for lunch at my office, but she'd done it anyway. Every single day since we'd had dinner together at my place a week ago. And she always included lunch for Ian, too.

I'd only run into her once here in the office when she'd delivered food.

Today, I'd been tied up in a meeting, but my secretary had informed me that my lunch had arrived as soon as I'd left the conference room.

Unfortunately, Ariel had been long gone, off to run other errands.

"I have no idea what you're talking about," I said to Ian as I reached into the hot bag and claimed my warm sandwich wrap that Ariel had made at my house.

I smiled when I realized there were no chips. Instead, she'd made a side salad filled with fresh vegetables that she'd stored in another bag.

I popped off the lid and started with the salad.

Since we'd decided to become friends instead of just boss and employee, Ariel had felt free to nag me half to death about my nutritional habits and my unhealthy relationship with takeout junk food.

Like the woman had any right to lecture me when she hadn't eaten enough to maintain her weight just a few weeks ago?

I'd learned a lot about Ariel, and although she loved junk food, too, she'd almost never given in to the urge to consume it during her dancing years. She'd always been on a strict regimen to nourish her body without extra calories.

Now, she seemed to be hell-bent on feeding me things that would fuel my body without the junk and to make sure I got food on a regular schedule.

In her mind, it wasn't healthy for me to down a protein shake, work out every morning, and then not eat until evening.

Hell, she was probably right, but I rarely thought about food after I arrived at Blackwood. My work here had always been all-consuming.

Maybe it was a little pathetic, but it actually felt good to know someone cared whether or not I was eating right.

I wasn't paying her to give a shit about my nutritional habits, and I'd never asked her to bring me lunch, yet she still did it every single work day.

Ian helped himself to a bottle of water as he said, "Bullshit. You know exactly what I mean. I saw the way you looked at Ariel the other day when she brought lunch. While I commend you on the way you're helping her with this assistant job, I'm not sure it's strictly business for you."

It wasn't.

Never had been, and never would be.

Not with Ariel.

But I wasn't sure that was something I wanted to share with my older brother.

Ian was in a committed relationship with Ariel's best friend, and I was pretty sure that Ian shared everything with Katie.

At this point, I didn't know if revealing my situation was a good idea.

Dearest Protector

"We're friends, too," I hedged, hoping he'd drop this line of questioning.

Hell, I barely understood my feelings for Ariel myself. I sure as hell didn't think I could explain them to anyone else.

They didn't make sense.

They weren't logical.

They weren't rational at all.

But they were there, whether I completely understood them… or not.

Unfortunately, becoming her friend hadn't stopped my dick from getting hard every time I saw her.

I wanted her.

The problem was, I'd actually come to like her and admire her, too, which had screwed up my head even worse.

It would have been easier if she'd ended up being a total bitch or so self-absorbed that she was totally unlikeable.

Unfortunately for me, that wasn't the case.

She was real.

She was trustworthy.

She didn't give a shit about my family name or my vast fortune.

She was the kind of female I could talk to about anything, which was rare in my world.

She was the sort of woman a guy wanted to see every damn day.

Ariel cared, and I was quickly realizing how good it felt to have a woman in my life that saw me as a regular guy.

She fussed over me sometimes, and God help me, but I actually *enjoyed* that.

I looked forward to leaving the Blackwood offices because I hoped she'd still be at my place when I got home.

I now had something other than more work waiting at home, and that entire concept was foreign to me, but I was getting addicted to having her around.

Ian took a break from wolfing down his food to grumble, "Do friends always look at each other like they wish they were naked and alone together? I fucking recognize that look, Ben. I look at Kate the same way."

Normally, I'd probably tease Ian about the fact that he was the only one who referred to Katie as Kate, but I didn't.

I was too concerned that Ian could apparently recognize exactly how I felt about Ariel.

Fuck! My brother was on to me. He knew just how much I wanted Ariel, and it wasn't going to be easy to convince him otherwise.

And really, did I want to attempt to convince him that Ariel meant nothing to me?

Ian and I were getting tight again, and we hadn't been this close for years. I didn't *want* to lie to him.

We were running Blackwood *together* now. He spent time in the robotics lab in the mornings, but he was here physically in the executive offices, the way it always should have been from the beginning, the way my dad had wanted.

I didn't want to fuck that up now that I had my older brother back again.

I scrutinized his expression, barely noticing the lingering scars on his face from the accident that had killed my father and had left Ian broken.

Truth was, Ian was damn happy these days because of Katie, and that made *me* ecstatic.

I answered noncommittally, "I'm not going to say that I'm not attracted to her, but all she needs is a friend right now, Ian. I'm going to be that friend. I'm going to help her get her life back together. What happened to her was not her fault. She lost everything when she was hit by that taxi in New York."

Ian snorted. "Yeah. And how is that friendship thing working out for you? Been there and tried something like that myself, little brother. It's pure hell to want a woman you can't have."

I dropped my empty salad container back into the bag and opened my sandwich wrap. "Not...so great," I confessed. "But for now, I have to suck it up. She's been through hell, and *her* needs come first."

Dearest Protector

Being Ariel's friend wasn't exactly a hardship, even if I did want more. When it came to relationships, she gave far more than she was willing to take, and having *anyone* like that in my life other than family was…unusual.

She saw *me*, not my money or power. When we were operating in the friend mode, she saw me as just a normal guy.

Ian frowned. "Seems to me you've already done way too much of that 'sucking things up' for most of your adult life, and that's my goddamn fault. I wished to hell that I could make that up to you. I haven't been there for you for a long time as an older brother. But I'm here now, Ben. You can talk to me. I'm back, and I'm not going to abandon you to run the headquarters by yourself again. If I would have pulled my head out of my ass earlier, I would have realized how hard it was on you to be the only one here. Hell, do you honestly think I don't realize that every single day now?"

We'd had this discussion before, and the last thing I wanted from Ian was another apology. "Don't, Ian," I said gruffly. "I don't know now and will never know what you went through. I wasn't in that car with you and Dad."

Ian had always blamed himself for not being able to save our father, despite the fact that he'd been gravely injured himself.

"But you picked up all of the pieces. You ran your ass off to accomplish my obsessions about Blackwood," Ian acknowledged. "Don't ever think that I don't know the hell you've been through, too. You look like shit, even if you are one of the most sought-after bachelors in the world. I know you, Ben. Those years of running Blackwood alone physically and taking care of Mom's emotional needs have gotten to you. I never stopped working in my lab at home long enough to realize how much I was putting on you. I demanded, and you carried things out on your own. And you were mourning Dad, too. Hell, I'm happy that Ariel is looking out for you. I'm just worried because I don't want you to end up hurt. Thank fuck that she looks at you the same way you look at her."

"I've never seen that look," I admitted in a disgruntled tone as I reached for my water.

~ 63 ~

Ariel mothered the hell out of me despite the fact that I was six years older than her, but I'd *never* seen the same need in her eyes that ate at my guts every single day.

Being close to her was both heaven and hell.

I wanted her close.

I wanted her near me.

I had a connection to her that I'd never experienced with another woman.

But hiding just how much I wanted her was getting damn near impossible for me.

Ian sent me a disgruntled expression. "Then you're fucking blinded by your own feelings, brother," he warned. "My only request is that you make sure you know what you want before you change this so-called friendship into something else entirely. Ariel is vulnerable. You're right, she needs a confidante and someone to help her. What happened to her is completely fucked up, but she's more like a sister than a friend to Kate. It would destroy her to see Ariel hurt again."

I took a slug of water before I asked, "And if I end up being the one who's hurt by this relationship?"

"That would gut me, too," he answered. "You haven't even had the time to look for the woman who will make you happy for the rest of your life. I'm pretty sure you're serious about Ariel. I can't exactly fault you on the fact that you haven't known her for long, either. One look at Kate and I was obsessed. It didn't matter that I was damaged. All I wanted was her, and I did whatever it took to make sure she was safe. Maybe the way I approached that with the whole stalker thing was wrong, but it was really my only option at the time."

I smirked. Ian's method of keeping track of Katie while she got her college education and afterward was wrong, but I definitely understood that compulsion.

"Then maybe you'll understand why I feel the same protectiveness toward Ariel," I replied. "Dad used to say that when you meet the right woman, you'll know it almost immediately. He never really

Dearest Protector

explained how, but I guess it's really hard to explain until you experience it yourself."

Ian nodded. "It is, and I know he was right. So that's it? Ariel is the one?"

Fuck! How could I deny the fact that I'd completely lost my mind when I'd seen Ariel for the first time? And how was I supposed to explain why I'd left her if I'd already suspected that she was special?

I couldn't express in words how much I really hated myself because I'd left her when she'd needed someone who cared the most.

I nodded slowly as I chewed and swallowed the last of my sandwich. "I didn't want this. I didn't ask for it, and I don't like it. But yeah, she's the one woman who can make me lose every rational thought in my brain without even trying. It would be a hell of a lot easier if I *could* just be her friend and maybe her protector. I'm trying, Ian, but I can't fucking do it. Being close to her makes me completely insane."

He grinned. "Give it up. You can try all you want, but it will never work. If you keep attempting to rationalize the way you feel, it will drive you crazy."

Christ! Like I didn't already know that?

I really wanted to talk to my older brother.

I wanted to tell him what happened.

This whole situation with Ariel had been eating me alive, and I wasn't sure what the hell to do.

Truthfully, I was winging this friendship with her, when I wanted something completely different.

Problem was, if I pushed too hard, too fast, I was worried that I'd screw up the second chance I'd been given to make things right with her—if that was even possible.

"I never expected to see Ariel here in Florida," I explained. "Or to get another chance to get to know her. And I had no fucking idea that I could feel this way about *any* female. I can't fuck this up, Ian. I've been thinking about her for months now, and it's been driving me completely insane."

"Months? You just met her a few weeks ago at Mom's birthday ball, right?" Ian questioned, his voice puzzled.

"It's kind of a long story," I said reluctantly.

Maybe this wasn't something we should discuss while we were in the office.

Now probably wasn't the time to spill my guts.

We both had things we needed to get done before the end of the day, and I wasn't sure I could even explain what had happened months ago.

Ian rose, walked to my office door, called out to my secretary that we weren't to be interrupted, and then firmly closed the door behind him.

Once he was seated comfortably again in his chair, he insisted, "Tell me, Ben. Nothing is more important right now than this situation. Fuck the business stuff for a while. I have a feeling this is more important than anything else to you, and you've never had anyone there to listen. Right now, I'm just your older brother ready to listen to whatever is bothering you."

I swallowed hard. It had been a long time since I'd put anything before Blackwood or my family, and it had been even longer since I'd had an older brother to talk to about anything.

Jesus! I'd missed Ian.

I'd really missed the close relationship we'd had when we were younger.

We'd been slowly rebuilding that trust and that comradery again, and I was grateful every single day that I had my older brother back again.

Sure, he could end up repeating whatever I said to Katie, but I was positive that he wouldn't.

Ian would keep my confidence unless it was absolutely necessary to spill my personal shit or until I decided to tell Katie myself.

He had the same sense of family and loyalty that I did. We were both raised that way.

Ian folded his arms across his chest as he waited.

"I fucked up pretty badly," I cautioned him.

Dearest Protector

"Yeah, well," he started drily. "I'm not exactly one to judge other people about their mistakes. I've made way too many of my own. Shoot."

If I couldn't trust my own brother, who could I trust?

Relieved that I could finally talk about it, I took a deep breath and told Ian *everything...*

Chapter 7

Ariel

"This condo is adorable," Katie commented as she finally finished walking the space and plopped down in a chair at the breakfast bar. "You can't quite see the water, but it's like a minute walk to the beach."

I nodded as I slid a glass of wine to her and picked up my own from the kitchen counter. "It's so different from my old place. I love it here. I just wish I could express that gratitude to Ben. He acts like this perk is no big deal. It's huge for me."

It was the first time Katie had actually seen my place. Since she lived on Sanibel Island, we usually met someplace in between. But she'd been determined to see my condo today.

She'd left work in the city and had driven down to the beach right after she'd left the huge Blackwood Technologies laboratory earlier.

I released a long sigh of contentment. There were times over the last few weeks that I felt like I was living an entirely different life than I had been weeks ago, but I also felt like I still couldn't completely let my guard down.

Dearest Protector

I tried not to dwell on the negative, but no one knew better than me that bad things happened when you least expected them.

It had felt really good to pay Katie back for the groceries she had paid for right before Ben had stepped into my life.

She'd argued about taking the money, but when I'd told her that it was important to me, she grudgingly accepted.

God, how my life had changed since I'd taken this job with Ben.

It wasn't just the financial improvements, either.

I felt more alive than I'd felt in a long time, and so much of that was because of how close I was getting to Ben.

My friendship with him had made me realize how alone I'd been before we'd met.

Maybe I hadn't totally allowed myself to believe things could stay this way, but I was trying hard to make sure I never went back to the dark place I'd existed in not so long ago.

I spent most of my spare time taking photos, and working on my business.

My website was almost ready to go live, and thanks to Ben, I was learning everything I needed to know to be successful.

He'd helped me incorporate, and with all of the other details that had to be handled before I could launch.

Katie shrugged. "To him, giving you this condo as a perk *isn't* a big deal, Ariel. It's one tiny place in a very large portfolio of worldwide real estate investments. He has other places in the area where he can put up new employees or visitors if he needs to. Please tell me you don't feel guilty about taking him up on this benefit."

"I do," I admitted. "I feel guilty about this whole arrangement most of the time."

"Don't," Katie insisted. "You're doing a lot for him. God, you even drop off lunch for him and Ian every workday, and don't think I don't appreciate the fact that you come drop off something for me, too, in the tech lab. Just the fact that you're getting his house in order has to be valuable to him. It's an amazing place, but it's always needed more than to just be furnished."

Ben's home was just as spectacular as Ian's, but Katie was right. "It's sad that he only used it as a place to sleep," I commented. "It would be anyone's dream home. I'm not sure he's ever gotten into that beautiful pool or hot tub, and I don't think he's ever taken the time to notice that all he has to do is take a few steps outside and he's on the beach. I think the only rooms he used for years was the gym, the living room, his home office, and the master bedroom."

Katie shot me a speculative glance as she said, "It's almost spring. Maybe you should teach him how to appreciate that beachfront he owns, the pool, and most especially that hot tub before it gets too warm and humid."

I snorted. "What do you want me to do to convince him? Take off my clothes, jump in the jacuzzi, and tell him to join me?"

Katie chuckled. "I doubt very much if he'd mind if you did. He does come to the tech lab sometimes. I don't think he even realizes how much he talks about you, and he looks pretty damn happy with this whole arrangement. It's obvious that he cares about you, Ariel, and *not* just as a friend. I think you care about him, too."

I nearly choked on a sip of wine. "I do. But Ben does not want carnal knowledge of my body, Katie. He's just…a friend."

Everything had changed since the evening that Ben and I had sworn to be friends.

I no longer guarded my words. Well, unless those words had something to do with the way I wanted to get him naked.

Ben talked to me openly, too, and we had no problem teasing each other mercilessly at times.

Getting to know him as a friend in addition to being his employee had been both easy *and* complicated.

The problem was, the closer we got, the more difficult it was to hide my attraction to him.

I still felt that sexual tension in the air whenever we were together.

I'd almost gotten used to the never-ending longing, and the fact that we were just friends.

But there were times, especially when we were physically close, that I couldn't ignore it no matter how much I tried.

Dearest Protector

I'd thought that maybe treating him as a friend would keep my heart from stuttering every time I saw him.

It hadn't.

Because I liked him so much, the urge to be closer to him in a much different way had just gotten more powerful.

"Ariel Prescott, I've known you since we were kids," Katie admonished. "Don't try to tell me you're not interested in Ben as more than a friend. I can see it written all over your face, even though you're trying to hide it."

I swallowed a mouthful of wine and let out a long sigh. "How could I not be?" I asked. "He's ridiculously hot, successful, more intelligent than any guy should be, and extremely kind. But he's not interested in me that way, Katie. I know he cares about me, but Ben Blackwood could have any woman he wanted. I've never been beautiful, and my foot is a total mess. Some of my other scars from the accident have yet to fade, and other than anything that has to do with dancing, I'm completely uneducated. I didn't even go to college. I went straight from high school to a dance company in New York to continue training. I'm not nearly as worldly as some of the women he's probably dated, either."

"That's complete bullshit," Katie said with a frown. "You went to learn and perfect your dancing in New York on a scholarship that you earned, and you're far from unaccomplished. You're far more sophisticated and accomplished than I was when I came straight out of the university. Hell, you still are, even though you don't see that. You circulated with the rich and famous, Ariel."

I had. It had been part of my job to deal with donors and the rich fans of ballet, but… "Yeah, but I was never one of them, Katie. It was all…an act. I didn't live in that world."

"Furthermore," Katie continued, totally ignoring my comments. "You *are* beautiful and elegant. Do you have any idea how long I wished I was a gorgeous blue-eyed blonde with a slim body like yours? Thankfully, you're almost back to your normal weight. You already look much healthier."

I smiled. I had put on a few pounds, and could probably use a few more. Better nutrition had made me stronger, but even before the accident, I'd never been beautiful. "I never felt attractive unless I was in heavy stage makeup and dancing."

Makeup had transformed my look into something dramatic, and dancing well had made me forget that I was nothing special.

If I forgot that for a single second, my mother had always been there to remind me that I was worthless without ballet.

That I was nothing without my dancing ability.

That my nose was too big for my face.

That I was too pale.

That my lips were too full.

That my blonde hair was too curly and not straight and elegant.

That my posture was abysmal when I wasn't dancing.

That I wasn't smart enough to do anything *except* dance.

That every ounce of creativity I had needed to be focused on dancing because I had no other talents.

All those statements had stuck with me, and I swore they were ingrained in my psyche.

Maybe I was slowly learning that I could be more without dancing, and that I wasn't a totally ugly idiot without it, but it was hard to get over the things that had been ground into me since childhood.

Really hard.

"Then your self-esteem needs work," she observed. "Not that I have any right to judge since mine has always sucked, too, but you have a lot to offer any guy. And I have no doubt that Ben has noticed the same thing. He's a really good guy, Ariel. You couldn't do any better than my stepbrother."

I laughed. "You don't have to sell me on Ben Blackwood. He's ridiculously perfect. I noticed that before he and I met in person. He's incredibly photogenic, and women pant over him every single day."

"I don't see him chasing any of *those* women," Katie mused. "He's not interested. I think he wants a lot more than to just get laid. Like maybe, a woman he trusts? Or a woman he can talk to about anything and not feel judged? Or a female who looks at him without seeing dollar signs? It sounds to me like you two already have that. He's not superficial enough to give a shit about your scars. Any of them." In a softer voice, Katie added, "I know your mother was always critical, but she's gone now. She died before you went to New York. You sounded like you'd regained your confidence and sense of self after you got to New York. You became successful beyond your wildest dreams without her constantly nagging you. I thought you realized that you were beautiful and unbelievably talented without her constantly reminding you that your only asset was your dancing ability."

I shook my head slowly. "Maybe I did feel better for a while, but after the accident, all of the things she said came flooding back to me. Even though she's been gone for years, that voice is always present in my head."

Katie's face expressed her horror. "Well, she was wrong. She was *always* wrong. You're kind, smart, thoughtful, an amazing friend, and a woman who is as talented as she is beautiful."

God, I wanted to believe that, but those were things I'd never been able to internalize about myself, no matter how many times Katie had said them.

I let out a pent-up breath. "You've haven't seen my foot. It looks really bad."

"Then show me," she said stubbornly and waved me over to her. "We're best friends for God's sake. You don't ever have to hide it from me."

I balked even though I knew she was right. Katie had always been my biggest supporter. "It's nasty," I said, not moving from my position.

Katie stood, walked around the breakfast bar and into the kitchen. "I wish I could have been in New York more often. When I was, your injuries were mostly covered except for the laceration on your head. You looked worn out, but you were just as gorgeous as you've always been, accident or no accident. Scars or no scars. You're the bravest, strongest woman I've ever known."

Honestly, Katie was at the hospital with me more often than she should have been considering she'd had a waitressing job and a full-time workload at her university in Massachusetts.

She'd come to visit as often as she could to support me after the accident.

Still, she'd never seen all of my scars.

"Take my word on it, you don't want to see this foot," I said drily as she arrived at my side.

She put her hands on hips. "Seriously? Are you telling me you're going to walk around in socks in the summer in Florida? Bare it, sister. I never realized you were that self-conscious about it, but maybe I should have."

Yeah, wearing socks for the rest of my life had pretty much been my plan, even in the summer in South Florida.

No one needed to see my foot. It was painful for me to look at it myself.

"Katie, you know I've had more surgeries than I can count," I warned.

"Just take your damn sock off, Ariel," she demanded. "Would you want me to hide something like that from you? I should have asked to see it a long time ago."

I winced. We'd never hid much from each other. Ever. And I'd never want her to feel like she couldn't show or tell me anything.

I bent down and slowly took off my sock.

I lifted the leg of my jeans as she took in a sharp breath.

"I told you that it was ugly," I reminded her.

The crestfallen look stayed plastered on Katie's face as she dropped down to touch my mangled foot. "Oh, Ariel," she breathed out. "It's not ugly, but it does remind me of just how much you went through and how strong you are. They're just scars from your surgeries. You're not deformed, nor should you be walking around in socks all the damn time."

I let go of a sigh of relief, realizing I'd taken a small step forward by letting Katie see my foot, even if I thought it was horrifying.

Dearest Protector

"Are you really trying to tell me that this foot wouldn't scare any guy away?" I asked skeptically as Katie straightened up.

She looked me directly in the eyes as she replied, "Yes, that's exactly what I'm telling you. Those scars are just remnants of a horrible accident that you managed to live through. You battled your way through all those surgeries and then painful physical therapy to walk again. Every time you look at this foot, it *should* remind you of how far you've come after that accident. Does it still hurt?"

I couldn't be anything but honest with Katie as tears filled my eyes.

"Not really," I said. "It's just a little irritating sometimes. My doctor said I might need to get some of the hardware removed in the future, but I didn't have insurance, so I've waited to see a specialist. I can't think about that, Katie. I can't stand the thought of going back into surgery again."

Maybe the previous surgeries should have gotten easier with time, but they never had.

My time in the hospital had made me phobic about ever going back there again.

Tears started to flow down Katie's cheeks. She wrapped her arms around my shuddering body and squeezed.

"Yes, you can, Ariel. You won't be alone anymore. I promise. If that surgery has to happen, I'll be right there beside you. My situation is totally different than it was a year ago. There's no reason I can't stick to you like glue now. I wish you hadn't been alone in New York when all of the other surgeries took place. I completely understand why you're hesitant to ever do it again. I wish I hadn't been so strapped for money that I couldn't always get to you in New York, but it doesn't have to be that way anymore. Ben gave you medical insurance as part of your job, right?"

I clung to Katie more than I should have at the thought of doctors, hospitals, and surgery.

I wasn't sure how I'd ever force myself to walk into a hospital so soon after the terror of being confined to one for so long.

My road to recovery had been long, painful, and terrifying.

~ 75 ~

I choked back a sob as I finally released my best friend. "Please don't tell Ben," I pleaded. "I like this job, and I'll need recovery time and probably some physical therapy if they remove the hardware. I'd have to take time off work, and it's really not painful right now. I need some time to get up the nerve to do it, and I have things I still want to finish for him. And then there's the business I'm just starting. If nothing else, I do think there's a chance I can succeed at switching careers. I can't—"

"Ben would completely understand," Katie scoffed. "He's not about to fire you, Ariel. I'll give you one week before I put my foot down and make a doctor's appointment for you. If this needs to be done, it has to happen. Couldn't you end up with an infection if you don't?"

"It's possible," I waffled, trying to prolong the inevitable. "But not likely right now. I'd know if it was infected. The hardware is a little uncomfortable, and I've been noticing it a little more lately, but the removal isn't something that has to get done *right now.*"

"Then it should happen sooner rather than later so it never gets infected," Katie insisted. "Tell me the truth, are you okay financially?"

I'd already gotten two ridiculously large paychecks from Ben, and I wasn't paying much in expenses. "I'm good. Honestly. I'm not stretching the truth this time, I promise. I haven't had this much money in my bank account for a long time. It's not just the money, Katie. I'm happier than I've been in such a long time. I panic at the thought of going back into the hospital for anything."

That was the honest truth.

Maybe after my prolonged stint in the hospital, and with so many surgeries under my belt, it probably should feel routine to get the hardware removed from my foot. But it wasn't. It was frightening. I'd barely made it through my last surgery without having a complete meltdown.

I wasn't really *that* brave.

I'd had no choice back then but to continue my treatment, fear or no fear.

Katie wrapped an arm around my shoulders as she said earnestly, "We'll handle this together, Ariel. But you'll have to tell Ben. We'll all give you whatever support you need to finish this painful part of your life."

I nodded. "I just want it to be over. I want to put the past behind me. Just...give me a little time to deal with it."

I wanted just a little bit more freedom before I had to be laid up all over again.

"Not to change the subject, but have you ever considered counseling?" Katie asked gently. "You know I'm doing it to try to banish my issues from the past. It's helped tremendously, and if your insurance is anything like mine at Blackwood, it will cover the majority of the expense. I know someone good. Do you want me to give you her information?"

I surveyed my best friend for a moment, suddenly realizing how much she really had changed.

And it was much more than just having an amazing man in her life.

She was emotionally stronger, more confident in who she was, and comfortable in her own skin.

God, how I wanted that for myself, too.

I wanted to banish the ghosts of my past once and for all.

I slowly nodded. Maybe I could use some help to figure out who Ariel Prescott really was and what I wanted now that my dancing career was over. "Give me the info before you leave. I'll make an appointment. It certainly can't hurt."

Katie shot me an approving smile. "It will help, but honestly, you're stronger than you realize, Ariel. There aren't many women who could deal with what happened to them like you have."

Stronger than I realize?

Hell, someday I really hoped I could have as much faith in myself as Katie did.

Chapter 8

Ben

"Do you really think I can sell these limited edition prints for these prices?" Ariel asked doubtfully.

I watched her chew on her bottom lip as she looked over her website in preparation for going live tomorrow.

I'd taken her out to dinner to get her mind off her business launch, and now she was back at my house, fretting over her decisions as she sat on my living room sofa with her computer in her lap.

Fuck! I hated how unsure she was of her future success. Although her confidence was slowly improving, she still had no clue how good her artwork really was or how it touched people in a way that very few artists or photographers could.

Ariel saw the world in a very honest, vulnerable way that was expressed in every piece she created.

She didn't think about the things she created. They came directly from her heart and soul, which explained why she had so many fans.

She'd decided to start by loading a small collection of work to her website, even though I'd offered to foot the price of all the prints if

Dearest Protector

she wanted to begin with more. It was an offer that was quickly and adamantly refused.

Now, she was worried that the small collection she was putting on her site would never sell at the prices I'd talked her into asking for her work.

Hell, I honestly thought she could get double those prices, but I knew she'd never go for that right now.

She genuinely had no idea how amazing that artwork was, or how fast her followers were going to scramble to get one of those limited prints that she'd just received yesterday from a specialty printer.

"Yes, I think they'll sell," I told her firmly from my seat in a recliner. "I think you'd better get ready to order and load up some more. I'm glad I snagged a few of my favorites."

Not only had Ariel given me original pieces that she was never going to sell to anyone else, but she'd also gotten them framed and had put them on my walls.

I'd jumped at the chance to get one in particular, a piece she called *The Lonely Ballerina.* I couldn't look at the print now without sensing the emotion that had gone into the creation. The original digital image had featured only the back of a blonde dancer during a stage performance. I knew the performer in the original photo hadn't been Ariel, but I knew it was a self-portrait all the same. The costumed ballerina was electrifying and riveting, bathed in a very small circle of light, but her surroundings were stark and desolate.

I'd scooped it up immediately because of the vulnerability it had taken to create the image, and the emotion it would manifest in any viewer.

I'd needed to own it because of the personal emotion and creativeness that Ariel had put into it, and because I wanted to be the only one who saw the conflicting emotions that Ariel had experienced while she was working on the piece.

It was a heartbreakingly beautiful image that no one should own but…me.

Thankfully, it was now hanging in my home office.

I'd been even more grateful to own it when Ariel had told me that it wasn't a work that she would have ever sold to anyone else because it was so personal.

Maybe she only saw me as a friend, but at least she'd trusted me enough to share the image with *me*.

She was seemingly sharing everything with me now. She'd even informed me that she'd started counseling to work on sorting out some issues from her past. She'd also confided that she wasn't quite over the accident and the trauma it had caused, which was another reason she'd started working with a therapist.

It was humbling that she could allow me to see her vulnerabilities now, but it also made me feel guilty as hell that I was hiding a number of my own secrets from *her*.

It was rather ironic that her vulnerability made me even more protective of Ariel when I was actually the guy she should be watching out for because I wasn't being completely honest with her.

She was so fucking brave. She was confronting her fears head-on.

Meanwhile, I was still the coward who couldn't bring myself to tell her everything because I thought it was too soon.

I wished I'd been the one to suggest counseling in the first place, but it had been Katie who had encouraged her.

She shot me a dubious look. "You have to say that I'm going to sell like wildfire because you're my friend. And you know I'll always give you any print that you want."

Christ! There it was…that giving, innocent quality of hers that made me want her more than I'd ever wanted anything or anyone in my entire life. One of the things that had my dick hard every time I was with her and most of the time when I wasn't, too.

She'd become a hell of a lot more than just a friend to me. Maybe I'd never realized how much I needed Ariel until I'd seen her again, but my obsession with her grew stronger every single moment of every day.

I had to wonder just how long I could manage to keep my distance since it was getting more and more difficult as time passed.

Dearest Protector

The fact that I wanted more from her than just a fuck was the only thing keeping me sane at the moment.

Ariel was *mine*, and yeah, I wanted every man in the world to know it, but if I fucked this up, I'd be a sorry bastard for the rest of my life.

I shook my head. "I'm saying it because it's the truth. Stop worrying. Your social media followers are in a frenzy right now to finally be able to buy some of your work."

She snorted. "If I sell all of those prints, I'd be rich. I'd have enough money to take *you* out for dinner."

She wouldn't be rich. Not really. But it would definitely be a nice chunk of change to put into her bank account, which would make her feel more secure.

I'd never blow smoke up Ariel's ass, no matter how gorgeous that ass might be. Her skill was unique, priceless, and extraordinary.

She'd sell everything so fast that her head would swim.

The buzz for her work was real, constant, and continually growing on social media.

Her creations were stunning, riveting, and emotional. I'd been her biggest fan since I'd seen her portfolios for the first time a month ago.

"I accept that invitation. Where are you taking me for dinner?" I asked, teasing her to try to distract her from her anxiousness about her success.

In her case, worrying really wasn't necessary. I was willing to bet my entire company that she'd sell beyond her wildest dreams.

"If, by some miracle, I sell all of these prints, I'll take you anywhere you want," she said sincerely and shot me a nervous smile. "You get to decide."

Fuck! She absolutely meant that, which stunned me.

To her, it didn't matter if I was one of the richest guys in the world.

She'd happily spend her hard-earned money on me because I was her *friend*.

Would I let her do it?

No. There wasn't a chance in hell that I'd take anything from her that would reduce the amount of money she could spend on herself or save. Because we talked, because I knew her, I realized what having some security meant to her after everything she'd been through.

But just the fact that I knew she was willing to do that for me was enough to turn my guts inside out.

The way her mind worked fascinated the hell out of me.

She was the sweetest, most thoughtful, and giving woman I'd ever met.

That didn't mean she couldn't be stubborn as hell when she wanted to be or when she thought it was necessary.

Unfortunately, all of those traits, including her tendency to be obstinate when she was adamant about something, just seemed to get my cock harder. Even her occasional hardheadedness was sexy as hell to me.

In fact, there wasn't a damn thing about Ariel that *didn't* make my dick hard, which was unfortunate for me since I was currently securely entrenched in her friend zone.

My brows furrowed as I watched Ariel run a hand over her right foot for the third time since she'd sat down on the couch.

When it came to her, I was observant, and I'd never seen her do that before.

I nodded at her foot as I asked, "You okay? Is something wrong with your foot?"

Her head jerked up from her computer, and her expression changed to a deer-in-the-headlights look.

That was a sure sign that something was definitely *not* right, and she didn't want to tell me.

Okay, so maybe she *didn't* tell me *everything*.

I found that strange since she'd shared some fairly personal stuff.

She quickly let go of her foot as she said a little too brightly, "I'm fine."

Bullshit! She *wasn't* fine. I knew her well enough to spot a fabrication when I saw one. "Ariel," I said in a warning voice.

Her overly bright expression dimmed. "Okay, okay," she said grudgingly. "My injured foot is a little uncomfortable sometimes. I'm going to see a doctor tomorrow. It's not a big deal, Ben. I still have hardware in my foot from my surgeries for the fractures. It was crushed and broken so badly that they literally had to piece the bones back together. I think some of that hardware is intruding a little into a tendon. The specialist in New York mentioned it might have to be removed at some point. Maybe a year or so after the initial surgeries so it had enough time to completely heal. I'm getting close to that date. I won't know much until I see a doctor. I'm really sorry. I should have told you that I might need to take some time off to get that done, and I feel totally guilty about that because I haven't worked for you for long."

Christ! Why hadn't I known that earlier?

Like I gave a flying fuck about her taking time off?

I felt like I'd just been sucker-punched in the gut.

Did she really have no idea what my priorities were when it came to her?

If not, it was about time to make myself perfectly clear. Maybe I'd taken this whole *giving her some distance and acting like a friend* thing a little too far.

Screw the entire idea of staying impartial.

I didn't have that kind of control when it came to Ariel.

"Why in the fuck didn't you tell me that you weren't done with your medical treatment? You told me you'd gotten your follow-up care," I grilled her, pissed that I'd never dug deeper into her injuries.

I should have, knowing what I knew about her accident.

The powerful protective instincts I'd always had toward Ariel, the obsessive feelings that I'd managed to keep a handle on until right now, came roaring to the surface.

I hated all of the fucking pain Ariel had been through, but I couldn't keep ignoring it and telling myself it was over for her. It was beyond time for me to deal with the past, at least to some extent.

"I'm fine, Ben," she said in a soothing voice. "It's one last thing that will probably need to be done, and it usually takes a year to get to the point where the hardware can be removed. Technically, I did do all of my follow-up care."

Her rational response didn't help me at all.

"That doesn't mean that you shouldn't have been following up on this, goddammit!" I said impatiently, irritated with myself for not realizing that Ariel's medical treatment wasn't *completely* over. Her eyes widened at my tone, but I didn't give a shit. I was done trying to pretend that her well-being wasn't my first and only priority.

I moved over to the couch and sat beside her. I slammed her laptop closed before putting it on the coffee table.

Despite her protests, I swung her around so she could put her feet in my lap.

I suddenly realized that one other thing I should have noticed is that Ariel always—every moment we were together—had her socks on her feet.

"Either you take off these socks or I'm doing it for you," I told her gruffly.

"No," she squeaked, obviously alarmed. "It's just my right foot, and it's ugly, Ben. Really ugly."

I froze and slowly turned my head to look at her face.

"Do you honestly think I give a fuck what it looks like?" I rasped, trying to keep my tone measured so I wouldn't reveal just how irritated I was at the moment. "Do you really think I'm that damn superficial? We're supposed to be friends, Ariel. Do you think I care if you have scars from your surgery?"

Hell, I wasn't mad at *her*.

I was furious because this accident had happened to her in the first place.

I was also terrified that something else bad might happen to her if she didn't take care of this issue as soon as possible.

She shook her head. "I don't think that. I know we're friends. I don't want *anyone* to see it. Katie only recently saw it for the first time. It's not something I want everyone to see."

I scowled. "I'm not *everyone*. I'm your friend, the guy who doesn't give a shit about what your foot looks like. I just need to understand what you're dealing with, Ariel. I can't really understand if I don't see it."

Dearest Protector

Her scars from her accident were part of her, part of her past, what had made her into the incredible woman she was today.

Everything about Ariel was beautiful.

The only thing that bothered me about her having scars was the fact that she'd suffered a great deal of pain before those injuries had healed.

I pulled off her left sock first, and then her right.

Ariel's expression was filled with anxiety and horror, but she didn't fight me.

My gut tightened as my gaze stayed locked on her right foot.

Not because it was a horrible sight, but because it brought back way too many memories that I'd tried like hell and failed to scrub from my memory.

It reminded me of how much agony she'd obviously endured for months on end.

Most of the time, she'd gone through all that on her own.

Alone in the hospital with no one who really cared.

"I told you that it was ugly," she said in a soft, tentative voice that was barely audible.

She obviously did hate anyone seeing her scars, but I wasn't just *anyone.*

Maybe she didn't realize it, but I was the guy who wanted to comfort her more than I wanted to take my next damn breath.

I ran my hand over her injuries, as if I could absorb all the pain they had caused her.

"How painful is it exactly? And don't bullshit me, Ariel," I said through my clenched jaw.

"It's just irritating. It always has been. I think that's pretty normal, but as time passed, I felt the irritation of the hardware more," she replied in a matter-of-fact voice that I hadn't heard from her before.

She was trying to blow off the discomfort she'd probably experienced for months now, but that bullshit wasn't going to fly with me anymore.

And I wasn't going to pretend like it had never happened.

"Why haven't you seen a doctor before now? You can't tell me that your specialist in New York didn't suggest that you find a specialist here to keep an eye on this while it was healing," I questioned, trying to hold back my frustration.

I *needed* her to talk to me.

She sighed. "After I was injured, I lost my medical insurance. I had to officially quit the ballet after I finished my physical therapy and got my final prognosis. Maybe I should have followed up once I got to Florida, but I couldn't. Leland didn't offer me insurance. I was barely surviving, Ben. It wasn't a priority."

Rationally, I understood that.

But I was far from levelheaded at the moment.

"As of right now, *this* becomes priority number one," I said in a low growl.

She tried to tug her foot away. "I'll let you know what the doctor says."

I shook my head and refused to let her pull her feet out of my lap. "You won't have to. I'm going with you. How involved is the removal surgery?"

"Ben, my appointment is at four. You'll be working, and—"

"I'll be there with you," I interrupted. "The surgery?"

Fuck! I was going to lose it if I didn't get some answers.

"I don't know if they'll even do it right now," she said, her voice more relaxed. "If they do, I'm going to need a little time off work. I'm sorry."

If she apologized one more time, I was absolutely going to lose my shit. I'd show her exactly what I wanted from her, and how little I cared about what her scarred foot *looked* like.

"You'll get all the time off you need," I said tightly. "Is there anything else I should know?"

"No," she answered, her tone remorseful. "My foot has always been the biggest problem. Everything else healed months ago."

I finally turned my eyes away from her foot to meet her gaze, and it floored me when I saw that there were tears swimming in her beautiful blue eyes.

Dearest Protector

That completely gutted me.

Thoughts of my own displeasure suddenly fled. "Ariel? You okay?"

She shook her head slowly. "No," she croaked. "I think I've developed some kind of phobia when it comes to hospitals. I'm not sure I can go back to another one again this soon. I know that may sound silly since I was in the hospital for such a long time, and I've gone under anesthesia many times, but just the thought of doing it again terrifies me."

The raw, sheer terror in her gaze completely broke me.

Jesus! It wasn't hard to understand why that fear was so real for her.

She'd nearly...died.

She'd also been to hell and back in the hospital...all alone.

Ariel had done every single battle for her life *by herself.*

I knew Katie had gone to New York as often as she could, but other than the occasional visits from her best friend, Ariel *had* been on her own.

I gently dropped Ariel's feet from my lap and lifted her into my lap.

The need to be there for her, to physically comfort her, was something I couldn't ignore right now.

I closed my eyes as I wrapped my arms around her and felt her soft, pliant body against mine for the first time. I completely ignored the physiological reaction of finally having the woman I wanted more than life itself in my arms. Right now, my main objective was to shield her. Protect her. Alleviate the fear that was eating her alive. "It will be different this time, Ariel. I won't allow you to be alone or terrified all by yourself. Ever. Do you understand?"

I knew she was desperate for comfort as she willingly wrapped her arms around my neck and laid her head on my shoulder.

Ariel wasn't the type of woman who broke easily, but I could sense that she was currently at her breaking point.

I shuddered as I held her a little tighter and ran my fingers through her silky curls.

I savored being this close to her, yet I cursed the damn circumstances.

Mine!

This woman was *mine!*

Instinct had always told me that was true, but I'd never felt it clear to my bone marrow like I did right now.

Ariel was mine to protect and shelter from the fears that were gnawing at her psyche.

She always had been.

And this time, I was going to do it right.

I was going to be by her side every step of the way, the way I always should have been.

I didn't give a shit if the way I felt about Ariel didn't make sense right now in my analytical brain because it felt just as natural and just as necessary as breathing to me in this moment.

And I was never going to leave her alone when she needed me again.

Chapter 9

Ariel

Over the next few weeks, my relationship with Ben completely changed.
I couldn't hide *anything* from him.
He wouldn't allow it.
He not only encouraged, but he insisted that I share all of the details of my accident, both emotionally and physically, which was something he'd never done before.
A big part of me wanted to bury that painful time of my life, but it was also therapeutic to have someone who listened and concerned himself with my recovery like it was his own.
Ben never judged or made fun of my irrational fears of hospitals.
In fact, my long discussions with him about it made me feel almost…normal.
His constant presence at any appointment or diagnostic procedure was slightly uncomfortable at first, but I'd come to depend on him lending me some of his strength when I had none myself.

Having someone with me who cared when I had to go to the hospital for diagnostics and appointments had been the only thing that had propelled me through that damn hospital door.

My counselor had helped me talk through some of my fear, and I practiced my yoga and meditation every day.

But holy hell, every relaxation technique I'd tried flew out the window the second I saw that damn hospital.

Maybe Ben's extreme bossiness and tenaciousness should have irritated me, but it didn't.

The fact that he cared about me, worried about me, pretty much made up for his overprotective behavior.

Honestly, I was grateful that I was never alone.

Most likely, if I'd gotten *any* time alone during those appointments, my ass would have fled those medical facilities like it was on fire.

Yeah, it felt weird to have a constant, comforting presence beside me after fighting so many healthcare battles on my own, but it also felt good to know that Ben was *always* there for me.

Luckily, there was no infection to the bones in my foot, but the hardware had to come out because it was constantly irritating my tendon.

I still had over a week of freedom before I'd have to go under the knife again, thank God.

My fear of surgery was still highly irrational, but I was pretty sure I could get through it now because I'd have Ben and Katie there beside me this time.

"This is so amazing," I told Ben with a sigh as we relaxed in his hot tub after dinner. I'd just gotten my surgery date in the afternoon, but I wasn't sweating that information nearly as much as I would have been if I'd gotten the news alone. "I can't believe you didn't use it every single night in the winter."

I'd lost my discomfort about leaving my feet bare whenever he was around. Probably because he'd insisted that there were no socks allowed in his house unless my feet were actually cold.

Dearest Protector

I'd known that he was trying to get me used to not focusing on my foot and not seeing it as something ugly.

Strangely, his tactics had worked. The constant exposure to that horrible looking extremity had forced me into acceptance. Since I never saw a single sign that he found that foot offensive, I wasn't self-conscious anymore.

My body had filled out a lot because I'd been eating better, so I even thought that I looked okay in my black one-piece bathing suit.

Maybe I didn't fill the garment out like some big breasted, gorgeous females would, but I was slowly starting to be okay with the way I looked.

Granted, it had been difficult not to drool at Ben's muscular bare chest and torso when he'd walked outside in swim trunks earlier. I really wanted to fondle those six-pack abs of his, but knowing he didn't want more than a close friendship helped me keep my hands to myself.

For me, the longing to be closer to Ben hadn't faded over time. If anything, I yearned for it even more than I had before.

We had a tighter physical relationship because Ben comforted me whenever I got scared. He touched me sometimes, and he even held me in a calming embrace when I needed him. But that didn't mean he wanted carnal knowledge of my body.

Dammit!

The relentless desire to touch him, be even closer to him, was practically killing me.

Even in the dim light of his massive patio, just looking at him made me want to crawl inside him.

"I really never thought about taking the time to get into the hot tub before," he said with a nonchalant shrug. "There were always other things to get done when I was home."

I rolled my eyes. His sudden motivation to try out the massive hot tub had been all about me and my curiosity.

The only reason he was lounging in this hot tub right now was because of *me*. Because he thought it might chill me out.

~ *91* ~

"Do you ever do anything just because *you* want to do it?" I asked him, only partly teasing.

When Ben wasn't working he was focused on other people.

When he wasn't focused on other people, he was working like a maniac.

Did he ever give any thought to what *he* wanted to do?

He paused for a moment before he answered, "Not very often."

Why am I not surprised?

"You should," I advised. "I think you need to get selfish sometimes. Do something you really want to do just because *you* want it. Sometimes I feel guilty because you do way too much for me."

"I don't think you have the right to talk about that," Ben observed. "This house actually looks like a home now, and my home office has never been more organized. You make sure I eat well, and you've done all that on a foot that needs further medical treatment."

"That's what you pay me to do," I argued.

"You do far more than I pay you for," he balked.

"I'm your friend. I care about you," I told him.

"Ditto," he shot back.

I moved closer and slapped him on the shoulder. "Don't even try to pretend that what you're doing for me right now isn't extraordinary."

I sighed. Despite my protests, he'd already arranged to pay whatever didn't get paid by my insurance for my surgery and treatment.

While it was a relief that I wouldn't have that financial burden, it was kind of annoying that he took on that responsibility like it was his own.

Ben Blackwood had already saved my ass, and he was still doing it.

"I'll pay you back for all of this someday," I promised, grateful that I was selling my artwork like wildfire.

Ben had been correct, and he had no problem about smugly reminding me about that every single day since my website had gone live. I was going to need to upload more pieces, and eventually, I'd owe him that dinner I'd promised him as well.

Unfortunately, I was fairly certain he'd never let me actually buy him that dinner, no matter how much he teased me about it.

Dearest Protector

Things weren't slowing down for me businesswise, either. As people discovered my work on the net and through social media, my website got busier and busier.

Ben snaked an arm around my waist and pulled me close faster than I could blink.

"You've paid me back just by being in my life, sweetheart," he said hoarsely.

I shivered as our bodies made contact. God, I loved it when he used terms of affection with me, even though I knew he didn't mean it like a lover.

I wrapped my arms around his neck and closed my eyes, relishing every nanosecond of skin-to-skin contact.

It was literally torture not to touch him the way I wanted to touch him, but I savored his embrace anyway.

Maybe I was a fool to allow myself a moment of pure fantasy, but I craved Ben so badly that I couldn't stop myself from giving in to that temptation.

It was difficult being this close to Ben and not wanting…more.

His hard body was just begging to be explored, and my fingertips were itching to feel more than just the nape of his neck.

"Ben," I murmured in a needy voice before I could catch myself.

"Ariel?" he replied gruffly. "You okay?"

There it was, that constant habit he had of checking in with me that I completely adored.

He was always tuned in to my emotions. Always making sure that I wasn't in emotional or physical pain.

At moments like this one, we were so damn connected.

I felt like there was more to his concern than just being a friend, but I also knew that I was probably just trying to convince myself of that because I wanted it so badly.

Our gazes collided, and I could see the concern in his eyes, even though the light was sparse on the patio.

I'd seen that expression so many times over the last few weeks, and it still made me want to cry because it reminded me that I wasn't alone.

~ 93 ~

Ben…cared.

He gave a shit, even if it wasn't in exactly the way I wanted.

He ran a comforting hand up and down my back, and I had everything I could do not to rub against him like a cat in heat.

I wanted Ben Blackwood.

I had since the very first time we'd met.

And that longing was getting harder and harder to control.

I nodded to let him know I was okay, the lump in my throat keeping me from speaking.

I really needed to get a grip.

Even though I knew he cared, Ben didn't want me *that way*.

"Ariel?" Ben queried in a fuck-me baritone that sent a flood of heat between my thighs. "Do you really want me to do something I want just for myself, something selfish?"

I nodded again, puzzled by the heated look in his gorgeous hazel eyes.

The hand he had on my back moved up sensually until it was at the nape of my neck, and then urged my face closer to his.

My breath caught and my heart skipped a beat. We were so close that I could feel his warm breath on my lips.

My eyes fluttered closed.

Oh, God, yes. Kiss me.

How long had I wondered what it would be like to kiss this beautiful man?

Caught up in the moment, all I could do was feel, and I craved the touch of his lips on mine like a highly addictive drug.

"Then you're in big trouble, sweetheart," he warned in a throaty, lust-filled voice that I'd longed to hear since the first time we'd met. "Because the only selfish thing I want right now is *you*."

I had no time to think about his words.

His mouth covered mine so fast that there was no time to consider what we were doing.

He swallowed the moan of satisfaction that escaped from my lips as he plundered.

Dearest Protector

It wasn't just a simple embrace. Ben's kiss was total devastation, a conquering, a claiming that set every nerve ending in my body on fire.

He demanded, and I gave, opening to him like it was the most natural thing in the world to do.

Completely lost, I threaded my fingers through his damp hair and held onto him to ground myself.

I didn't just *want* this man.

I *needed* him, and I couldn't get close enough to satisfy that craving.

A whimper tried to escape from my throat, but Ben had total control, and nothing was going to stop his exploration of my mouth or his marauding tongue.

Not that I wanted him to stop.

I felt like I'd die on the spot if he suddenly ceased giving me this kind of pleasure.

I urged him onward, kissing him back with a fierceness that I couldn't contain.

Closer! God, I need to get closer!

I moved enough to straddle his body, and when I ground my hips against his groin in my attempt to fuse our bodies together, there was no hiding how much Ben wanted me, too.

His cock was big, hot, and so hard that it made me almost frantic to find out what it would feel like if he fucked me.

"Christ, Ariel, you're killing me," Ben rasped as he released my mouth so we could both take a breath.

"Yes," I panted as his lips trailed from my temple to the sensitive skin at my neck. "More."

Against all odds, Ben Blackwood actually *wanted me*, and I was drowning in the joy that knowledge gave me.

This was *better* than my fantasies, and I couldn't bear to lose the heady sensations.

My nipples were so hard that it was almost painful every time I moved against his bare chest, and my core clenched with a desperate need to get him inside me. It was the only thing that was going to satisfy the yearning that had swallowed me whole.

I reached between us, desperate to touch his cock, to explore the hard length of him.

"Don't," he commanded as he grasped my wrist, his voice harsh.

"I want to touch you," I whispered in a shaky voice full of desire.

"If you do, I'm fucked, and you will be, too," he said tersely against my neck. "And this is not going to happen like this. Relax, sweetheart."

How in the hell could I possibly relax?

My body was on fire, and Ben was the only one capable of extinguishing the flames.

He wrapped his arms around me protectively and just held me, staying immobile, his mouth near my temple.

I could feel the harshness of his breath against my face in a ragged tempo that matched my own.

I wasn't sure how long we stayed like that, Ben simply holding me tightly until my body stopped shuddering with desire.

Finally, once we were breathing normally again, he grumbled, "Be careful what you ask me to do next time. I might not be able to stop."

A few minutes later, he gently lifted me off his body, held out a hand, and helped me out of the hot tub like that earth-shattering encounter had never happened.

Chapter 10

Ariel

A half-hour later, the near silence between Ben and me was so uncomfortable that I wanted to weep. We'd been so close, but suddenly, it was as though we had absolutely nothing to say to each other.

We'd both showered and changed after we'd gotten out of the hot tub, and we were currently having a drink on Ben's patio in side-by-side comfy lounge chairs.

I had a glass of wine.

Ben had opted for something stronger.

It was a beautiful evening, and I could hear the sound of the waves lapping onto the beach.

The peacefulness of the night should have relaxed me, but the tenseness between the two of us made every muscle in my body tight.

Eventually, I couldn't stand it any longer, so I asked hesitantly, "Did I do something wrong?"

Ben turned his head and our gazes locked.

I couldn't really read him, but the intensity in his eyes stunned me.

Ben generally wasn't a broody type of guy, but he definitely had something heavy on his mind.

I was just hoping it wasn't regret over the fact that he'd kissed me like that in the first place.

For me, that embrace had been life-altering.

For Ben, maybe not so much?

"You did absolutely nothing wrong, Ariel," he said roughly, his eyes still glued to mine. "I fucked up. Why would you even think you did anything wrong?"

Flustered, words left my lips without even thinking about them. "God, I don't know. You're barely talking to me. I'm not exactly worldly when it comes to sex or making out, but I would have sworn that you wanted me, too. I don't have much experience. It's not like I've never been kissed or that I haven't messed around a little, but I've never had sex before. I don't really know what to do after I kiss a guy. I have no idea what turns you on."

That fiery expression of his turned molten as he asked huskily, "Ariel, are you saying that you're a...virgin?"

Great! Why in the hell did I just admit that to a guy that I really, really want to have sex with?

I felt like a total idiot.

Then again, Ben *was* my friend.

Yes, I wanted a lot more from him, but I couldn't discount how close we'd become or how much I valued him as a confidante.

"Yes," I confessed, and then broke eye contact because I was suddenly embarrassed to be telling a sophisticated guy like Ben Blackwood that I'd never had sex.

I was twenty-three years old. Most women my age weren't inexperienced. They'd been with multiple guys. They'd even been in multiple relationships. Some of the women I'd gone to school with were now married, engaged, or involved in a committed relationship.

"Why?" he asked in a graveled voice.

I sighed and said a little defensively, "Is it a crime that I've just never found anyone that I wanted that way? My entire life was

Dearest Protector

devoted to dancing. My schedule was so damn rigid that I never had time to really…date."

"Men had to be falling at your feet in New York," he stated.

I snorted. "I never looked down and saw a bevy of men at my feet. And I knew better than to date someone in my profession. If a relationship doesn't work out, you could end up dancing with your ex-boyfriend, which definitely makes your professional life uncomfortable. It's not a big deal. I'm not saving myself for marriage or something. I just wanted it to feel right. That just…never happened. Maybe that's weird at my age, but I never worried about it. I was perfectly capable of getting myself off. I've always had a pretty vivid imagination."

Ben reached out, snagged me around the waist and hauled me over to his chair and onto his lap.

"You didn't need to worry about it, and no, it's not a crime to be a virgin," he growled. "I'm just stunned that every man in New York wasn't trying to be the guy you wanted."

I still avoided eye contact with him as I shared, "They weren't. There are a lot of beautiful, well-educated women there, and I wasn't exactly seeking out a relationship. Dancing was emotionally and physically draining sometimes. I was usually more interested in soaking my aching feet after a really long day."

Now that I'd met Ben, I realized that my general disinterest in dating and sex in New York had nothing to do with my sore feet and busy schedule.

I would have wanted *him* under *any* circumstances.

But the man who could make me crazy with lust and need had never materialized while I was dancing.

He tilted my chin until I was forced to meet his gaze before he said, "I would have been fighting to be *that guy*. Nothing that happened between us was wrong, Ariel. Fuck knows I'm attracted to you, but I shouldn't have taken advantage of that moment. Not right now. You're still vulnerable from everything you've been through, and you still need to get through this upcoming surgery. Your artistic career is just starting to take off. It's just…fucked up timing on my part."

Relief flooded through my body as I realized he was telling me the truth.

He *was* attracted to me.

And that kiss had been more than just a momentary amusement for him, too.

I searched his face, but there was nothing except genuine emotion, albeit somewhat conflicted, in those beautiful hazel eyes of his.

"I don't care if the timing wasn't right," I said in a barely audible voice. "I could never regret what happened. That kiss was one of the best things that has ever happened to me. I never knew it could be…like that. You're right. Maybe it was bad timing because I'm not the woman I want to be yet, but I could never wish it had never happened, Ben."

If nothing else, Ben *was* my friend, and I couldn't tell him anything but the truth.

He ran a frustrated hand through his hair. "Fuck! I don't really regret it, either, even though I probably should."

Emboldened by his words, I also admitted, "I would have had sex with you and never regretted *that*, either."

He sent me warning glance as he said gruffly, "You should never tell a guy that."

I shrugged. "You're not just some guy. I care about you, and I've always told you the truth. You're also my friend, and I don't ever want to lose that."

Ben released what sounded like an irritated breath as his arm tightened around my waist. "I don't want to lose that, either, Ariel. But never doubt that I want a whole lot more than that. It's just not the right damn time for this."

He was right.

I knew that.

I wasn't completely healed emotionally from all the sudden changes in my life.

Ben deserved a woman who had her life and her head together, which I didn't. I might be getting closer to that healing every single day, but I wasn't…whole.

Dearest Protector

"On the other hand," he added roughly. "I doubt very much that I could tolerate seeing you date anyone else, either. If some other man ever touched you, I'd completely lose it."

My heart somersaulted inside my chest.

Like *that* was even likely to happen?

Ben Blackwood had turned my whole life and my emotions upside down. Never in my wildest dreams could I have even imagined he'd be interested in…me.

I put my palm to his cheek and savored that rough stubble beneath my fingers. "That's not going to happen," I assured him honestly. "I haven't thought about any other man except you. Not since the moment we met. Why do you think I'm still a virgin. You make me feel things I've never felt before."

His expression turned hopeful as he replied, "Damn good thing you haven't looked at another guy. I guarantee I wouldn't have handled that very well. This attraction isn't exactly new for me."

Okay, that surprised me. He'd never given me a single clue that he was physically attracted to me.

I smiled at him because I couldn't help myself. "Not new for me, either."

Maybe I still had a long road ahead of me, but knowing Ben might be there when I was done traveling that road made my heart soar.

"So friends for now?" I asked breathlessly. "Until I can get my life together again?"

He shook his head slowly. "This isn't about your state of mind right now or your circumstances. You've always been a beautiful, amazing woman. There's nothing wrong with you, but I do think you need your time to heal. And we're definitely friends. For now. Just promise me that I'll get my chance first before you decide you're ready for a relationship."

Really? Did he honestly think I could just turn this connection between us off and on that easily? Maybe some women could, but not me. "I promise."

I sighed. I knew I didn't have the mindset to be a good partner to him at the moment. I had a surgery to get through, a business to focus on, and issues to conquer in counseling, but once I felt like I could be the equal partner Ben needed, I'd be there for him in a heartbeat asking for more.

Until I could be more than a broken prima ballerina, I'd suck at being a girlfriend, especially to someone like Ben Blackwood.

"All I really want is to be with you, Ben," I said honestly. "I don't want anything else. Just...be with me."

I couldn't ask him to wait for me until I could put all of the pieces of myself back together again, but I secretly hoped that he would.

"I'm not going anywhere, Ariel," he replied hoarsely as his arms tightened around me. "In fact, I'm hoping that after you recover from your surgery, you'll quit this gig as my assistant so you have more time to work on your business. Maybe you still don't believe it, but this career is going to fly for you. And I'll be here to help financially and emotionally until it does. Let me help you find your new dream."

I blinked back the tears that were forming in my eyes.

I was enormously torn.

God, yes, I wanted to pursue my fine arts photography. It was my heart's desire now, and I needed more time to make a full-time income, but the money *was* coming in. I was starting to believe I could actually make it my next career.

All because of Ben.

Still, I hated to take advantage of Ben's generosity in order to make my new career fly.

If my work is ever going to support me, I might have to agree to let him help me for a little while.

Really, I wouldn't need to take a handout from him monetarily. I was used to living on a budget, and if things continued like they were now with my business, I could easily survive. All I'd really need was the use of his condo.

He'd always been willing to give me his emotional support.

And God, I really *needed* to feel like a whole person again.

Really, wasn't he already assisting me by giving me this job in the first place?

Maybe I had helped him make his house more like a home, and lightened his load, but my position wasn't something critical to him.

I could still help him out as much as possible while I was building my own business, right?

"Only if you agree to let me keep helping you out," I said, my mind made up.

He frowned. "Helping me out how…exactly?"

I could tell he wasn't crazy about my idea, but Ben was a fixer, and right now all he wanted to do was help me get through my surgery.

Well, that's just too bad, Mr. Blackwood, because the only way I'll agree to this uneven proposal is if you let me do something for you.

"Cooking dinner. Bringing you lunch sometimes. Making sure you're taken care of personally, too," I insisted. "You don't need to pay me to do those things, but I'll probably need the condo for a while if that's okay with you. Your business is a lot more brutal than mine right now, and you never stop to do anything that's good for you."

"I'll consider it after you can get around while you're staying with me," he mused. "The condo will be there for as long as you need it. But you're not lifting a damn finger until you're on your feet again physically."

My eyes widened as I asked, "Staying with you?"

He lifted a brow. "Surely you didn't think I was going to let you stay alone in your condo after your surgery. You won't even be able to bear weight on your foot or drive for two weeks, Ariel. After that, you still have to be extremely careful. I've already informed Ian that he's on his own at the office for a while. I'm taking some time off to take care of you after your surgery. I'll work remotely if necessary, but I'm not going into the headquarters. The whole idea is to have someone with you in case something happens while you're laid up."

My mouth dropped open, and I simply stared at him in astonishment.

"That's completely non-negotiable, Ariel," he added in a no-non-sense voice. "You cannot be by yourself at your condo after your surgery."

"I'll have crutches. I can get around, Ben," I argued, still flabbergasted that he'd actually planned on taking time off and putting up with a helpless houseguest.

"Not happening," he said in a graveled voice. "You're staying here where I know that you're okay. I even have a damn elevator. And you can do your post-surgery physical therapy in my home gym. I already set it up."

"You're absolutely insane," I told him.

Maybe I should be pissed that he'd made all of my recovery plans for me already, but it felt so good to have someone care about me that much that I really wasn't angry.

Ben wasn't a control freak.

He was motivated by fear of something happening to me.

After being pretty much alone in the hospital in New York, and then worrying about how I was going to get around on my own there, it hit home how much my life had changed since then.

Ben cared.

Katie was close by and in a situation where she'd be around much more often, too.

It would make all the difference in the world.

And I was so grateful that I wanted to cry.

"If you refuse, then I'll be at your condo all of the time, and I'll be sleeping in your spare bedroom," Ben warned. "It would make my life easier if you don't get stubborn about this. I have a well-equipped and very well-organized home office now, thanks to you. It would be a lot less complicated for me if we were here."

An errant tear spilled onto my cheek as I stared at his handsome face and obstinate expression.

Ha! And this man had the audacity to call *me* stubborn sometimes?

I nodded slowly. "Okay," I said in an emotional whisper. "But I'll return the favor someday."

Truth was, I actually had been a little fearful after all of my previous struggles with immobility alone in New York.

I dreaded this upcoming surgery, but knowing Ben would be there made it a hell of a lot easier to face.

Dearest Protector

Ben's eyes softened as he kissed me on the forehead and commented simply, "Sweetheart, maybe you don't realize it right now, but you've already paid me back."

Chapter 11

Ben

I'd taken a long run on the beach after I'd walked Ariel safely back to her condo, but I was still so fucking edgy that I couldn't sleep.

I stepped into the shower, wondering what in the hell I'd been thinking when I'd decided to kiss Ariel like a man starving for sustenance.

We were supposed to remain strictly friends until Ariel was in a better headspace and until I could finally drum up the nerve to tell her the whole truth.

Her sweetness and those damn beautiful, ocean blue eyes had gotten to me.

After that, her soft curves and luscious mouth had completely destroyed me.

Fuck! I'd wanted Ariel Prescott since the first second I'd seen her, and that want had turned into a relentless obsession since that day.

Stronger.

Harder.

More tormenting every single day.

I hadn't told her the truth, either, and until I did, I had no business starting any other kind of relationship with her.

Dearest Protector

As every opportunity to tell her about our first meeting had passed by without me saying anything, I knew I was digging myself deeper into a hole I wouldn't be able to climb out of again.

I have to let her get through this upcoming surgery first. After that, I'll tell her.

She didn't need any additional stress at the moment.

Yeah, asshole, then maybe you shouldn't have kissed her in the first place.

It wasn't like I hadn't known that once I'd touched her, I'd be completely screwed.

Still, I'd given into temptation, dammit!

Now, I had no idea how I was going to go back.

I couldn't put that fucking horny genie back in the bottle again.

I'd at least needed to make my intentions clear so she'd never think I didn't want her.

Just the thought of her going out with another guy made me feel like a lunatic.

Virgin! Virgin! Virgin!

I forced myself to listen to that chant in my head like it was actually going to make a difference, like it was going to keep me from ever touching her again in the near future.

It wouldn't.

All I could think about now was the fact that I was going to be the man who taught Ariel about carnal pleasure someday.

I'd be her first.

Damned if *that* didn't give me some kind of crazy, primal, and intense caveman satisfaction that I didn't fucking understand.

Not that it really mattered if Ariel *had* been with other men before me.

I'd be just as determined as I was now to be her *last and only* from this day forward.

I scrubbed my hair a lot harder than I needed to wash it. Maybe I wanted to punish myself for ever laying my hands on her.

"Friends, my ass," I grumbled.

That wasn't going to fly for long.

Ariel was mine, and I wanted to claim her.

I'd eventually tell her the truth, and then I'd prove to her that no other man could possibly ever care about her and fucking adore her the way I would.

And then what?

I was assuming that she'd be okay with the fact that I'd been concealing something important.

There was no telling what Ariel's reaction would be when I did find the balls to tell her the truth.

And how long could I keep my dick in my pants when I was around her?

It would be easy while she was recovering from surgery.

But after that…?

"Son of a bitch!" I spat out as I rinsed my hair.

Hell, who was I fooling? I'd do whatever was necessary not to hurt her, even if my balls did turn blue.

She was still fragile.

She was worried and afraid of her upcoming surgery.

She'd had way too much pain in her life already.

Virgin! Virgin! Virgin!

Nope! That idiotic chant still wasn't helping.

Someday, Ariel Prescott *would* be mine, even if I had to wait to make that happen.

Any other possibility was intolerable to me.

That casual little comment she'd made earlier about getting herself off certainly hadn't helped my peace of mind.

Immediately, I'd seen that fantasy play out in my head.

Over and over again.

And God help her if she'd managed to reach my cock before I'd stopped her in the hot tub.

All of the promises I'd made to myself that I wouldn't take advantage of her vulnerability would have flown away in the breeze once her fingers had wrapped around my dick.

I needed her.

Dearest Protector

And every primal instinct inside me when it came to Ariel had been urging me to satisfy her, morals and scruples be damned.

I let out a strangled groan of frustration as I wrapped my hand around my cock.

Every muscle in my body was tight as I stroked up and down the shaft.

I closed my eyes, and my head hit the shower enclosure with a loud *thump.*

My thoughts immediately focused on an image of Ariel, completely naked on her bed, stroking herself to climax. It was an erotic fantasy that had been haunting me all evening.

I wondered how long I'd be able to watch that happen in my mind before the primitive urge to satisfy her myself would take over.

Or...maybe I wouldn't interrupt.

Maybe I'd just be an observer because watching her reach her orgasm would be the most riveting sight I'd ever seen.

Christ! She was beautiful for so many reasons, and not all of them had to do with her curly blonde hair, her supple body, those amazing baby blues of hers or those plump lips that I desperately wanted wrapped around my cock right now.

Yeah, I wanted her like I'd never wanted any other female, but the attraction went well beyond physical desire.

I wanted to fucking claim her, protect her, and make sure she never knew another moment of pain or uncertainty in her life.

My hand got rougher on my dick as I imagined Ariel, her fingers in her wet pussy, running over and over her clit.

Of course, while she was doing that, she was thinking about me and only me.

Hell, it was *my* fantasy. I could imagine whatever the fuck I wanted.

And I did. I let my imagination run wild.

She was thinking about how good it would feel if I had my head between her thighs, eating her out until she was on the brink of her climax.

"Ben," I imagined her moaning, her head thrown back, her fingers moving faster over her engorged clit.

She was hungry. She needed satisfaction, and my girl was going to get it one way or the other.

A thin sheen of perspiration was making her skin glow, and her race to satisfaction was etched into her expression.

Christ! She was fucking stunning, and the way she went after what she wanted made my cock twitch as I jerked harder and harder on my cock while my sexual fantasy continued.

Her hips moved as her desire took hold of her body, her small but perfect breasts bouncing up and down as she writhed on the sheets, lost in her fantasy about…me.

Wanting…

Needing…

Me!

"Fucking hell!" I cursed out loud, wanting to insert myself into the image as she thrust a finger into what I already knew was her very tight pussy.

"Ben!" she crooned, and my balls tightened.

"Go after it, sweetheart," I demanded, fisting my cock harder to do the same.

She fingered her clit faster and faster, until suddenly, she broke.

Her back and neck arched, and the tormented expression on her face turned to total ecstasy.

"Oh, God, yes, Ben. I'm coming," she screamed.

"Me, too, beautiful," I groaned back to her artificial image.

As I watched Ariel tilt over the edge in my mind, I went with her, coming harder than I could ever remember.

Maybe it was somewhat twisted that a fantasy about Ariel was better than any of the sex I'd ever had, but for once in my life, I definitely wasn't in control of the way I felt.

My chest heaved as I tried to hold onto my fantasy Ariel, but she faded away as I caught my breath.

I turned and slammed my fist against the shower enclosure. "Not. Real," I said in a tormented voice. "Not. Fucking. Real."

Dearest Protector

The irritating voice in my head cajoled. *It could be! She's willing!*

"Not. Yet," I argued back.

As much as I wanted her body, I still wanted…more.

With Ariel, I had to have it all.

Then you'll have to tell her the truth!

Disgusted about arguing with *myself* like I was a crazy bastard, I ignored that taunting voice and cleaned myself up before I stepped out of the shower.

No more fantasies about Ariel.

That shit was dangerous.

I toweled myself dry and tossed the towel into the hamper before I made my way into my bedroom.

I got into my bed, determined to get some sleep since I had an early meeting in the morning at Blackwood.

But I still didn't sleep.

My eyes stayed wide open as I stared toward the ceiling.

I desperately wondered how in the hell a guy told a woman he cared about that everything that had happened to her, all the pain she'd been through, was essentially *his* fault.

Chapter 12

Ariel

I knew I was dreaming.

Yet I couldn't yank myself out of my slumber.

I was familiar with this particular nightmare, but I hadn't experienced it since I'd first gotten out of the hospital.

The dream always began and ended the same way.

I was laying on the pavement, trying to breathe, right after I'd gotten hit by the taxi.

The ambulance was coming.

All I had to do was keep breathing until the paramedics arrived.

"Talk to me. Stay with me. Talk to me, Ariel," a deep baritone voice cajoled, preventing me from falling into the darkness that was beckoning.

The pain was so excruciating that all I wanted to do was fall into the welcoming abyss.

But fear and that calming voice kept me awake.

"I can't see. Everything is blurry. Can't breathe. Am I going to die?" I asked, my voice weak and wheezy.

Dearest Protector

I'd voiced the question, but I wasn't sure I really wanted an answer.

Somehow, even though I was confused and in more pain than I'd ever experienced, I could sense that I was teetering on the brink of death.

The sense of impending doom was undeniable.

The body that matched that soothing voice bent over me. I could feel his warm breath on my face as he said, "You're hurt. I'm not going to lie to you. But you are not going to die."

Strangely, I felt better because he was telling me the truth about my injuries.

Was he lying about the not dying part of it though?

I could hardly breathe, and I wanted to sit up to help get oxygen to my lungs, but gentle hands held me in place.

"Don't move," the voice demanded. "If your neck and back are injured, you could make things worse. Just breathe, Ariel, and stay with me."

I wanted to tell him I couldn't breathe.

I wanted to tell him that I'd never felt this kind of pain.

I wanted to tell him that I'd never been so terrified in my entire life.

In the end, I simply gasped, "Hurts! Bad!"

"I'd be shocked if it didn't," he said brusquely. "But the medics are coming. Just hang in there and breathe. That's your only job right now. Understand?"

It helped, him telling me what I needed to do because I couldn't put two thoughts together on my own.

I breathed.

In.

Out.

In.

Out.

In.

Out.

"Good girl," he crooned in a low baritone, putting his face closer to mine so I could hear him.

I couldn't make out his face because my vision was so blurry, but his words were comforting.

I knew every breath I took was short and shallow, but I kept working to get air in and out of my lungs.

"Scared!" I managed to huff out between those shallow breaths.

"I know," he said in deep, rumbly voice full of concern. "But I'm here with you, Ariel. I'm not going to leave. I'm going to stay right here and remind you to keep breathing. We'll get through this together, okay?"

I didn't know who this person was or how he knew me.

All I knew was that his gruff, reassuring voice was my lifeline, my only grip on sanity.

"Don't. Go," I gasped, desperate to hold on to the only thing keeping me conscious.

"I'm right here," he said reassuringly next to my ear. "Just keep breathing, and stay with me, Ariel."

I felt gentle fingers on the pulse at my neck as I kept breathing.

In.

Out.

In.

Out.

Oh, God, it hurt like hell to breathe.

The sharp pain in my chest and shoulder nearly made me pass out with every inhalation.

Still, because he told me to do it, I breathed as deeply as possible.

"You're doing great, Ariel. Keep going," he encouraged.

I didn't want to.

Everything hurt so damn bad that I wanted to give up.

"Don't do it," he commanded as my eyes began to flutter closed. "Stay with me."

The alarm in his voice made me open my eyes with a painful groan.

He was no more than a blurry form above me, but something made me want to stay connected to this voice.

I didn't want to leave him, and even worse, I didn't want him to leave me.

"You're. Bossy," I said, every word excruciating.

His warm hand held my neck and head still, and I felt gentle fingers brush the hair from my forehead. He leaned close to my ear and warned, "I'll do whatever it takes to keep you with me until the ambulance gets here."

He would.

I could sense it.

And knowing he was here, willing me to keep breathing, was more comforting than he'd probably ever know.

"Thank fuck! I can hear the sirens," the voice informed me.

In moments, I could hear them, too, as they came closer and closer.

Rather than relief, the only thing I felt was sheer terror.

I needed that voice.

I needed this man's reassuring presence.

"Don't. Go," I said again as I tried to lift a hand to reach for the male form towering over me.

He instantly took my hand and threaded our fingers together. "I'm going to need to fall back so they can do their work. But I won't leave, Ariel."

"Promise!" I insisted in a weak voice.

"I promise," he said huskily as he squeezed my hand gently. "I'll be right here. Let them take care of you. I'll stay close."

Suddenly, the paramedics were there.

Finally, I closed my eyes, and the mystery man let go of my hand as EMS took over.

Organized chaos ensued, but I sensed that even though I could no longer hear him, that my voice of reason hadn't gone far.

God, I really hoped I was right and he hadn't left me…

I sat up, gasping for breath as I awakened.

Shit! Shit! Shit!

I swiped my hand over my face, trying to wipe the dream about what had happened after I'd been hit by that taxi out of my memory.

I took a deep breath.

And then another.

No pain.

I was awake, and I could breathe perfectly normally.

It had been so long since I'd dreamed about what had happened that day.

Why now?

I ran my hands up and down my arms, suddenly cold and afraid, even though I had no reason to be anymore.

I slowly calmed myself, waiting until my pulse had stopped hammering in my ears so I could think clearly.

Yes, I knew a supposed bystander had been on the scene with me right after the accident.

He'd helped stop the bleeding by cutting up his own shirt and bandaging some of my wounds that were bleeding profusely.

I'd had so little blood left in my body after that initial bleeding that the Good Samaritan had probably helped save my life.

He'd kept me calm during my confusion. He'd kept me from hurting myself even worse by keeping me still. The taxi driver had given a thorough statement about the events that had followed the impact.

The police had helped me fill in the blanks as much as possible with the driver's testimony.

Still, I had no idea exactly what had really transpired right after that accident. All I knew is what I'd been told.

The dream I'd just experienced, a dream that I'd had frequently in the days after the accident, was probably nothing more than my imagination.

I knew the basics from the police, but I really didn't *remember* it.

Obviously, when I was asleep, my subconscious wanted to fill in the blanks.

In reality, my actual memory was a total blank about that period of time right after I'd been hit by a taxi.

Dearest Protector

Later, while I was healing, I'd wanted to thank the man who had apparently helped me, but no one had gotten his name.

Apparently, he'd said he was family, so the medics had let him ride with me to the hospital.

Unfortunately, he hadn't stayed long enough at the hospital for the police to catch up with him and question him, too.

Everything I knew about the mystery man was due to thirdhand information.

Hell, I didn't even know if I'd really spoken to him or what he had really said on the scene.

I sighed and rolled out of bed to use the bathroom.

For the most part, I was okay with the memory lapse.

Honestly, I hadn't really wanted to recall *anything* about the accident that had nearly taken my life and robbed me of a long career as a ballerina.

Not back then.

It had hurt too much, and it was too traumatic to dwell on.

But now, I had to wonder if, deep down, there was a part of me that *wanted* to know the truth.

It would probably be a hell of a lot better than dreaming about something that had likely never occurred.

I reached for the light switch in the bathroom and flipped it up.

Crazy as it might seem, that soothing presence I'd conjured up in my dream reminded me an awful lot of...Ben Blackwood.

I shook my head as I saw my own baffled image in the bathroom mirror, and nixed that thought almost as quickly as it had floated through my mind.

What in the hell was wrong with me?

That had to be the most ridiculous thing I'd ever imagined in my entire life!

Chapter 13

Ariel

"Thanks for all of the distractions this week," I told Ben as we walked on the beach the Saturday evening before my surgery.

I was now settled into one of several suites in his home, with everything I could possibly need for the next…year or so.

Honestly, the amount of stuff he'd hauled over to his place was ridiculous, but I knew he was trying to make sure I'd be as comfortable as possible.

"I have no idea what you're talking about," he answered nonchalantly and grabbed my hand as I stumbled just a little.

It was pretty dark out on the beach, but I'd wanted to be outside as much as possible since I'd be confined to the indoors after my surgery on Monday.

The weather had totally cooperated with my wishes.

It was hot for early spring, and had been all week long.

We'd used that gorgeous pool of Ben's after work yesterday, and I'd probably be in there all day tomorrow if I could swing it.

Dearest Protector

I let out an exasperated breath as I walked beside him. "Please," I said drily. "You've either been home early from work every day or on time. You've taken me out for two movie nights and we had a pool night last night. You've also taken me out for dinner twice. I know they're distractions so I don't have time to think about the surgery Monday morning. Admit it."

"Nope," he said succinctly. "I would have taken you anywhere you wanted to go, regardless. They weren't necessarily *distractions*."

I bumped his shoulder in reply.

Yeah, he probably would have taken me anywhere I wanted to go. But it hadn't been me who had suggested these evening outings.

His desire to make me forget that I was going under the knife on was glaringly obvious.

"But," he added. "If these were, in fact, supposed to be distractions, are they working?"

I snorted as I let him change directions so we were headed back toward his house. "I knew it," I said with a chuckle. "They were distractions, and yes, they're working. It's been a very entertaining week. Now can I thank you for them?"

"Not necessary," he said abruptly. "We're friends. You'd do exactly the same for me."

I definitely would, but I wasn't Ben Blackwood, busy CEO of Blackwood Technologies.

I knew it wasn't easy for Ben to break away from work, but he was doing it.

Every day.

For me.

And he never accepted a thank you for any of the nice things he did.

"It is necessary," I argued as I relished the feel of the cool water on my bare feet. "I never want you to think I don't appreciate you or the things you do for me. This whole surgery thing is a major inconvenience for you."

He suddenly stopped and turned me toward him, his hands on my shoulders as he growled, "Don't ever say that. You are not and never will be an inconvenience. Ever. Christ! I care about you, Ariel. I care what happens. I care if you're in pain or uncomfortable."

His fierceness threw me off-guard for a moment, but it probably shouldn't.

This was Ben, and going out of his way for someone he cared about was never a pain in his ass.

I couldn't see his eyes. In fact, I could barely make out his face in the dim light, but I knew from his tone of voice that he was tense.

Sometimes, I got the feeling he was almost more worried than I was about my upcoming procedure.

"I'm sorry," I said, instinctively reaching out to run my palm along his jaw. "I shouldn't have said that. You've never made me feel that way. I guess I'm just not used to having someone this supportive beside me. I've never had to rely on someone to help me get through fear. I'm probably not comfortable with it, either, even though I couldn't have gotten through this without you. I'm used to taking care of myself."

It felt amazing to have someone care about me, but there was also a part of me that felt incredibly...guilty.

He put his arms around my waist and tugged me close to his hard body.

I relaxed and put my head against his shoulder.

"Get used to someone giving a shit," he grumbled and ran a rough hand through my curls. "It's not something I can control when it comes to you. You make me a little crazy sometimes."

I smiled against the thin cotton of his shirt, knowing he meant every word he said.

This whole situation seemed to be driving him crazy, and that's probably why I felt so guilty.

I put my arms around his neck and hugged him, wishing he'd kiss me again, but I knew that wouldn't happen.

Other than his concern about my well-being, Ben had a tight rein on his emotions right now.

He was incredibly affectionate, but he hadn't let things get out of control since that night in the hot tub.

Dearest Protector

Rationally, I knew it was better if he didn't kiss me, but I couldn't help myself from wanting...more.

"I care about you, too, Ben," I murmured against his shoulder before I reluctantly released him and continued walking. "I just really wish you'd let me thank you once in a while."

He kept a tight grip around my waist as he replied grumpily, "Someday, I'll be more than happy to let you thank me. But not with words."

My heart skipped a beat, and I nearly tripped over a small rock on the sand...again.

Luckily, I didn't go far since he had a firm hold on me.

Shit!

He couldn't just say those kinds of things to a woman and expect her not to react.

I took a deep breath and let it out slowly.

Things had changed since Ben had kissed me.

Yeah, we could still be friends. We could still banter like buddies and have a good time. We could talk about nearly anything.

But now there was always an underlying electricity and heat that smoldered between the two of us whenever we were together.

Sometimes, I could manage to ignore it because I knew nothing could happen.

Other times, I just couldn't forget it was there beneath the surface.

I didn't know if Ben felt the same way, but I had to assume that he felt it, too.

It really made me want to get my shit together sooner rather than later so we could explore that attraction more thoroughly.

Financially, my situation was definitely improving.

My work was drawing more attention, and I'd just received a larger batch of prints for a bigger selection of my work that I'd uploaded to my website.

I'd also added more work to my portfolios now that I was more relaxed and inspired to create.

Just recently, I'd even been offered large sums of money for commissioned pieces.

"I officially owe you dinner next time," I informed Ben. "I sold the last of my original uploads today. I just finished putting up a larger collection. I can hardly believe I sold them all so fast."

"I knew you would," he answered smugly. "There was never a doubt in my mind."

I sighed. "I have to admit, I had my doubts. Now, I get up every single day thinking about what I can create next instead of worrying about how I'm going to eat. I won't thank you because I know what you'll say, but my life has changed so enormously, Ben, in such a short amount of time."

"Are you happy?" he queried.

"Yes," I answered honestly.

I was so happy that it was almost frightening.

Despite my counseling, which was helping, part of me was just waiting for the other shoe to drop.

Maybe that was ridiculous, but for a woman who had struggled a lot over the last year, maybe it wasn't so weird that I felt that way.

"That's really all that matters," Ben replied as he cut away from the water and headed up the beach toward his home.

I opened my mouth to remind him that being happy wasn't my only concern. That I had to make enough money to eat and pay my bills long-term, but I closed my mouth again without speaking those words.

My work *would* pay for all of my bills and more very soon if I stayed on the same trajectory.

Maybe my problem was that I was never taught that my personal happiness really mattered, but Ben was right. It *did* mean something.

I'd spent my entire life trying to be more, do more, reach for more.

Happiness had never really been part of the equation for me.

I wasn't supposed to be happy.

I was supposed to be successful as a dancer.

All my life, I'd put everything else aside to reach the top of that never-ending ladder of success one rung at a time.

I'd never really thought about what would happen after that because there was no end to the rungs I could climb in my former career.

Dearest Protector

I'd reached a certain platform by being a principal dancer in Swan Lake in New York, but there would have been other mountains to conquer after that.

Nowhere in my schedule had there ever been time to be happy, even when I'd reached a goal.

"I'm not sure I even knew what real happiness was before," I mused, sharing my thoughts with Ben.

His brows furrowed as we arrived on his patio.

He pulled out a chair at the table and motioned for me to sit as he requested, "Explain that."

I smiled as I watched him grab us both a water from his outdoor fridge before he sat down next to me.

Ben knew about most of my past and my childhood. He knew about my mother and her constant criticism.

He listened now as I tried to explain my currently jumbled thoughts. I tried to sort them out as I told him what I'd been thinking.

"I had absolutely no balance in my life," I finished after telling him everything I'd been thinking about on our way back to his house. "Do you understand?"

He frowned. "I get it," he confirmed. "And I think you already know how unhealthy that was. You had no childhood, Ariel. No young adult or new adult life. Just work and that constant pressure to be more and do more. Maybe I have no room to talk since I let myself get caught up with work after Ian's accident, but I had a great childhood and early adult life. And now that Ian is back, I'm slowly learning to relax a little more, especially now that I have you in my life. Now, I want to be someplace other than work all the time."

My heart squeezed until I was almost breathless.

It was hard to believe that I was Ben's motivation to slow down and enjoy life a little more, but I'd happily accept what I considered a major compliment.

I shrugged. "Maybe we both deserve a little more balance. Maybe we both deserve to be…happy. I nearly died, Ben, and the only thing I could have said about my life was that I'd danced the principal role in Swan Lake. I'm not saying that wasn't a great achievement, but other than Katie, there was no one in my life who would have actually missed me if I had died on that pavement that day."

It was a sobering thought, and one I'd never really considered.

For the first time in my life, reaching the pinnacle of work success wasn't my priority anymore.

Yeah, I had to meet my financial obligations, but I wanted so much more than that now.

"Don't say that," Ben growled.

"It's true," I argued as a tear rolled down my cheek. "But I plan on changing that. I want to enjoy life. I want to learn to live in the moment. I want to know more people who will genuinely care about me, and I want to give that caring back to them. After nearly losing my life, it's not enough for me to live on ambition anymore. I've been without family and people who care about me for a long time."

Ben scooted his chair right up next to me, wrapped a strong arm around my shoulders and pulled me against his strong form as he said huskily, "I once told Katie that you can make your own family and that blood wasn't everything. I meant that. I'm lucky. I have an amazing mother and older brother, but I also have Katie now, who's like a little sister to me. Blood doesn't always love you back, but you can choose your own family. You don't just have Katie anymore, Ariel. For what it's worth, you also have me."

Every lonely moment of my life suddenly hit me as I let my tears soak his shirt.

I'd loved my mother because she'd been my parent, and as much as she was capable, maybe she had loved me, too. But it was *always* conditional, *always* reliant on how well I could perform at ballet.

She'd had no patience for a daughter who was less than perfect, and I'd always tried my best to perform to keep that twisted love because it was all I'd had.

After she'd died, I'd had…nothing. Only my ambition and my desire to keep performing because I'd still wanted to please her, even after she was gone.

Katie had been the only one who had cared, even when I was less than perfect.

I wrapped my arms around Ben's neck and sobbed out all of my fear and desolation because I knew that when I was finally done, he wouldn't judge me for it.

He'd just hold me until I could stand on my own.

That's how much he cared about me.

As the torrent of tears subsided I murmured against his neck, "For what it's worth to you, having you care about me even when I'm not perfect means everything to me."

Ben might never understand what it meant to me that he didn't seem to see any of the imperfections that had previously crushed my soul.

He kissed the small scar that was barely visible below my hairline as he grumbled, "You'll always be perfect to me, Ariel. I don't give a shit what kind of flaws you think you have."

I let out a shaky breath as I rested my head on his shoulder, emotionally exhausted.

This man's acceptance, kindness, and patience completely floored me, and it was helping me heal.

And the truth was, in spite of every flaw Ben Blackwood thought he had, the man was beyond perfect to me, too.

Chapter 14

Ben

"Christ! How much longer is this going to take?" I said irritably as I looked at my watch for about the fiftieth time in the last ten minutes.

"Relax, Ben," Ian said patiently from his seat next to me in the small waiting room. "It's not open heart surgery. Ariel will be fine. They've only been in the OR for fifteen minutes."

Yeah, easy for *him* to say. It wasn't his woman going under the damn knife.

Katie was perfectly happy, healthy, and sitting right beside him.

My mother, who had insisted on being present during Ariel's procedure, was sitting next to Katie.

My mom had said if Ariel was important to me, then she was important to her, too. Mom had shown up with Ian and Katie way before Ariel had been taken into the OR.

It wasn't like Mom didn't know about Ariel, and she'd met her at the birthday ball. I also talked about Ariel every time we saw each other or spoke on the phone.

Maybe it should have been awkward that my mother had seen Ariel for the second time when she was lying on a gurney and ready to be wheeled into surgery.

But Mom being Mom, she'd treated Ariel like the long-lost daughter she never knew, and Ariel had seemed to thrive on that maternal concern.

That probably shouldn't have surprised me considering how her real mother had acted.

I'd nearly lost it when Ariel had tried to thank me one more time right before she'd been wheeled away.

If she knew the truth, she'd realize that I didn't deserve her thanks for anything I did for her.

I let out a long breath, trying to force my body to relax. Hell, I was supposed to be *the fixer*, and I couldn't even control my own impatience right now. "You wouldn't be saying that if Katie had been on that gurney," I answered Ian hoarsely.

"You're right," Ian replied, sounding somewhat remorseful. "I'm just trying to get you to calm down. She *will* be fine."

"She looked like she was going to her own execution," I told him, my last glimpse of Ariel still haunting me.

She hadn't looked like she'd been ready to hop off the gurney and flee, but the small smile she'd shot me as they wheeled her away was hardly reassuring. Smiling or not, she'd been terrified. I knew her well enough to sense exactly how she'd felt.

"She's nervous," Katie piped in. "Not that I blame her. She's been through this way too many times. But I agree with Ian. She's going to be okay, Ben. Once it's over, she'll be even better. It will help a lot that she'll get to go home later tonight as long as she's feeling okay."

I swallowed hard and nodded.

I needed to remember that just hours from now, Ariel and I would be able to head back home.

She'd be relieved that it was over, and I'd be able to breathe again.

Unfortunately, right at this moment, that hopeful departure seemed like it was a long way away.

Jesus! I was losing my shit.

I was usually calm under pressure.

I'd been my mother's rock after my father had died and while Ian laid near death in a hospital.

I'd been devastated about my dad, but I'd never let my family see that I was destroyed because they'd needed me.

Now, all that emotional control had been blown to hell because I couldn't control what was happening to Ariel.

"Did you get a chance to tell her the truth?" Ian asked in a low voice as my mother and Katie chatted.

I shook my head as I answered quietly enough so Katie and my mother couldn't hear me, "Now isn't the time. She needs to get through this surgery first."

"Yeah, I get that," Ian mumbled. "But I think it needs to happen soon. I think that shit is eating you alive, and the longer you wait, the harder it will be."

Like I didn't already know that?

Ian slapped me on the back and rose from his seat. "Katie and I are going to the cafeteria for coffee," he told me. "Can we bring you anything?"

Hell, I could use a very large glass of whiskey right now, no water and no ice, filled to the brim.

"Water," I said instead, knowing the last thing I needed was more coffee at the moment.

Ariel was always on my ass about hydrating. Maybe slugging down some water would make me feel better.

Mom asked for coffee and moved into Ian's seat once my brother and Katie had left for the cafeteria. "Are you okay, Ben?" she asked in a concerned voice as she put a gentle hand on my arm.

There wasn't another soul in the waiting room, but I still kept my voice low. "You don't have to tell me that I'm overreacting. I already know that, Mom. But Ariel has already been through so much. She was terrified. She put on a brave face, but I could tell."

She smiled as she put her hand on my back and rubbed it like she'd done to comfort me as a child. "I'd never criticize you for caring about

Dearest Protector

her well-being, Ben. I just wanted to know if *you* were alright. And you're right, she did look worried, but I think the drugs helped."

Ariel had been honest with the doctor about her anxiety, and they'd given her something to relax before they'd taken her into surgery.

"I hate seeing her like that," I admitted as I tried to chill out.

"I'm sure you do," my mother replied. "Should we stop all this nonsense about the two of you being close friends. I can see right through you, Benjamin. I'm your mother. You're crazy about, Ariel, and you're not *just* her friend."

I cringed. I hated the fact that I'd been a grown man for years, and I still couldn't hide anything from my mother.

Yeah, I'd given her that story about Ariel and I being friends when we were on the phone, but even then, I wasn't sure she'd bought the bullshit.

She *always* knew the truth, even when I didn't want her to know. She'd always had scary intuition like that when it came to her sons.

"I've never seen her as just a friend," I told her honestly. "But she's not ready for anything more right now. She has way too much on her plate."

I wasn't about to tell her *everything*, even if she could read me like a book.

There were some things a guy just didn't confess to his mother.

"Maybe she's not ready because she's still healing from her losses and her accident," she said thoughtfully. "But she certainly looks at you like she feels the same way."

"She looks at me like she adores me because I'm her *friend*," I said, nearly grinding my teeth because I was really starting to hate that F word. "That's it, Mom. That's all there is at the moment."

There would never be more until I could tell her the whole truth about our past.

Had it occurred to me that I could just stay silent about it?
Well…yeah.
Ariel didn't remember a thing about what had happened.

- *129* -

It would be easy to just let it go and pretend like it had never happened.

I'd thought about that solution for all of five seconds or so, but I wasn't the kind of guy who didn't own up to his mistakes... eventually.

The truth would eat me alive, and it would erode any relationship I had with Ariel. Hell, that was already happening. I wasn't the guy she thought I was, and that gutted me every single day.

I wasn't about to inform my mother that Ariel and I were not only friends, but that we lusted after each other, too. She *was* my mother for Christ's sake.

"And in the future?" she asked curiously.

"Mom," I said in a warning voice.

I didn't want to get into what my future with Ariel might look like right now.

I just wanted to see her wide awake and done with this fucking surgery.

"What?" she said innocently. "You can hardly blame me because I want both of my boys to be happy. It's obvious to me that Ariel cares about you for all the right reasons. I think Ian seems to think so, too, and she is Katie's best friend. Katie wouldn't be that close to Ariel if she wasn't a genuine person. She sees *you*, Ben, not your money. Even though she was frightened about the surgery, she was trying to keep her cool for you. Because she could sense that you were uncomfortable, too."

I wanted to deny that Ariel truly saw me because she didn't know everything, but in some ways, she actually did see me.

My wealth and power meant nothing to her.

She had absolutely no issue with getting in my face if she thought I needed a lecture on something or if she thought I needed to be protected from some unknown foe.

To her, I wasn't the figurehead of the largest tech company on the planet who had almost an unlimited amount of money.

I was simply a person she cared about, and someone she never wanted to take for granted.

Dearest Protector

She'd probably never know how rare that was for me or how much it meant to me.

It was one of the many reasons I needed her so damn much.

I took a deep breath and let it out before I asked, "You think she was trying to protect me? Hell, she just looked terrified to me."

"Probably because you see her, too. You sense her emotions, even when she's trying to hide them. But I like the fact that she seems to put you first. She cares about how *you're* feeling. I don't think she cares about your billionaire status. There's an absolute devotion in her eyes that can't possibly be faked, no matter how much you profess that you're just friends. To be honest, I was relieved. I had a feeling you weren't telling me everything, and Ian has been disappointingly silent about most of your relationship with Ariel. Katie hasn't said much, either. Tell me everything I don't know about her," she prodded.

I would have laughed if I wasn't so uptight.

My mother hated to be kept in the dark, and obviously, no one was talking enough for her.

I started to tell her some things about that she didn't know because I needed the distraction.

My mother already knew the basics, but I told her more about Ariel's accident and all of her shattered dreams.

It helped calm me to talk about Ariel, and I had a feeling my mother knew it would stop me from checking my watch every other second.

"That poor girl," my mother said when I finished. "She's so young to have so many bad things happen to her. I'm glad you were there for her, Ben. I know her heart must be broken over the ballet, but Katie has shown me Ariel's artwork. It's brilliant. She has so much talent."

"She does," I agreed. "She's about the only one who doesn't see how unique her talent really is."

"Her sales should convince her," my mother said firmly. "I wanted a few of her prints myself, but they were sold out when I went to her site."

I smirked. "I have plenty of the originals hanging in my house. One of a kind pieces that no one else will ever own."

"Smart boy," she teased as she patted my shoulder affectionately. "You know a good investment when you see one."

I knew she was teasing me, and that she understood the sentimental value of those pieces to me, but she was probably right. Considering how fast Ariel's work was selling, those pieces she'd gifted me would be worth a substantial amount of money in the not so distant future.

I shook my head. "She just...gave them to me, Mom. Any originals I wanted, and she'll never sell any prints of them in the future. That's Ariel. That's just her nature. She'll just hand them over because I'm her friend and she cares about me."

My mother let go of an elegant snort. "How does that feel? I doubt you're used to anyone giving you anything for free. Especially not something that may very well be even more valuable in the future. Her work is already raising a lot of eyebrows in some serious art communities and establishments."

Since my mother was a lover of a wide variety of art, I wasn't surprised that she already knew how well things were going for Ariel.

I shrugged and thought about her words for a moment. "It was actually pretty humbling," I finally answered honestly. "I've helped her in some small ways that she thinks are monumental, but she's helped me, too. And having her just hand over her art like it was nothing was a little mind-blowing."

"It sounds like you two are very much alike," she contemplated.

"We're not," I insisted. "She's willing to give a lot more than I am."

Hell, I didn't want my mother to think I was a saint in this situation. She'd be extremely disappointed if she found out the real truth.

She shot me a dubious look before she said, "She might be confused right now, but I think she knows a good man when she sees one."

I wanted to tell her that if I was really a good man, I would have been as honest with Ariel as she'd always been with me, but I didn't.

"It's...complicated," I stated flatly.

"Most worthwhile relationships are, Ben," she commiserated without asking any additional questions that she probably knew I wouldn't answer. "Don't forget that I'm here if you want to talk, and I'd very much like to visit Ariel while she's recovering to see if I can do anything to help."

"I'm sure she'd like that," I said truthfully. "Her own mother wasn't exactly warm and fuzzy, and her childhood sucked."

"I hate knowing that she didn't feel loved," Mom said with regret in her tone. "A child should always know they're loved unconditionally."

"Agreed," I said as I took her hand gently in my own. "I've probably never thanked you enough for being a mother who loved her sons no matter what."

It was so damn easy to take a parent who loved unconditionally for granted.

Probably because Ian and I had never known anything but loving parents who had always supported us.

Her eyes lit up as she smiled at me, and I couldn't help but grin back at her.

My mother was a beautiful woman who had aged well and gracefully, but her true appeal was that genuine, generous smile and her emotional strength.

She'd been there for me and Ian.

Always.

Even when we'd made mistakes.

"You were always there for me, too, Ben," she reminded me sternly. "And it's my job to worry about my boys, even though they're all grown up and they're very capable of taking care of themselves. Although I do wish Ian would get on with it and ask Katie to marry him. She's young, and I'm not asking for grandchildren *right now*, but it would be nice to know that's going to happen in the future."

"You just want to help Katie plan her wedding," I teased.

My mother would be ecstatic if she could help Katie seal the deal with Ian, and not just because she wanted grandkids.

She adored Katie, and I was pretty sure she just wanted to make sure that she'd never lose her.

I also knew she was relieved because Katie had drawn her son back into the land of the living when we'd both failed at the same goal.

"Maybe I do. I'd love to see Ian marry Katie," she said without an ounce of shame or remorse. "She loves him, even though he's insufferable sometimes."

I squeezed her hand. "She knows exactly how to handle Ian, even when he's insufferable."

"Thank God," my mother said in a relieved voice. "My goal is to see both of my sons happy."

"I am happy, Mom," I told her. "Maybe my relationship with Ariel isn't exactly what I want it to be, but I'm happier than I've been for a long time."

I hated to see my mother worry, and I wasn't exactly stretching the truth.

Ariel *did* make me happy.

"Do you think I haven't noticed that?" Mom asked. "You paid dearly for your father and Ian's accident, even if you weren't in the car with them. I hate the fact that you had to grow up so fast while you were still in college and that it changed your life so profoundly."

"I'll never know what Ian went through," I told her stiffly.

"But I know the price *you* paid, even though you weren't in that car," she replied in a no-nonsense tone. "Ian is happy now, Ben, and he's back at the helm with you at Blackwood. It's time for you to please yourself. Everyone is fine, including me. It's time for you to be selfish for a change."

I ran a hand through my hair, suddenly remembering where I was and what I was doing here.

Hadn't Ariel said almost the same thing about me being selfish? The woman had no idea how selfish I was sometimes.

"I'd be ecstatic if the damn doctor would get in here and tell me that Ariel was fine," I grumbled.

"It won't be long now," she said in a soothing voice.

~ 134 ~

Dearest Protector

I looked at my watch and realized that only another ten minutes or so had passed.

Ian and Katie reappeared with drinks in their hands and a supportive look in my direction.

My brother slapped me on the back again as he said, "The doctor should be out shortly. Hang in there just a little longer."

I gulped down my water, but every muscle in my body was still tense.

I crossed my arms over my chest and waited, my eyes glued to the door of the waiting room, hoping like hell that Ariel's doctor would walk in soon.

Rationally, I knew she'd be okay. It was a routine surgery. But when it came to Ariel Prescott, I had absolutely no reasoning ability anymore.

All I really wanted was for all of this bullshit to be over so I could take my girl home where she belonged.

Chapter 15

Ariel

"The gang is all here and Ian is grilling steaks on the patio," Ben remarked as he came through my open bedroom door. "You okay? Are you ready to eat?"

I smiled up at him from my position on the bed.

I'd just finished carefully packing all of my prints that had sold for shipment.

It had been eleven days since my surgery, but Ben was *still* checking in with me constantly, even though my stitches had been removed yesterday, and everything had gone really well with the hardware removal.

The first three days had been rough, but things had gotten much easier after the initial pain and swelling had lessened.

I'd be starting physical therapy shortly, which would get me back on my feet fairly quickly.

Compared to some of the pain I'd experienced in the past, this procedure had been relatively easy.

"I'm ready and I'm starving," I told him eagerly. "Is your mom here?"

He grinned. "Of course. You don't think she'd turn down an invite, do you? I think she likes you more than she likes me."

He was being absurd, and he knew it.

Marilyn adored her boys, and she never stopped talking about Ian and Ben whenever we spoke.

I sighed. "I'm glad she's here. She's been really good to me."

I adored Ben's mother.

She'd come over several times during my recovery, and we'd gotten to know each other pretty well. Marilyn Blackwood was probably the sweetest woman I'd ever known, and it was very clear to me why Ian and Ben loved their mother so much.

Ben shot me a grin. "I'd say you've been good to her, too. She was thrilled when you offered her that original print she admired."

I shook my head. "I was happy to give it to her. It was no big deal."

Ben's grin grew wider as he swept me off the bed and picked me up like I weighed next to nothing. "You, Ariel Prescott, are a very big deal. You're turning down offers for commissioned pieces right now that are coming from some very reputable places."

I swatted him playfully on the arm after I'd quickly put the other one around his back to keep my body balanced. "Only because I have to. I can only do so many commissions and still keep turning out new original work myself. I'm also not quite used to doing something that didn't originate in my own brain. God knows I'd like to do them all. Everyone is offering me a small fortune just for one of my pieces. Ben, I am capable of getting downstairs on my own."

I couldn't bear weight on my foot quite yet, but Ben did have an elevator and I had crutches. It wasn't like I hadn't had plenty of practice getting around on crutches after my accident.

"They're offering so much because your work is unique and out-standing," Ben said matter-of-factly. "And I know you can get around if you have to, but you don't have to. I'm here, and I don't want to chance you getting another injury. We don't need to go through that again. *You* would probably get through it, but it would probably kill *me*."

I laughed. An honest to goodness, carefree laugh that had been coming out of me a lot more often lately.

I knew Ben was joking...mostly. But he was so deadpan that his comments about my surgery and recovery were thoroughly amusing.

Had he been overprotective with me? Had he been as worried as I was in the beginning?

Yep. Definitely.

Had he been a bossy pain in the ass sometimes?

Absolutely.

Had he made me crazy with his demands and his over the top concern?

Truthfully? No. Because I knew he was genuinely worried.

However, I had teased him to death once I was feeling well enough to give him a hard time.

In all honesty, Ben had been amazing.

He'd doted on me like a man who cared, and I couldn't chastise him for *that.*

I would have been the same way if our positions were reversed.

"I'm fine now, Ben," I said softly as he walked to the elevator. "It doesn't hurt like it did in the beginning."

"And I'd really like to keep it that way," he answered succinctly. "Don't get me wrong. I want to see you walking again. I just don't want anything to happen to that foot before it's strong enough to handle the stress of walking."

I hit the elevator button for the downstairs automatically since we'd done this so many times before.

And then I hugged him, closing my eyes as I savored his masculine scent. I stopped myself just short of burying my face in his neck so I could absorb that clean, tantalizing smell of man, musk, and some kind of mysterious pheromones that sent my female hormones into a frenzy.

God, he smelled good.

He looked good, too, even dressed casually in the jeans and the navy blue Henley he was wearing.

Dearest Protector

Maybe I should be used to him carting me around by now, but I wasn't.

Every time I got this close to him, I wanted to wrap my legs around his waist and beg him to fuck me.

I wanted Ben Blackwood with a need that bordered on desperation, and it got harder and harder to ignore those carnal instincts every time I got close to him now.

I wasn't in constant pain anymore.

Well, not from my foot surgery anyway.

Now, it was getting to the point where my longing for Ben was almost worse than the physical pain I'd been through.

While I probably could complain about that unsatisfied desire, I didn't.

It was difficult to be this close to him, but I wouldn't trade it just to be comfortable again.

The way I felt about Ben made me feel...alive.

I wasn't going to bitch about the most amazing sensations I'd ever experienced, even if they were also somewhat painful.

"Thank you," I murmured next to his ear in a breathless voice. "And please don't say all of this is nothing. Just say *you're welcome.* Don't blow me off this time. It's important to me. I want you to know that I couldn't have done this without you."

Katie and Ian had been here.

Ben's mother had been here, too.

I'd been grateful for their constant reassurance and help, but Ben was the one who had been my constant caretaker, seven days a week, twenty-four hours a day for the last eleven days.

He hadn't left the house at all. Not even once.

God, he even anticipated most of my needs so I never really had to ask for anything.

Ben hesitated for a moment before he answered huskily, "You're welcome, sweetheart. If it's important to you, then I'll always say that. It's not that I don't hear you. I just really don't think it's a big deal to take care of you when you need me."

I was stunned into silence for a moment.

~ *139* ~

God, he truly meant those words, which completely blew me away.

I smiled as I let go of my death grip around his neck and ended my prolonged hug.

"You're the most amazing man I've ever known, Ben Blackwood," I told him.

"I hope you always feel that way," he rumbled as he stepped out of the elevator and carried me outside.

My smile receded as I wondered exactly what he'd meant by *that* comment, but I never had a chance to ask.

He put me gently into a chair at the outdoor table and pushed it in until I was comfortable.

Katie and Marilyn beamed at me from the other side of the table while Ben joined Ian at the grill.

"You look so much better," Katie said. "How's the pain?"

"It's so much better," I shared. "And the swelling is gone. My sutures came out yesterday afternoon. I'll start physical therapy soon. I can't wait to get around on my own again."

Marilyn smiled. "It looks my son is still taking good care of you."

Still dizzy from Ben's scent that wouldn't fade away, I answered distractedly, "I couldn't ask for a better man."

Marilyn's smile grew, and I suddenly realized what I'd said. "I mean, I couldn't ask for a better *friend*," I corrected hastily, hating the fact that I was actually blushing.

Crap! I'd been so dazed from being close to Ben that I'd screwed up in front of his mother.

"I know what you meant, dear," Marilyn replied serenely.

I wanted to hug Katie when she rescued me from the awkwardness by saying, "Marilyn and I were just talking about my graduation in Massachusetts at the end of next month. I just wanted them to send my diploma, but Ian is insistent that I walk for it in person. Do you think you and Ben could come?"

"She's the valedictorian," Ian commented from his place at the grill. "That's a huge accomplishment and they want her to speak. She needs to go in person. That's a big deal, whether she thinks so or not."

Dearest Protector

I nodded, agreeing with Ian completely. "Oh, Katie, you have to do it in person. That's huge, and you deserve to have your moment, even though I know you hate public speaking."

Katie held up a hand. "I'm going. Ian already convinced me. I might hate public speaking, but it won't be so bad because I'll have all the important people in my life there with me if you and Ben can join us."

Obviously, Marilyn would be there, and I wanted to go. I wanted to be there to support my best friend during her big event.

I couldn't speak for Ben, but I instinctively knew nothing would stop him from being there for Katie. She was family to him.

I nodded. "It's still a month away. I'll be walking just fine by then, and now that I'm making really good money, getting a plane ticket isn't a big deal. I'd love to be there. You worked so hard for your degree."

Katie coughed before she said drily, "Um…a plane ticket isn't necessary since Ian has a private jet that would probably accommodate an entire football team."

"If your departure time doesn't work for Ariel, I can fly her in my jet," Ben offered, obviously keeping track of the conversation. "You know I'm going to be there, Katie."

I swallowed hard as I saw the moisture form in Katie's eyes.

My best friend very rarely cried, but I knew she was feeling overwhelmed.

Just like me, she'd been raised by a single mother who had already passed away.

She had no other close family, so I knew it meant a lot that she was going to have all of her chosen family with her at her college graduation.

She nodded. "Then I'll have absolutely everyone I want with me."

The conversation quickly changed to another subject, but I couldn't get over the fact that we'd be flying in a private jet out of my mind.

Both Ian and Ben had *private jets*.

Yeah, I knew they were ridiculously wealthy, but that fact hadn't slapped me in the face very often.

- *141* -

I'd never asked Ben if he even had a private jet, but it should have been obvious, right?

Ian and Ben certainly weren't going to fly commercial.

"Hey, you okay?" Ben asked as he bent close to me to deliver my plate with my steak and baked potato. "You got pretty quiet. Are you hurting?"

"No!" I denied emphatically. "I was just lost in thought for a moment. I'm good."

Sometimes, I just couldn't see Ben as the powerful billionaire that I knew he was, especially when he never flaunted it.

He didn't have an overinflated ego.

He was just…Ben, the hottest, most handsome guy on the planet. And the kindest, most thoughtful guy I'd ever met.

There were other facets to his personality.

There had to be.

I'd just never seen the rest of them for any period of time.

Or maybe I just didn't care because I knew the real Ben Blackwood, and the rich, powerful billionaire that he had to portray at times was merely a façade.

Oh, I knew he could play that game, but I'd never really seen him in action when he had to play the part of a badass business tycoon.

"Eat," Ben grumbled as he dropped his own plate in front of him and sat down beside me.

Okay, so maybe his bossiness *was* real, but it was far from intimidating.

Not to me.

Underneath his gruff attitude was a guy who had an amazing heart.

As I began to eat, it made me a little sad when I realized that probably very few people could see the man that I saw every time he walked into the room.

Then again, women already fell over all over him because of his wealth and his hotness.

Did they really need other reasons to pursue him?

Dearest Protector

Ben sent me a shit-eating grin that nearly made my heart stop as he saw me tear into my food because I was starving. *Nope.* Nobody needed to see the same Ben I saw and adored. Especially not the females who wanted nothing from Ben except his money, his gorgeous body, and his handsome face.

They could all just suck it.

They'd had their chance and they'd blown it.

I was always going to appreciate every asset Ben had, and I'd keep those more endearing qualities of his all to myself.

Chapter 16

Ben

"I've been thinking a lot about what happened right after my accident lately," Ariel shared as we sat in the loungers on the patio after all of our company had gone. "I've told you before that I don't remember what happened right after I was hit by that taxi, but I dream about it. Maybe I blocked it all out, but I wish I knew what really happened."

My body tensed, and I threw back a large swallow of the whiskey I'd been sipping slowly just a few minutes ago.

I didn't really want to pursue this subject, but I couldn't just cut her off, either. Not when it was something she probably needed to talk about.

"Why now?" I asked carefully. "And what's the dream about?"

Ariel set her empty wine glass on the side table as she replied, "Someone was there right after the accident. He helped me, but I don't even know his name, and I have no idea if what I'm dreaming is even remotely based in reality. For a long time, I didn't even want to recall what happened, but I have to admit that I'm curious. It's a time period that's totally blank for me. I guess it's starting to bother me now that I'm not afraid to think about it anymore. Counseling has really taken away a lot of the anxiety I had about the accident."

"What's the last thing you remember?" I asked, my concern outweighing my apprehension.

"I was standing at a light, waiting for it to change so that I could walk across a busy street safely. I was happy and flying high because I'd done my first performance as a principal dancer. I was on my way to some boring but necessary afterparty that I had to attend because the gentleman hosting the event was a big supporter of the ballet. All I really wanted to do was go home and soak my aching feet, and I was late, which I hated. After that…I don't know what happened. I was in an induced coma for several days in the ICU after my initial surgeries. The next thing I remember is days after the accident, after they started waking me up again in the ICU. I have a huge hole in my memories. The only data I can fill in is whatever the police could tell me way after the fact, which is really kind of vague."

That wasn't at all surprising because she'd sustained so many injuries.

Maybe she was better off *not* remembering any of it.

"Who was there when you finally woke up?" I asked curiously.

"By that time, Katie was there. She'd heard about it on social media," she said slowly, like she had to force her memory to catch up the information. "And my dance partner, Erik, the guy who played the prince in Swan Lake. He was the only dancer I was close to at the time, but he could rarely stay long, and he didn't drop by that often. The Swan Lake show had to go on without me. He was busy practicing and performing with my understudy, which I completely understood."

Fuck! I hated thinking about how Ariel must have felt about that back then.

Rationally, she probably did understand that the show had to go on, but there was no way that didn't hurt her at that time. Not only was she gravely injured, but she'd had to come to terms with the fact that someone had taken her place in the Swan Lake production, and that she might never dance that ballet ever again.

"Don't tell me that it wasn't painful knowing that the show was happening without you," I said.

"It was painful," she agreed, her voice melancholy. "To be honest, I encouraged Erik to just stop visiting because I couldn't stand to hear about it. I regret that now because I pushed someone away who cared about me as a friend, but it was the only way I could get through it. He even tried to call me once I left the hospital, but I just couldn't return his calls. That part of my life was over, and I wasn't dealing with my depression well back then."

"Don't feel bad," I insisted. "You did what you had to do to survive, sweetheart."

"Maybe," she said, sounding totally unconvinced. "But it was a dumb thing to do. I was even lonelier on my own."

Her words gutted me, but I tried not to let her see my reaction as I asked, "Do you think you'll ever remember what happened?"

"I'm not sure," she answered softly. "The doctor said there's a chance that I won't ever recall getting hit by that taxi. He also said that I'd never recover what happened in the ER and in ICU while I was in the induced coma because I was so heavily sedated during that period of time. I think I'd really like to recall exactly why I walked out in front of that taxi. The light hadn't changed yet according to the police, so the taxi wasn't at fault. It was me who did something stupid enough to nearly kill me and caused my whole life to be turned upside down. I was always so cautious in New York. It wasn't like me to do something that idiotic, but all I was thinking about was how late I was for that afterparty. I was distracted and wound up, which is probably why I did it, but I don't exactly know for sure."

"You're not stupid, Ariel," I said, my voice rough and graveled. "We all make mistakes."

"But I was usually so careful, Ben, especially with my physical safety because I always had to be in optimal condition to dance. Then again, I wasn't myself that night."

"Can you live with not remembering?" I questioned.

~ 146 ~

Dearest Protector

She sighed. "I guess I'll have to because there's no other option. I thought I'd already gotten over all that. I thought I was okay with not remembering, but these stupid nightmares just bring it all back."

Every muscle in my body tight, I finally pushed her harder, "Tell me about the dreams."

"There isn't a lot to them," she answered. "I never dream about why I walked in front of that taxi. Things always start after I'd been hit. I dream about the pain, the confusion, and how hard it was to breathe. It was so horrible that I just wanted to give up, but a male voice just keeps talking to me, forcing me to keep breathing and not to give up. So, I keep trying. God, I know that's probably not what happened at all, but when I'm dreaming, it all seems so…real. Maybe because I *know* what my injuries were, I'm able to conjure up a believable scenario. I couldn't breathe, but I know I had a collapsed lung. My vision is really blurry in the dream, but I also know that I had a concussion and that my head was split open from the impact."

I watched as her hand went to her barely visible scar near her hairline.

It was a reflexive move, and I doubted whether she even knew she was touching the healed scar.

My gut started to roll as I took her hand and entwined our fingers. "Obviously, it's very real for you, Ariel. When was the last time you had this dream?"

"Last night. Maybe that's why I'm thinking about it so much today," she said. "It's sporadic. Before we met, I hadn't had that dream for months. Now, I'm dreaming about it pretty often."

"What can I do to help?" I questioned, my voice husky.

Hell, if I could turn her brain off at night, I'd do it.

I hated watching her struggle for the truth, especially when I knew I could fill in a few blanks for her, but not without her knowing about everything.

It's too goddamn soon for that.

She can't stand up and leave at the moment, no matter how much she might want to do exactly that after she knows what really happened.

It was killing me not to blurt out information just so she no longer had to wonder about some things that had occurred that night.

Ariel shook her head slowly. "There's nothing you can do unless you're psychic, and you can use those powers to tell me what happened," she teased.

Fuck! Other than this discussion about her nightmare, Ariel had sounded so damn happy lately.

She was over the moon about going to Katie's graduation, and her delight and absolute astonishment about her successful new business was intoxicating to watch.

Ariel was taking her life back and living it exactly the way she wanted.

She was letting the people she cared about in, and she was speaking her mind without hesitation.

It was more than obvious that she was leaving her old life behind and embracing a future without ballet wholeheartedly.

Maybe she still didn't completely understand why people wanted her artwork, but with every sale, her confidence in what she was creating grew.

Even though she was still laid up, her joy and exuberance about living her life in the moment was infectious.

More than anything, I wanted things to stay just like this.

I wanted to watch her keep blossoming every single day until there was nothing but excitement and amusement left in her beautiful eyes.

Until every bit of her previous wariness and disillusionment were nothing but a memory.

Until every dark shadow that had lingered in her gaze was completely obliterated.

Hell, I wanted to wallow in that kind of happiness with her, but there was one very large roadblock looming ahead of me.

I was waiting for a perfect time to tell her, even though I knew that time would never come.

Okay, so maybe it was better to wait until she was fully recovered from her surgery, but even then I knew I'd be hesitant to tell her

Dearest Protector

the truth because there was always going to be that risk that she'd walk away.

Oh, hell no.

That was never going to happen.

Even if she walked out on this relationship once she knew the truth, I'd follow her.

She was mine.

Unless she told me to fuck off someday and I thought she really meant it, I'd be by her side, even if she was pissed off.

Letting her go was never going to be an option.

You don't have to tell her the truth. Most likely, she'll never find out. Who's going to tell her?

I grimaced.

Not telling her was also not an option since *I'd* always know, and not sharing everything with Ariel at some point would eventually destroy both of us.

It had never been my intention *not* to tell Ariel about the past.

I just hadn't wanted to do it at a time when she was so damn vulnerable.

I'd balked at the possibility of her walking away when she needed someone to lean on.

However, now that she was rapidly approaching the point where she didn't need *me* anymore, I'd discovered that I needed *her* so damn much that I was hesitant to tell her everything.

But I *would* tell her as soon as she was recovered from this surgery and back on her feet.

She deserved to know, and I'd waited long enough.

Finally, I replied, "I'm afraid being a psychic isn't one of my many talents."

She squeezed my hand. "And here I thought there was nothing you *couldn't* do," she joked.

Hell, there was plenty I couldn't do.

Most importantly, there was no way I could go back in time and make sure we'd never crossed paths until I'd seen her at my mother's birthday ball.

- *149* -

But we *had* crossed paths.

And there was nothing I could do to change that fact.

I'd fucked up badly with Ariel Prescott the first time, which would inevitably affect our relationship in the future.

Fuck! For a man like me who hated uncertainty and liked to know exactly what odds he was facing going into any situation, the thought of jumping in completely blind was torture.

This isn't a goddamn business deal.

I could afford to lose a few of those business ventures if the odds weren't in my favor.

But Ariel?

Fuck, no!

Losing her was unfathomable now and pulling her closer to me by telling her everything was going to be the biggest risk I'd ever taken.

Maybe the odds weren't in my favor, but I'd jump in anyway, headfirst if necessary.

There were no other alternatives for me.

Chapter 17

Ariel

I yawned as I closed my laptop and put it on the bedside table. I'd gotten a lot of work done on a commissioned piece I was doing for a large company, but it was after two in the morning now, and I was exhausted.

It was weird how time could fly by when I was working on something.

Ben had turned in a long time ago, but I hadn't been able to sleep, so I'd opened my laptop. What seemed like a few minutes had actually turned into two hours.

While commissioned works weren't my favorite thing to do, they brought in a lot of income for me. And even though I knew what theme I was working on for a requested image, it still took a lot of creativity to reimagine those pieces.

I glanced down at my legs and smiled when I finally got to the painted toenails I'd polished earlier this evening.

I flexed my right foot without a single twinge of pain.

The incision where they'd removed the hardware was just one more scar that was a little angrier than the rest of them, but I'd accepted the fact that they were never going away completely.

That scar would fade just like every other scar on my body.

When I looked at my foot now, I no longer saw the shattered dreams that had haunted me before, so it wasn't nearly as unsightly as it had been.

It's just...a previous injury. Not ugly. Definitely not a reason to sweat my feet with socks all the time just because I hate looking at it.

Maybe my change in attitude had to do with the fact that I didn't see myself as a loser or a failure anymore.

Did I occasionally doubt myself still?

I did, but those thoughts were getting less and less frequent.

I was happy with my life, probably happier than I'd ever been before. I had a new career that I loved, and the circle of people who truly cared about me was getting larger. I also had people to care about in return.

No one who really cared about me gave a damn about those scars, so why should I?

I'd still have to keep doing the physical therapy I'd started about a week ago, but I was walking, which was all that really mattered to me.

Yeah, I still had to baby that foot until it was stronger, but any discomfort I'd felt with the hardware in was now gone.

Now, if I could just figure out what in the hell is wrong with Ben, my life would be nearly perfect.

He'd insisted that everything was fine, but it wasn't.

Something was eating at him, and I was determined to get to the source of his quietness and broodiness.

Ben had started going into the headquarters now that I was able to get around on my own, but I was pretty sure his issues weren't about work.

Work had never gotten to him like this previously.

"Ariel!"

My body stilled as I heard the strangled shout coming from Ben's room.

He sounds like he's in some kind of pain!

His bedroom was right next door to mine, which had been something he'd done on purpose so he could be close to me after my surgery.

He'd wanted to be within shouting distance for me, just in case I needed something at night when I'd been unable to bear any weight on my foot.

I scrambled out of bed, my heart racing.

"Ben," I said breathlessly.

Something was wrong.

I didn't stop to worry about the fact that I was in my pajamas, which consisted of a skimpy, thin pair of black sleep shorts with a matching scooped neck tank.

My only thought was to make sure that Ben was okay.

His tone when he'd called out my name had been urgent and tormented.

I flew to his bedroom as quickly as my healing foot would take me there, and then pushed the door completely open that he'd left ajar.

The lights were all off in his room, but his shutters were open. When I turned on the light in the hallway, it completely flooded his bedroom. I could see him lying in the middle of his enormous king-size bed, fighting with his covers like they were his enemy.

"Ariel! No! Don't!" he cried out urgently.

"Ben?" I questioned softly as I approached the bed, suddenly realizing that he was dreaming.

Or was it a nightmare?

Apparently, whatever he was dreaming about wasn't pleasant, and it obviously involved…me.

I turned on a soft light on the bedside table and climbed into his bed without a second thought. I touched his shoulder gently as I said a little louder voice, "Ben! Wake up."

I couldn't possibly leave him like this.

When he didn't wake, I stroked a hand through his hair, like I could calm him down that way.

God, even in his tortured dreams, he was gorgeous. His ripped upper body was completely bare.

He tossed onto his side, his face far from serene in sleep.

Stop gawking and wake his ass up, Ariel! Whatever he's dreaming about isn't pleasant.

I stopped all attempts at being gentle as I shook his shoulder roughly. "Ben!" I said in a more demanding tone. "Wake up!"

He suddenly sat up in the bed and took a heaving breath, "Fuck! Ariel?"

I watched as confusion flooded his expression, and then finally… relief.

"I'm here," I told him as I wrapped my arm around his massive shoulders. "Everything is fine. I think you were having a nightmare."

"You're here. You okay?" he asked grimly as he wrapped an arm tightly around my waist and pulled me in closer until he was cradling my body against his.

I put my arms around his neck and hugged him. "I'm fine. It was just a dream, Ben."

I'd had heard the stress in his voice, but as usual, his first thought was to check in with me.

His body shuddered as he wrapped both arms around me and pulled me into his lap. "Jesus, Ariel!" he rasped against my temple. "I thought you were hurt."

"It was just a bad nightmare," I crooned as I threaded my fingers into his hair.

He rocked me for a few seconds, not saying a word, like he had to convince himself that I was in one piece and perfectly fine.

Then, a heartbeat later, he pulled my head down and started to kiss me like a madman.

Maybe I should have stopped him because it was uncertain whether he really knew what he was doing, but I couldn't.

I'd waited too damn long to feel his lips on mine again.

I moaned into the heated embrace, savoring the intimacy, taking what I'd endlessly craved.

His tongue traced the seam of my lips, and I opened for him almost immediately.

Ben explored my mouth like he was claiming what had always belonged to him, and I responded with the same urgency.

Dearest Protector

Running my hands down his naked back, I shivered at the feel of his hard muscles covered by very warm, soft skin.

Yes!

God, how long had I wanted to explore this man's body in a sensual way?

Maybe it hadn't been all *that long*, but it felt like I'd waited an eternity to be this close to Ben.

I swung my leg over his body and straddled him.

Ben never released my mouth.

He let me take an occasional breath, but his pursuit of my lips was completely relentless.

Desperate and completely intoxicated by the feel of Ben's hard body and his rough, desperate, claiming embrace, I melted into him, my hands moving restlessly to touch every inch of him.

I squirmed in his lap, feeling like I was going to die if I didn't get the hard cock beneath me into my body.

I ached.

God, I ached.

"Fuck!" Ben cursed as he released my lips and then began leaving a heated path of fiery kisses down my neck. "This has to stop, Ariel."

"No," I insisted, eyes closed, my head tilted to give him whatever access he needed to keep going. "Don't. Stop."

I needed *this.*

I needed *him.*

I had for a very long time, and I'd be damned if I was going to stop now that I had him exactly the way I needed him.

Hot.

Demanding.

And completely out of control.

I could sense his need to possess me, and it made me crazy.

I panted as he continued to explore the skin at my neck while his hands slid beneath my tank and ran up my bare back.

Every fervent touch ramped up my heated body until I felt like I was going to spontaneously combust.

My back hit the mattress before I even realized that Ben had moved.

He held my wrists over my head, his big body looming ominously above me as he rasped, "I am not going to fucking take you like this."

"Why?" I panted as our eyes clashed and finally locked together. "You don't hear me complaining. I've wanted this for a long time, Ben, and I think you know I want it. I think you want it, too. Just put us out of our misery for God's sake."

I tried to pull my wrists free from his grip so I could touch him, but those attempts were futile.

"Do you think for even one second that I *don't* want you?" he said in a raw, tormented voice that I'd never heard before.

I shook my head slowly, my eyes never leaving his. "Then why are you stopping?" I questioned, my tone confused.

If he wanted me, I was all his. I thought I'd made that pretty obvious.

"You're a fucking virgin, Ariel," he grunted. "And we really need to talk. There are some things I have to tell you."

"I'm probably the horniest virgin on the planet right now," I shot back at him. "I'm not completely innocent, Ben, and I've been on birth control for years because I have rough periods when I'm not on the pill. Use a condom if you want, too. I don't care. And whatever we need to talk about can happen later."

I wanted him.

Right now, nothing else mattered.

"Christ, Ariel, do you really think I'm worried about myself right now? I'm clean, and I haven't been with another woman for over two years, but it's not me I'm concerned about. There's something we definitely need to discuss *before* this happens. I'm also a big guy. I could easily hurt you if I don't get a damn grip, and I have zero control at the moment."

This was a side of Ben that I'd never seen before, and seeing him this uncontrolled and wild for *me* was my undoing.

"I doubt it would hurt more than it does right now," I told him.

Ben's chest was still heaving as his eyes ran over my face like he was searching for the truth. "Is this really what you want?" he asked gruffly.

Dearest Protector

"You already know it is," I answered breathlessly. "I don't care if it hurts a little the first time."

"I'll make sure it's minimal," he vowed. "But once this happens, there's no going back for me to the friendship zone, Ariel. So be certain you know what you're asking for."

"Let me go," I said as I jerked hard at my wrists.

If he thought I'd want to go back to being *just friends* after this, he was out of his mind.

The loss of this kind of intimacy would kill me.

He frowned, but he finally released me.

I reached out and put one hand on his shoulder and ran the other along his stubbled, hard jawline as I murmured, "I've never wanted any man but you, Ben. You're the only guy who has ever made me this crazy. Let go of your need to take care of everyone else and take what *you* want. I guarantee that I want exactly what you want."

Maybe it was still hard for me to believe that Ben wanted me this way, but the physical proof was obvious, and his desire was written all over his gorgeous face.

"You'll be stuck with me, Ariel. I mean that," he warned.

I smiled. "Oh, poor me. Stuck with the hottest, most amazing man on the planet? Whatever will I do?" I teased.

God, didn't he realize how badly I wanted to be his? How badly I wanted to be connected to him and only him?

I craved him like a parched individual who desperately needed water.

I'd never be *stuck* with Ben Blackwood.

I'd be the happiest woman on the planet.

"You just sealed your own fate, babe," he said harshly as his hands moved down to the hem of my tank and tugged it up and over my head. "I'm about done talking."

I lifted my arms so he could pull my shirt off as I shivered with anticipation.

Because my need for him was so raw, and because I'd waited for so damn long, I couldn't get the two of us naked fast enough.

Chapter 18

Ariel

There was no virginal shyness for me as Ben tossed my shirt to the floor and his eyes raked over my small breasts.

Maybe my lack of hesitation was because I saw nothing but fire in his molten gaze, and that hungry look was infectious.

Or maybe...it was just because this was *Ben*, the man I'd come to know so well. He seemed to like everything about me, even if I wasn't perfect.

"Beautiful," he said in a fuck-me baritone as he put a finger at the base of my neck and lowered it slowly to my breasts. "You're so fucking beautiful, Ariel."

At that moment, I *felt* beautiful, because Ben made me feel like a damn goddess.

How lucky was I to have a guy like this one for my first time?

I wasn't afraid.

I wasn't apprehensive.

I was much too hungry for this man to give a shit about anything else but...him.

Dearest Protector

I wanted him right now with a need that crossed the line into obsession.

All I could think about was how desperately I needed to be as close to Ben as I could possibly get.

He lowered his head and took one nipple into his mouth and strummed the other with his fingers.

My eyes closed with a tortured moan. "Ben," I crooned as I threaded my fingers into his coarse hair, relishing his touch.

My back arched as he bit down erotically on my sensitive nipple, and then soothed it with his tongue.

He teased and stroked until I was half out of my mind.

"Ben," I said sharply, my body burning. "Please. Fuck me. Don't make me wait any longer."

I was squirming, aching to have him inside me.

But apparently, he wasn't done tormenting yet.

He took my mouth without stopping that sensual touch on my breast.

After kissing me until my head was spinning, those talented fingers moved slowly down my abdomen.

My belly tightened in anticipation as Ben nipped at my earlobe and rumbled right next to my ear, "Don't rush me, beautiful. You have no idea how long I've wanted to touch you like this."

I wanted to touch him, too, but he was making it very clear that he was completely in control.

And this time, as my body shook with desire, I was completely okay with that.

I wanted, but I wasn't entirely sure how to get exactly what I needed.

But *Ben* knew.

Oh God, *he knew,* and I had no doubt he was going to eventually satisfy the desperate longing that was eating me alive.

I tensed a little as Ben's hand breached the elastic of my sleep shorts and then edged beneath my saturated panties.

He briefly explored the small landing strip of blonde hair before he finally ran a finger over my slick clit.

"Yes," I whimpered. "Touch me."

"You're so fucking wet," Ben said hoarsely against my ear before he slid down my body and deftly removed my panties and sleep shorts. He spread my legs apart and inserted his shoulders between them. My hips nearly lifted off the bed as he got the access he wanted, and his fingers delved deeper into my pussy.

I'd already known that he was probably going to put his mouth on me, but I wasn't prepared for exactly how good that would feel until his tongue boldly licked and stroked over my clit.

It was hotter and more pleasurable than anything I could have conjured up in my sexual fantasies.

My back arched at the mind-blowing sensation. "Oh, God, yes," I moaned.

That was all the encouragement Ben needed to start devouring my pussy like a man who needed what he found between my thighs for his basic survival.

I'd heard women talk about oral sex.

Hell, I'd even fantasized about Ben doing it.

But nothing could have prepared me for this kind of sensual devastation.

Because I listened when women talked about sex, I'd always gotten the sense that men didn't like to go down on women all that much.

Apparently, Ben *wasn't* one of those men who didn't enjoy it.

He ate me like he thoroughly relished the task and savored the taste.

He groaned deeply against my slick flesh, and the vibration rocked my entire body.

My legs started to shake as his tongue lashed mercilessly over my clit.

Over and over.

Until I wanted to climax so badly that I could barely think.

"Please," I begged, my hands moving to fist in Ben's hair.

I wasn't sure whether I wanted to push him away because this was all too much or pull him closer, harder against me, which was probably exactly what I needed.

Dearest Protector

I couldn't take it, yet I still needed…more.

I gasped out loud when he slid a finger inside me without missing a beat on my clit.

I let out a needy moan as he added another finger, filling me, and then fucking me.

"I-don't-think-I-can-take-anymore," I babbled mindlessly as I started to feel the force of my orgasm begin to build.

And build…

And build…

Nothing quite like this had ever happened before, and it was almost frightening.

"Too much," I groaned before I quickly added, "More, Ben, please."

I wanted…

I needed…

He sucked the engorged bud into his mouth and bite down gently. Then he curled his fingers until he found my G-spot.

"Shit!" I squeaked as my climax started to roll over me like a tidal wave.

My back arched off the bed from the powerful spasms.

I couldn't control it.

All I could do was ride the enormous waves of pleasure as my entire body shook with the ferocity of my release.

By the time Ben climbed back up my body again, I was slick with perspiration and I was a total mess.

I couldn't speak.

I simply wrapped an arm around his neck as he lowered his head to kiss me.

His kiss was hot, hungry, sensual, and so passionate that my body ached with need.

I could taste myself on his lips, which only aroused me even more.

I'd climaxed. *Hard.* But it hadn't satiated my need for *Ben.*

Just the opposite, in fact.

It had just stoked my longing to the point where I felt like I was going to lose my mind.

"Fuck. Me," I panted as soon as he released my mouth. "I need you, Ben. Now."

I wrapped my legs around his hips, trying to urge him to give me the connection I really needed.

"You're so fucking tight, Ariel," Ben growled next to my ear.

"That will feel good to you, right?" I said in an urgent whisper, suddenly feeling a little inept.

I wanted to make Ben burn like I did right now, I wanted to please him, but I wasn't exactly sure how.

"Too damn good," he groaned. "I won't last long, and it's been a long time for me. Not to mention the fact that I've never taken a woman without a condom."

I stroked my hands down his back. "Then let's enjoy every second while it lasts."

"Fuck! You make me crazy, woman."

"Now you know exactly how I feel," I murmured as my fingertips caressed the top of his very firm ass.

Ben reached down and put the head of his hard cock against my slick opening. "I'm not going to prolong the painful part of this, sweetheart," he said in a warning growl.

I didn't have time to ask him what he meant.

With one powerful surge of his hips, he gave me exactly what I wanted in one swift motion.

It wasn't gentle or slow.

There was no hesitation.

He didn't creep into it slowly.

He just got the initial shock over with as quickly as possible.

"Yes," I hissed, ignoring the twinge of pain I'd experienced when he'd buried himself to his balls.

I'd been a ballerina for many years. That brief moment of pain was nothing next to ingrown toenails, dancing on top of blisters, and the plethora of other painful things I'd experienced during my dancing days.

And God, the satisfaction of feeling our bodies totally connected would have been worth a far greater pain.

Dearest Protector

Ben stilled, giving me a chance to get used to his size and girth.

"You okay?" he asked tensely.

I took a deep breath in and out as my internal muscles stretched to accommodate Ben.

He had to be dying to move, but he didn't.

He just waited, checking in with me to make sure I was alright, as usual.

Tears filled my eyes, but not from the pain.

They were tears of joy, tears from the bliss of being with Ben like this.

I finally felt like I was his, and that euphoria swamped me with a carnal pleasure I never knew existed.

"I'm...really good," I shared, my voice shaky with emotions I couldn't express in words.

He pulled his head back so he could look at me.

"Tell me that you're not bullshitting me right now, Ariel," he demanded gruffly. "Look at me."

Our eyes met and clashed.

I could see the passion and need burning in his eyes, and it intoxicated me.

"I'm not," I said accommodatingly. "I just want you to fuck me. I never knew it could be this...amazing."

"It gets a hell of a lot better. Are you crying?" he asked, his tone suddenly remorseful.

I nodded. "Only because it feels so damn good to finally be with you. Keep going. Please."

I pressed my hands against his ass, urging him not to stop.

I wanted to feel Ben moving inside me, possessing me, claiming me.

What had been a little uncomfortable at first was now starting to consume me.

There was absolutely no pain, and I needed to be closer to Ben.

Much.

Closer.

And more than anything, I wanted to see him lose himself to the pleasure he'd given me.

I closed my eyes as Ben slowly pulled back, and thrust back inside me again.

"God, that feels good," I purred.

As Ben did the same thing over and over again, his speed increasing gradually, I lost myself to the seductive rhythm.

Nothing existed anymore except Ben and me, and the exhilarating bliss of finally feeling him moving inside me.

I lifted my hips, moving with him, anxious for every thrust of his massive cock now.

"Harder! Don't hold back, Ben," I pleaded, wanting every bit of this fierce madness that only Ben could give me. "I need you."

Once I said those words, it was like Ben finally caved in and lost the last of his control.

He fucked me so deep and hard that it took my breath away, and I still craved more.

"Yes-please-just-like-that-Ben," I chanted, egging him on as our skin slapped together with every forceful drive.

I could feel my orgasm welling up inside me.

The feeling was different this time.

Slower.

More like a rough caress than a tsunami.

And deeper than the climax I'd had a short while ago.

I reached for that unfamiliar orgasm, but I couldn't quite capture it.

"Touch yourself, Ariel," Ben demanded with a lusty groan. "I can't last much longer, and I need to feel you coming around my cock."

Instinctively, I knew what he was asking me to do.

I knew what he needed because my body was begging for exactly the same thing.

Even though every thrust of Ben's cock was ecstasy, I didn't want to wait, and Ben *couldn't* wait.

I went off like a firecracker within the first few seconds of reaching between our bodies to stimulate my clit.

That was all it took to send my body reeling.

"Oh, God, Ben!" I screamed, my internal muscles clamping down on Ben as I came so hard I was seeing stars dance on the inside of my eyelids.

"Fuck!" Ben groaned. "You're mine, Ariel. Say it. Tell me you're mine. Tell me you'll never leave me."

Leave him? Is the man out of his mind?

He surged inside me one last time as my body clenched around his massive cock, milking him to his own release.

"You already know that I'm yours, and I'd have to be crazy to go anywhere," I choked out, my fingernails digging into his back because the pleasure was so damn intense.

The raw emotional and primal satisfaction that was pouring from my body was so powerful that my heart felt like it was going to explode out of my chest.

Ben Blackwood was mine as surely as I was his, and the satisfaction I got from that knowledge was profound and explainable.

He rolled and pulled me on top of him, his cock still inside me as he rasped harshly, still trying to catch his breath, "No going back, Ariel. We're never going back. I can't go through that kind of torture again."

"Is that supposed to scare me?" I asked, out of breath as I rested my head against his shoulder, my body as limp as a noodle. "Because it doesn't."

"It should," he grunted as he wrapped his arms around my body, one hand resting on my ass possessively.

I actually giggled right before I laid a sweet kiss on his lips.

If this was what it was going to be like moving forward, I was definitely looking forward to being his.

Chapter 19

Ben

I absolutely refused to touch Ariel again until I told her the truth. Okay, so maybe I *had* promised the same thing *yesterday* morning, too, but this time, I meant it.

I'd given myself one day yesterday to enjoy just being with Ariel, to savor the pleasure of being able to touch her. But it was Sunday morning, and I had to do what I should have done before I'd ever touched her.

Fuck! She'd handed me her virginity and had never looked back.

Guilt was devouring my soul right now, and I couldn't take it anymore.

I couldn't ignore what had to be done, and I felt like a fucking asshole for being so damn selfish.

Nothing would be absolutely right between us until she knew, and then decided if she could forgive me.

Christ! I *hoped* that was her decision because I didn't know what I'd do if it wasn't.

Now that I knew she was mine, now that I'd touched her, it made it even harder to contemplate *any* other outcome.

Dearest Protector

We'd done nothing but explore each other's bodies since I'd taken her virginity on Friday night.

Even though I wished we could do the same thing all day today, I knew that wasn't possible.

Time's up!

Moment of truth!

I closed my eyes and just enjoyed the moment, and the feel of Ariel's soft, sweet body in my arms, hoping like hell this wasn't the last time I held her like this.

She'd woken me up this morning to the feel of her gorgeous lips around my cock.

Inexperienced or not, the whole scene had felt like one of my hottest fantasies, only better and more intense than I'd ever imagined.

Because it was her.

Because it was Ariel.

Things had ended with her riding me until I'd finally lost it.

We'd showered together afterward, but somehow had still ended up back in my bed.

Not only could I *not* touch her again until I told her the truth, but also because she'd had more sex in the last thirty-six hours or so than any virgin should experience in one weekend.

She had to be sore as fuck, but she wouldn't admit to that, and her insatiable need to fuck me made me completely insane.

If she wanted me, I was always beyond ready to satisfy her.

I couldn't leave my damn hands off her.

"What were you dreaming about Friday night?" she asked curiously as she laid next to me in bed, her fingers toying with my hair. "Do you remember?"

Hell, yes. I remembered.

Her walking in front of a vehicle.

Her flying through the air.

Her landing on the pavement.

And *me*, being unable to stop it from happening.

I'd had the same nightmare a thousand times since her accident, and it always ended the same way.

With Ariel broken and bleeding in the middle of the street, bravely fighting for her life.

"I remember," I told her honestly as I opened my eyes. "You were in danger and I couldn't save you. I'm glad you woke me up."

"It's weird that you dreamed about something like that," she commented with a frown. "You actually saved me in real life. I'm not sure where I'd be right now if it hadn't been for you. I'm happy with my new career, my bank account is flush and growing larger every day, I have people I care about who care about me, and I'm now exclusive with the hottest guy on the planet."

"You really think I'm that hot?" I asked.

Okay, I sucked. I was a guy, and I wanted to hear about how much she wanted me before I had to break some bad news that might make her hate me.

If that made me totally pathetic, I didn't give a shit.

She raised an adorable brow before she answered, "Do you really need to ask that question after the last day and a half? Yes, I think you're smoking hot, Mr. Blackwood. I've been panting after you since we met that night of the ball on the patio. Happy now?"

Well, yeah. I was fucking ecstatic as a matter-of-fact.

"For now," I told her with a grin. "And I didn't save you, Ariel. You decided what you wanted and you went after it. All you needed was a small boost to help you out for a short time. You've been through more shit than most people could handle in a lifetime, sweetheart. Give yourself a break and the credit for your talent and strength."

How many people lost everything like she did, and didn't give up?

She smiled and kissed me softly before she rolled out of bed. "You've always been my biggest supporter, and you have no idea how much that matters," she said as she pulled on the same pajamas I'd taken off of her late Friday night. "I think I definitely need breakfast and coffee."

I got up and pulled on a pair of sweatpants so I could follow her to the kitchen.

We'd showered several times together, and we'd raided the kitchen for food, but this was the first time we'd actually surfaced for coffee or cooked anything since Friday.

Ariel made a huge pan of scrambled eggs and toasted us some bagels while I handled the coffee.

We scarfed down our food at the breakfast bar and took our coffee outside.

I waited until she was settled into the lounge chair next to me before I tried to ease into a discussion I definitely didn't want to have.

But I owed Ariel an explanation, and we should have had this talk before I'd laid my hands on her.

The fact that I hadn't told her was eating me alive.

Her first time should have been with a man she could trust with her whole heart.

Honestly, I had no excuses anymore.

She wasn't vulnerable anymore.

She was recovered from her surgery.

Her life was coming back together perfectly.

And her new career was wildly successful.

Ariel didn't *need* me anymore for anything.

She was a woman who was perfectly capable of taking care of herself.

"We need to talk," I started grimly. "I should have insisted that we had this discussion before anything happened between the two of us, but I couldn't fucking do it."

She took a sip of her coffee as she met my eyes over the rim of the mug. "That sounds ominous," she teased after she'd swallowed. "Talk. I don't think there's much of anything we can't or haven't discussed. I have to be honest, I kind of knew there was something bothering you. I figured you'd tell me eventually."

Oh, there was something we hadn't talked about, and I fucking hated myself for not mentioning it earlier.

Hell, Ariel knew me better than anyone ever would, so yeah, it didn't surprise me that she sensed something was eating me alive.

I broke eye contact.

I couldn't stare into those trusting, happy blue eyes and still tell her everything.

"I've had the same nightmare that I had on Friday night many times," I said stoically, forcing the words out of my mouth. "It's not something I made up in my imagination, Ariel. It's exactly what happened the night that you got hit by that taxi. I reached for you as you started to walk in front of traffic, but I missed grasping your arm by a matter of inches."

"I-I don't understand, Ben," she said, confused. "How can you possibly know exactly what happened? You weren't there. How could you have…reached for me?"

I gripped the handle of my coffee mug until I was afraid that it was going to snap.

I waited, knowing she was rolling over what I'd said in her head.

Any time now she'd figure out the obvious.

"Unless," she said hesitantly. "Unless you *were* there."

I nodded. "I *was* there. I was a total asshole. I came up next to you at the light while you were waiting for it. I was in a hurry, and I anticipated the light change. I stepped off the curb. I stopped before I walked into oncoming traffic. You didn't. That's why you stepped in front of that taxi, Ariel. You started going forward because *I did*. It was obvious you thought that the light had changed because I moved ahead. By the time I saw you going forward because I had, it was too damn late. You bolted, probably because you were worried about being late. I couldn't grab you before that taxi plowed into you. The whole thing played out just a few feet in front of me. Funny thing was, I was in a hurry to get to the same event you were headed toward, and the only reason I wanted to get there was to meet *you*. I never fucking noticed you were standing right next to me, and I didn't immediately notice you started moving ahead because I had. Not until it was too late."

"B-but we didn't even know each other back then," she stammered pensively, her tone completely bewildered.

I let out a frustrated breath. *Christ!* I knew I was doing a shitty job of explaining.

"I was at your premier earlier that night, Ariel. Generally, I'm not a huge ballet fan, but the business associate I was in New York to meet with had tickets, and he asked me to go with him. He's one of the donors for the ballet company. I was thoroughly enchanted from the moment you took the stage. I knew that I had to meet you in person. Although I was thoroughly gutted when Chris told me that he had a relationship with the principal dancer."

"Are you talking about Chris Longmont, the guy who was hosting the afterparty I was on my way to attend that night?" she asked.

"Yes. Chris was also a business associate of mine at the time. We weren't friends, and I knew very little about his personal life."

"He was *Erik's* partner, the dancer who played the *male* lead," she said. "He and I had no relationship except for friendship. It's hard not to be friendly when two people spend that much time dancing together. I'd never even met Chris in person before."

"That's a little fact I didn't know about until much later, after I discovered that you were back in Florida and my stepsister's best friend," I informed her. "But even though I thought *you* were exclusive with Chris at the time, that didn't stop me from wanting to meet you, wanting to know if you were just as captivating in person as you were on stage."

She was silent for a moment before she finally asked quietly, "Were you the guy who stayed to help me at the scene?"

"Yeah. Everything you told me that happened in your dream really did occur. After Ian's accident, I got certified in CPR and took some first aid courses. I didn't know a lot, but I did whatever I could to stop the bleeding and tried to keep you breathing and conscious until the paramedics arrived. I didn't have a lot of medical knowledge, but I knew enough to know that you were in really bad shape."

I had to force myself to dispel the image from my head of Ariel laying in the street, all of the blood pouring from her body because of her extensive injuries.

It was a picture I'd never been able to totally get out of my head.

"If what I dreamed is actually true, you helped a lot just by being there," she told me, her tone matter-of-fact. "No wonder I felt so connected to you when we met here. You *weren't* a stranger. God, I sensed that, but I didn't listen to my instincts. In my mind, it was impossible that we'd met before, but you were with me during the most traumatic event of my life. In my dream, I was absolutely terrified, and your voice was the only thing that made me want to try to breathe, which probably wasn't easy considering my lung was collapsed. Did you really lie to the medics so you could ride with me to the hospital? That's what I was told. A witness said that the guy who rode with me to the hospital said he was family."

"I did," I confessed. "I told them I was family. I promised you that I wouldn't leave you, and I didn't. Honestly, I couldn't. Not when you were alone, and no one was there with you. I had to ride in the passenger seat, but I stayed with you. You lost consciousness on the ride to the hospital. After you arrived in the ER, I wasn't allowed to go in with you because they had an entire trauma team that needed to be in that room. I waited in the waiting room until Chris and Erik arrived. Chris told me to leave, that he had everything covered and that he and Erik would stay there with you. I felt like I *had* to leave, even though my gut was telling me to stay. Chris knew that you and I had never met. Fuck! I thought he was your *boyfriend*, and that he'd stay with you every moment that you were there in the hospital. Had I known that Chris wasn't your significant other, and that he was only there because Erik was your friend, I never would have gone, Ariel. I would have stayed."

"Even though I was a stranger to you?" she questioned.

"You *never* felt like a stranger to me, and you felt even less like a stranger after you were hit by that taxi and asked me to stay near you," I answered hoarsely. "Ian once told me that Katie had knocked him on his ass from the second he'd seen her for the first time. I felt the same way about you. Christ! I wish things had been different. I wish I would have stayed. I wish I would have questioned who you'd have with you. I called Chris once I got back to Florida. It was a short call. I could hardly tell him that I was obsessed with his girlfriend, but I had to know whether or not you'd pulled through. He gave me a brief update, and told me it looked like you were going to make it, so I'm assuming that Erik told him how you were progressing. Once I knew that you were going to survive, I knew I had to stop

Dearest Protector

asking. Chris and I weren't well-acquainted, and our shared business interests ended soon after that call. Never once in that phone call back then did I think to ask about your relationship with him, and he said nothing that tipped me off to the fact that *Erik* was his love interest and not you. Maybe I didn't want to know because I thought you were seriously involved with someone else. Months later, when I realized that you were in Florida and that you were actually Katie's best friend, I called Chris again and asked him straight out if you and he were an item. That's when I figured out that you weren't, and that you'd mostly struggled through your recovery alone. I hated myself for that. There wasn't a single day that I didn't wonder how you were doing, and there were many nights when I had nightmares about what happened. You have no idea how much I looked forward to seeing you again at my mother's birthday ball. If that event hadn't already been planned when I figured out the truth, I would have found a way to meet you through Katie some other way."

"So you offered me that job because you felt guilty?" she asked, her voice completely flat.

"No," I said truthfully. "I did it because I gave a shit about what happened to you, and I knew you'd been through hell. Maybe there was a little—or possibly a lot—of guilt involved, too, because I was the asshole who made you walk in front of that taxi in the first place. I'm sorry, Ariel. I'm so fucking sorry that happened to you. Had I not been in such a hurry, we wouldn't be talking about this right now because you never would have had to give up dancing. That accident would have never happened if I hadn't made it happen."

She was silent, so I finally turned my head to look at her face.

Fuck!

Tears were streaming down her cheeks, but the expression in her eyes was almost lifeless.

It took everything I had not to lift her into my lap so I could hold her, but her body language and her expression told me that wasn't what she wanted.

She didn't want me to touch her.

~ *173* ~

Her arms were wrapped around her legs like she needed some kind of cocoon to protect herself.

Son of a bitch!

I'd done the last thing I wanted to do.

I'd hurt Ariel Prescott…again.

Chapter 20

Ariel

I didn't blame Ben for my accident.
He was taking on the guilt about what had happened to me for absolutely no reason at all.

People anticipated lights all the time, and everyone was in a hurry, especially in a city like New York.

I knew it was my own distracted brain that had caused me to walk in front of that taxi. I didn't remember Ben jumping that light, but I remembered having a million things on my mind that evening.

I was late, which I hated, and worried about getting to that after-party on time. That was my last true memory, and I wasn't surprised that I'd done something stupid.

Maybe it was his actions that had made me start moving forward, but ultimately, it was my impatience and my stupid obsession to stick to my rigorous schedule that had obviously caused me to do something completely out of character.

It wasn't like he'd *pushed* me in front of that taxi. I flown in front of it myself. I should have been paying attention to the light.

If what he said was really true, he'd actually tried to stop me, and I knew for a fact that he'd probably saved my life after I'd gotten hit.

He had no reason to feel guilty because he did something people did all the damn time.

What was *really* killing me right now was the fact that he'd lied to me.

I thought we'd been so close.

I'd trusted him so completely.

I was so shocked and confused that I didn't know who the real Ben Blackwood was right now.

Okay, maybe he'd never out and out said that he *wasn't* there.

I'd never straight out asked him if we'd met before.

But he knew that I had no memory of that period of time right before and after the accident, and he never spoke up to fill in the blanks.

He never mentioned that we'd had a previous encounter.

Nothing.

Not a single word.

Not even after we'd become close as friends.

I'd told him *everything.* Every single painful detail of my life, including my childhood.

I'd thought that I knew Ben, when, in fact, I'd never really known him at all.

The Ben Blackwood I thought I knew never would have held back this kind of information from me.

God, I feel like a total idiot.

I'd even told him how badly I wanted to know the truth about that night, and he *still* hadn't told me.

The fact that he'd been present at my accident was a pretty big exclusion for two people who supposedly knew and cared about each other.

"Why didn't you just tell me, Ben?" I asked tearfully. "Why did you have to lie? I thought we were close. I thought we told each other everything."

Dearest Protector

"If you had known the truth, would you still have accepted that job as my assistant?" he asked tersely.

I thought about his question for a moment before I shook my head. "I don't know. If I thought you were motivated by guilt, maybe not. Although, I was pretty desperate, so you may have still convinced me to give it a try. I guess we'll never know."

"It wasn't just *guilt*, Ariel. I wanted to help you. I wanted to get to know you."

I swiped the tears from my face angrily.

I had to wonder if he'd been disappointed once he'd realized that the dramatic ballerina he'd seen on stage was really just an illusion.

He'd been fascinated and momentarily infatuated with someone who had never really existed.

When I was dancing, it was a role. I was pretending to be someone else. For the most part, I actually lost myself when I was dancing. I took on the persona of someone else.

"Was any of this real, Ben?" I had to ask. "I'm not and never have been any of those characters I played on stage. Once the costume and makeup came off, I was just…me. If I caught your attention while I was on stage, you must have realized at some point that I wasn't really that person at all."

Maybe that was why I'd always loved dancing.

I could be someone else just for a little while.

My whole identity had been tied up in the ballerina back then because I'd never had one of my own.

My value as a person had always been dependent on my ability to dance and do it well.

When I'd lost that ability, I'd lost myself completely.

But I wasn't lost anymore.

I finally knew who I was without ballet.

I had to know that everything we shared wasn't about the woman on that stage that night.

"Do you honestly think that all I cared about was that woman on stage?" Ben asked huskily. "We all have false personas, Ariel. By now, you should know that I'm not the Ben Blackwood that people see in the media, either, or the guy who makes hard decisions and deals in a boardroom. The real me isn't that billionaire tech mogul and CEO of one of the biggest corporations in the world. That's just one part of who I am, but because it's the most provocative, sometimes that's all people see and the only part of me that anyone wants to know."

God, I understood that. I really did.

But did I really know the real Ben Blackwood?

I wasn't sure anymore.

I hadn't even had time to process the fact that Ben was the mystery man at the scene of the accident.

The guy who was probably the reason I was still alive right now.

The man in my dreams that I'd never been able to figure out.

One thing I would have bet my life on was the fact that Ben would never lie to me or withhold the truth on something this important.

Now I was questioning our entire relationship and wondering if I was a major fool.

"My accident was not your fault, Ben," I said, wanting to make sure he knew that. "Maybe I don't remember what happened after I was standing at that light, but I was extremely distracted. I was constantly stressed out about sticking to my schedule, and I was late. That after-party was an obligation, and all I wanted was to get through it so I could go home and soak my sore feet. I was exhausted and running on the high I'd gotten from doing my first performance as a principal dancer. I was wired and anxious, which is why I did something that stupid. Any guilt you have is completely unwarranted."

Maybe I was confused about a lot of things right now, but one thing was for certain, Ben *had* been there for me when I really needed him. He'd stayed to help save my life after I'd done something exceptionally foolish. He didn't need to haul any guilt around about the accident itself.

"Do you really think I can easily accept that, Ariel? It was my fault. There hasn't been a single day since it happened that I don't think about that. If I hadn't jumped that fucking curb—"

"Stop!" I insisted. "People jump curbs all the time. You didn't push me off that damn curb. I did it. I walked in front of a taxi because I wasn't paying attention. If you hadn't been there, I also may have bled to death right there on that street. You did everything you could to save me, and you didn't have to do it. I wanted to call you and thank you later, after I heard about the mystery man who had helped me, but the police hadn't gotten your name, and I never did meet Chris. It's highly possible that he was only there on the day of the accident. Erik was alone when he came to visit me after I regained consciousness. Those first days in the hospital are and always will be a blank to me because I was so medicated. Later, after you and I met at the ball in the most mortifying way possible, you helped me put my life back together, Ben. You gave me the support I needed to get me back on my feet again. I'll always be grateful to you for everything you've done."

"The thing I want isn't your gratitude, Ariel," Ben said in a graveled voice.

I shrugged. "Too bad, because you'll always have it, whether you want it or not. You have no idea what it feels like to be free and to know that I can pay my bills. I have more money in the bank than I know what to do with, and more cash on the way. Money may not be everything, but it means a lot when you've been in a situation where you can't even buy groceries. More importantly, the job you gave me got me out of a very bad situation with a horrible boss. I was finally able to breathe, which opened up a whole new world and career for me. That never would have happened for me if it wasn't for your generosity and your friendship."

"And are we still friends, Ariel?" Ben asked warily.

I shook my head. "I don't know. I don't know what to think right now, Ben. I don't blame you for what happened. At all. But I never thought you could keep something like this from me. That wasn't who we were as friends or as lovers. It makes me think everything was a lie, and that I was a fool."

Maybe I'd only had less than two days as Ben's lover, but that experience had rocked my entire world, and part of me still refused to believe that Ben had been playing me for some reason.

What we'd shared had felt so damn real to me.

~ 179 ~

Then again, I wasn't exactly experienced when it came to dating and relationships.

People lied.

Hearts got broken.

Even after knowing that other person for years.

"Nothing else was ever a lie, Ariel," Ben said, his tone raspy and insistent. "The way I feel about you was never some kind of joke. And it wasn't the ballerina persona that drew me in when I saw you. It was something else. I can't explain it, and it will probably never make sense. I still don't know how I just *knew* that you and I were somehow meant to be together, but I don't waste my time trying to find a rational explanation anymore. There is no sensible reason, but my instincts were right. That's really all that matters. Anything else I've ever said was the truth. At first, I didn't want to tell you because you had so much on your plate, and I wanted to help you. I didn't know if you'd ever accept a job from the guy who had caused you that much pain. I wasn't sure how you'd react if I told you the truth. I needed you to take the damn job."

"What prompted you to tell me now?"

Ben let out a huge breath before he said, "I had to, Ariel. I should have told you a long time ago. I could always think of a good excuse not to, but the honest truth is that I didn't want to lose you. I want more than some kind of friends with benefits relationship, and to get there, I had to tell you the truth. It's the only thing that I haven't been honest about. I had to come clean and hope you'd forgive me. I didn't have a choice. I couldn't live with myself if I didn't."

My heart skittered as I looked up and our eyes met.

He looked almost more broken than I felt right now, and I couldn't stop my tears from falling like a river down my face.

God, he looked so sincere.

Then again, I'd always thought he was genuine. I thought he'd never look me in the eyes and tell me a lie or that he'd omit something this important to me.

Was I being an idiot?

I suddenly realized that I was head over heels in love with this man, and I wasn't even sure if I could *trust* him.

If I did, and he turned out to be a complete liar, it would totally destroy me.

I stood up so fast that I nearly knocked the lounger on its side.

I picked up my empty coffee mug as I said, "I think I'd really like to gather my things and go back to the condo right now. I need some space to think."

I was barely keeping it together at the moment, and if I sat here for another moment, I'd turn into a hot mess that couldn't stop bawling like a child.

My hands were shaking, and I nearly dropped the ceramic mug I was holding as I turned toward the patio door.

Ben shot out of his seat and reached for my arm. "Ariel," he said, his voice raw with what sounded like emotional pain.

Don't do it, Ariel!

Don't turn to him like you always do!

He's not the guy you think you know!

You need to escape!

"Don't!" I said as I stepped forward. "I can't do this, Ben. Not right now. I have to think this through."

He couldn't have looked more crestfallen if I'd slapped him in the face.

I wanted to fall into his arms and forgive him, but I was too confused, too stunned because I'd just realized I was in love with a man I might not really know at all.

He dropped his arm to his side, his expression harsh with regret as he answered, "Take all the time you need. You know where I'll be. Right here waiting for you if you decide you want to come back. I'm not going anywhere, and I sure as fuck will never even look at another woman when the only one that I really want is you."

I shook my head, tears flowing down my cheeks as I replied as honestly as I could. "I don't know what I want right now. I'm confused. I thought we had something real, and now I don't know what to think. The Ben I thought I knew wouldn't keep this big of a secret from me."

His eyes darkened as he rasped, "It was all real, Ariel. This is the only thing I've ever lied to you about, and if I had to do it all over again, I'd probably do the same thing. There's no way I could take that chance of you turning me down flat on the job offer when you were desperate. The only thing I'd change is how long it took for me to tell you the truth. After what happened with Leland Brock, my primary concern was keeping you safe when you were vulnerable. Hell, that's probably *always* going to be my main concern. I'm fucking obsessed with your well-being and your happiness. Always will be."

I choked back a sob.

I couldn't allow myself to become a blubbering mess right now.

I needed time.

I needed to think.

I couldn't do that while my damn heart was breaking because Ben looked so troubled and devastated.

I didn't know what was real and what was artificial anymore.

I hated myself because I still ached for him, and it took everything I had not to reach for him because that's what I'd always done.

I'd been leaning on him and his strength for far too long.

"I'm sorry that I can't give you an answer right now," I told him. "I'm not sure what that answer is myself."

Like it or not, I could never hate Ben Blackwood. He'd been much too instrumental in helping me change my life, and he'd been way too kind.

Whether all of that was an act or not, he *had* been there when I'd needed him.

He shrugged, but his eyes were tormented as he answered, "I can wait. If you need to talk about it, or if you need anything, you know where to find me. I meant it when I said I wasn't going anywhere, Ariel."

I nodded jerkily because I couldn't speak.

Gathering every bit of strength I had, I turned and walked back into the house.

I really need space. I really need space.

Ben was giving me exactly what I'd asked for, just like he always did.

Given that fact, why was it so damn hard not to run right back to him because I felt like being with him was exactly where I belonged?

Chapter 21

Ariel

"This place is adorable," Katie said a few weeks later as she walked out of the bedroom of my new apartment. "And pretty close to your old condo."

I nodded as Katie sat down on the opposite end of my new couch. "I like it. I'm still close to the beach."

The apartment was small, but worlds away from the one I'd lived in when I'd first come back to Fort Myers.

I'd decorated it in a coastal vibe with furnishings that were beachy, light, and bright.

Lately, I'd been taking a lot of photos of seashells, boats, and other seascapes. I had a whole portfolio of pictures that I was currently working on for a new collection.

I'd also finished two more commissioned pieces that had more than paid for my move.

I looked around the cozy home with a sigh, still amazed that I could afford this kind of living space. There was something to be said about knowing I'd earned the money to buy every single new thing is this place.

Dearest Protector

I'd even replaced my old clunker of a vehicle. I hadn't gone crazy and bought something brand new, but the compact car that now sat in my parking space was reliable, and only two years old.

And I *still* had an amazing bank balance, and I was earning more every single day.

"You got a new haircut, too," Katie observed as she cocked her head.

I lifted my hand and ran my fingers through my curls.

I'd been on a mission to find myself, which included finding a hairstyle that suited me.

My unruly locks still hung to my shoulders, but the stylist had taken off a lot of the length. The new style had done wonders to help tame my crazy curls.

"It's a lot easier to handle these curls in a shorter style," I told Katie with a smile.

"You look beautiful, Ariel. I can tell you replaced your old wardrobe, too," Katie mused.

I nodded. "I have to meet with potential clients sometimes. I thought it was past time I took care of myself."

"It feels good, right?" Katie asked as she ran her hand through her own stylish cut. "I don't think my hair has been this healthy since I was a kid."

I smiled as I saw the glint of light from the large diamond that Ian had put on Katie's finger not long ago.

My best friend looked beautiful, too, but the most gorgeous thing about her was the happiness in her eyes.

We'd both known hardship and sacrifice.

We'd also known long periods of time when taking care of ourselves had been our last priority.

It was almost surreal that both of us were in a completely different place now.

I held my hand up to my eyes and said jokingly, "Stop! That ring is going to make me go blind."

She held her hand out and stared at her ring finger. "It was a little over-the-top, which reminds me very much of my fiancé. I love it."

- 185 -

She loved her fiancé even more than she loved that ring, and judging by the way Ian treated Katie, he felt exactly the same way about her.

My best friend had changed so much, yet she was the same Katie I'd always known and loved.

Gone was the woman who doubted herself and was socially awkward.

I'd attended her graduation on the East Coast, accepting the offered ride in Ian's private jet. Ben had followed a little later in his own jet, so I hadn't spent much awkward time together with Ben at the event.

Ben and I had been cordial, but we'd hardly had the opportunity to exchange a few words before the ceremony had started. He'd kept his distance afterward, obviously respecting my request for personal space.

He'd been a man of his word.

He hadn't called.

He hadn't texted.

He hadn't pushed.

Katie had performed her speech like a woman who had no problem being in the public eye.

No one would ever have known that she was self-conscious about being in front of a crowd.

"So," Katie asked in a pseudo casual tone. "What made you decide to move out of the condo? Spill it, Ariel. Ben told me what happened yesterday, but he didn't get any sympathy from me. He should have told you the truth. He's moping around right now like you died. It's completely pathetic."

I'd tried extremely hard not to discuss Ben with Katie because she was so close to him, but it hadn't been easy not to spill everything.

The only thing I'd mentioned was that I wasn't working for Ben anymore because I wanted to dedicate my time to my business now that it would support me.

Luckily, she hadn't asked for details because she'd been so busy... until now.

Dearest Protector

"It's not that I didn't want to tell you," I explained. "But you and Ben are close, and he's Ian's brother."

She lifted a brow. "And you're my best friend. I cried on your shoulder plenty of times when I was going through drama with Ian. I love Ben, but it's not like I don't know that men can be total jackasses. He shouldn't have kept that kind of information from you. God, I can hardly believe that he was actually there when your accident happened and he never told you. I've already lectured him about that and why he should have been upfront with you. Did you think I wouldn't stand up for you after everything we've both been through together?"

I shook my head. I knew Katie would always support me. "It's not that. I just didn't want to make things difficult for you."

"It won't," she insisted as she reached into her large tote bag, pulled something out, and tossed it onto my lap with a perfect throw. "I even brought candy, and we're already drinking wine. I'm staying for a while."

I laughed as I lifted the enormous bag of candy that had been handpicked and packed.

I already knew it was from our favorite candy store in the city, one that we'd rarely been able to afford when we were younger.

I'd never been allowed to eat sweets because of my dancing career and my rigorous diet, but Katie and I had snuck out to get some a few times. We'd been so stealthy that my mother had never found out.

"Thanks," I said as I removed the tie around the bag. "I probably don't need a lot of help filling out my hips now. I think I've already gained plenty of weight since I went to work for Ben, but I'm eating it anyway."

There was something very therapeutic about chocolate, especially when it involved men, disagreements, and broken hearts.

She folded her arms across her chest stubbornly. "You're like a sister to me. We've known each other since we were kids. I'm not leaving until you tell me everything."

I popped a chocolate into my mouth, tossed some to Katie, and then washed it down with a sip of my wine before I started talking.

~ *187* ~

I caught her up on what Ben hadn't told her, and I answered any and all of her questions.

"So, I guess the only thing left to do is to decide if you're going to eventually forgive him," Katie stated before she devoured another chocolate.

I sighed. "It's not like I don't want to do that," I confessed. "Maybe I'm still trying to figure out exactly what happened. We were really close, and then things turned sexual, too. I gave the man my virginity for God's sake, which is something I could never regret because it was amazing. Crap! I think I'm just afraid that he'll decide there's other things he thinks I'm too fragile to handle in the future, and he'll hide them. I know he didn't mean to hurt me. In his own, misguided way, I think he was trying to protect me."

I'd done a lot of thinking since Ben had told me the truth, and that was the only thing that really made sense.

I wasn't confused anymore, and I'd finally stopped thinking with my heart.

I *did* know Ben.

I *didn't* think he'd intentionally deceived me.

That just wasn't who Ben was.

I'd come to the conclusion that he'd been truthful about the fact that nothing else was a lie, but that didn't stop me from worrying about a possible future together.

I didn't need constant protection anymore.

I'd come a long way from the woman I'd been when Ben and I had first met.

"He was trying to protect you," Katie confirmed. "But that's really no excuse for keeping the truth from you. He had no idea back then how strong you are, Ariel. Your circumstances may have been dire, but that doesn't make you weak. I think you could have handled the truth much better before both of your emotions got involved."

"I probably would have still taken the job he was offering," I said. "Yeah, I might have wondered if he just felt sorry for me or guilty, but it wasn't like I had a whole lot of options at the time. I would have to be a total idiot to turn down an opportunity like that."

I'd had to get really honest with myself to come to that conclusion, but it was the truth.

Katie's eyebrows lifted. "I don't think that offer had anything to do with pity. At all. I think he took one look at you on that stage and decided he had to have you. Yeah, it's a caveman approach, but Ian did the same thing. Ian also lied to me, and I was in the same situation as you are right now. I had to decide if I was going to let those lies go and embrace the fact that he loved me like a madman. For me, Ian was worth that risk, and I know he'd never lie to me again because it would destroy our relationship. He loves me, and I love him. I don't think he'd ever be willing to jeopardize that love again. I've made it very clear that I'm willing to deal with his obsessive protectiveness, but I won't tolerate lies between us."

"In some ways, I understand why Ian felt like he had to lie," I pondered aloud. "His need to make sure you that you were financially okay while you were going to college overcame his desire to be honest."

She shrugged. "I could say the same thing about Ben. But hey, at least he didn't become your stalker."

I snorted. "He didn't have to. I was totally willing to be his assistant, his friend, and then his lover. I can't regret any of those relationships."

"He's a good man, Ariel," Katie replied in a more serious tone. "If it's any consolation, I think he struggled with his decision not to tell you, and I think he's living in hell because of it. In the end, I think he had to tell you because he couldn't live with himself anymore. He's crazy in love with you, girlfriend."

My eyes shot to Katie's face. "He never told me that he loved me."

"Well, he didn't tell me that, either, but it's so damn obvious. Do you really think he'd be acting like he was in mourning if he didn't?"

"How is he, really?" I finally asked, even though I probably shouldn't.

"He's hurting, just like you are," Katie said candidly. "But he's stubborn, just like his older brother. If he thinks you need space, he's going to give it to you for as long as necessary. But he's not going away."

"I don't think I want him to go away," I admitted. "I love him so much it hurts, Katie, but I want to make sure that I have my shit together before I try to talk to him. I might be strong, but in some respects, Ben was right about me being vulnerable. I was completely lost because I couldn't dance anymore, and after that I was in survival mode. Being an assistant for a slimebag like Leland was probably the straw that nearly broke me. I was pretty low at that point."

"I know you loved your mom," Katie said gently. "But she was a tough woman to please. I think you were still fighting with those demons, too."

"I know. I've been working through that in counseling," I told her. "I've totally realized that her love was always conditional and how dysfunctional that was. That's probably why I had such a hard time letting go of the fact that I couldn't dance anymore. My entire identity revolved around dancing and doing it perfectly. Dancing was the only thing that made me feel like I was loved and accepted. I think she loved me in her own way, but it was messed up. I'm not even sure if she was telling me the truth about my birth father. I sent in a DNA sample to see if I can find out who he was. She told me he died before I was ever born. If he's really dead, then I guess I'll have closure on that topic. If he's alive, I'm not even sure I want to approach him. I just want to know where I came from. That question has always been there. Does that make sense?"

"It makes perfect sense," Katie agreed. "I'd want to know. My father sucked, but at least I know who he was."

"That's all I really need to know," I explained. "I guess I just need to tie up some of the loose ends in my life. I don't associate my self-worth with my ability to dance anymore, and I'm really happy about my new career. There's just…"

"Ben?" Katie finished.

I nodded. "That's my most difficult challenge right now."

"Maybe you should just take things slow," she suggested thoughtfully. "Everything has happened pretty fast between you two, not

Dearest Protector

that I have any room to criticize about that, but I wasn't in an accident that almost took my life, either. But for God's sake, please talk to him. He's always been a workaholic, but he's even worse than he was before. He has no reason to work the hours he does right now, but I think it's his idea of a distraction. I'm pretty sure he never sleeps, and he looks like shit."

My heart squeezed at the thought of Ben going back to his old workaholic ways.

"I wonder if he's upset about the check," I speculated.

Katie sent me a questioning glance. "What check?"

I took another gulp of wine, unwrapped another chocolate, and told her about what I'd decided to do.

Chapter 22

Ben

"She sent me a goddamn check, like I was some kind of obligation that she had to pay off," I told Ian as we sat in my office at headquarters. "She even calculated the rent she would have had to pay for the condo, and she included the salary I paid her as my assistant. There was no personal note. Just a statement of what she was paying, the key to the condo, and the fucking check."

Yeah, I was pissed off, but honestly, *that* had hurt.

Like I wanted or needed her money?

Ian shrugged. "Maybe she just wanted to pay you back. Honestly, it's kind of sweet."

I glared at him. "There's nothing sweet about her telling me fuck off with a check."

"You have no idea what she was trying to tell you. She was nice enough at Kate's graduation," he reminded me.

Yeah, she was nice enough to me—if she was a stranger who was meeting me for the first time.

She wasn't.

Dearest Protector

"She hates me," I said in an emotion-roughened voice. "And she was distant at Katie's graduation. Well, to me anyway. She said a handful of words that she'd say to a stranger."

"Ben, give her some time. Do you think she's not struggling with this whole thing, too?" Ian questioned.

"I have no idea," I said honestly. "She's not exactly telling me how she feels."

"I don't think she sent you that check to hurt you. Ariel isn't spiteful or deliberately hurtful," Ian pointed out.

My shoulders slumped. "You're right. She's not. Maybe it's just driving me insane because I have no idea what's on her mind right now."

"Maybe you should just call her and ask her," he suggested.

"I can't do that," I said as every muscle in my body tensed. "I promised to give her some space. And I certainly can't stop by her place since I have no idea where she lives anymore."

I'd simply gotten the key to the condo with that damn check.

She'd moved, but I had no idea where she'd gone.

Fuck! It wasn't like I hadn't been tempted to call her.

Every. Single. Goddamn. Day.

"Katie knows," Ian informed me. "She's at Ariel's new apartment right now."

"I have no right to ask," I said hoarsely. "But just tell me that she doesn't live anywhere near the place she had before she came to work for me."

"Okay," Ian drawled. "She lives nowhere near the downtown area, and it's a good neighborhood. It's about a block from where the condo is. She's making very decent money now, and her business opportunities are enormous. She has no reason to go back to a place like that. Take a breath. She's okay."

My body relaxed a little. "Thank fuck!"

I'd told myself that it was none of my business where she chose to live, but I'd thought about it ever since I'd gotten that check and knew that she'd moved.

"So, about how long are you going to be able to wait?" Ian asked.

"As long as it takes for her to forget about the fact that I lied to her," I shot back.

Ian shot me a sympathetic look. "I don't envy you, brother. Been there myself."

I had to let Ariel come to me, whether I liked it or not.

I'd fucked up, and I was going to have to live with the fact that she needed space.

Maybe I just hadn't been prepared for exactly how much space she required.

Three weeks of total silence from her end was a little more than I could handle.

"There's every possibility that she'll never come back," I said tersely.

Ian shook his head. "That's not going to happen. I've seen you two together. She's crazy about you. It sounds to me like she's just trying to pull her life together. Katie said she's been working pretty hard, and she recently got herself a better vehicle. I think she's been pretty busy. It's not like she's out shopping for another man, Ben. She's been out taking a lot of photos. In case you haven't noticed, Ariel has changed. She took advantage of her opportunities and she's come a long way in just a matter of months."

She had. I knew that. But the way I cared about her hadn't changed at all.

It really sucked that my brother knew more about the woman who was making me crazy than I did right now.

I was used to being in Ariel's life on a daily basis.

We ate together.

Shared our day together.

Hung out together every single night.

And now...nothing.

Christ! I missed her. I missed every single thing about her.

Her scent.

The way her body felt against mine.

The way she laughed, and the way she tried to tease me out of my seriousness.

Dearest Protector

The way she gave me her total attention when I was talking, like nothing interested her as much as whatever I was saying to her at that moment.

Hell, I even missed the way she nagged me about eating healthier. My house felt empty and lifeless without her there.

And I'd give anything to know what she was thinking right now. But all I'd gotten was a fucking…check.

"She's fine, Ben," Ian said in a calming tone. "If anything was wrong, I'd tell you. I don't know how she's doing emotionally, but her life is good. Her career is good. She's got more offers for commissions than she can reasonably take on all at one time. Maybe she moved so she could take control of her own life. The condo was always going to be a temporary thing, right?"

"More or less," I said unhappily. "It was supposed to be hers until she no longer needed it. But she knew she could live there for as long as she wanted. It's not like I wanted her to find another place to live."

Unless she wanted to move in with…me.

If she'd wanted to move in with me, I would have happily taken that fucking condo back.

"But she knew that place wasn't really hers," Ian pointed out. "It was on loan to her temporarily."

"Honestly," I replied. "I would have given Ariel anything she wanted. If she'd wanted that condo to be hers, I would have signed the papers for that in a heartbeat."

"Luckily," Ian retorted. "She wasn't the kind of woman who would take advantage of that generosity. Mom's coming over to our place later for dinner. I think you should come. Get out of this damn office. Get out of the house."

"I'm not very good company right now," I said as I shook my head. "I thought I'd stay here for a while and go over the information for the meetings next week."

Ian shot me a disgusted look. "We've already gone over everything, and you don't need to stay late. It's almost five. I'm headed out in a few minutes. I thought we agreed that there are more important things in life than this company, and that we have a perfectly capable staff that can take some of the load off us."

He was right.

We didn't have to kill ourselves anymore. Ian and I had hired people together. Good people who were very capable of making things easier for both of us.

And yes, I had agreed with him that there were more important things in life than Blackwood Technologies, but that was before I'd lost the only woman I wanted to spend time with when I wasn't working.

Now, I didn't give a shit.

I didn't want to be home without her there.

It was better for me to stay busy.

I heard a notification go off for a cell phone.

"Mine," Ian informed me as he reached for his cell in his pocket.

I watched a happy smile form on my brother's face as he shared, "Kate. She's on her way home."

Another notification sounded.

"Must be yours," Ian informed me as he started to type a response to Katie.

I grimaced as I reached for my phone that was sitting on the desk.

Ariel: Katie invited me to her place for dinner tonight with your mom. You're probably going. Would it be really awkward if I go, too?

Fucking hell! It had never occurred to me that *Ariel* might be at my brother's house for dinner.

That changed everything.

If I'd thought there was even a chance that she'd be there, I would have accepted Ian's invitation.

Would it be awkward?

Hell, no. Not for me. Of course, I really wanted to see *her*.

I wanted to talk to her.

I wanted to spend time breathing the same air that she was breathing.

Obviously, she wasn't opposed to seeing me if she was asking, right?

I tried not to get my hopes up, but that was almost impossible.

~ *196* ~

Dearest Protector

It had been three weeks since I'd been with her.

Since we'd hardly had a chance to speak at the graduation, *that* encounter didn't really count.

I watched as Ian sent his response and stood up.

"I'm out of here," he said as he sent me an empathetic look before heading toward the door.

"Ian?" I called out before he had a chance to exit.

My brother turned after he'd opened the office door. "Yeah?"

"You're right. Life is too short to spend it all at work. I think I'll come by your place. It's been a while since I've seen Mom. I'll go home and change first. What time is dinner?" I asked.

Ian grinned. "You're so full of shit, little brother. Let me guess… you just figured out that Ariel might be there, right?"

I grinned back at him. "Maybe."

"Dinner will be around seven. Bring your suit. It's hot and Kate will probably want to go for a swim later," he instructed.

I nodded. "I'll be there."

"How disappointed are you going to be if Ariel doesn't show?" Ian asked cautiously.

"She'll be there," I informed him.

"Then you have more intel than I do," Ian observed. "All Kate told me is that she invited her. Later."

"Later."

The second that Ian was out the door, I started to text.

Chapter 23

Ariel

I stared at the message I'd just typed, wondering if I'd done the right thing.

Maybe I shouldn't have sent it.

But honestly, I needed the break, and I really wanted to see Marilyn, Ian, and...Ben.

God, I missed him.

I sighed as I put the chocolate Katie had left for me on the table beside the couch.

Unfortunately, the bag was nearly empty, and I was just finishing off the bottle of wine Katie and I had opened.

I held my breath when I realized that Ben was typing a response.

Ben: *Not awkward at all. I'd really like to see you, Ariel.*

I breathed a sigh of relief.

Me: *Thanks. I'd like to see you, too.*

Ben: *I'm headed home. Do you want me to pick you up? I'm sure there will be plenty of wine with dinner, and I know it gets to your head.*

I glanced at my half empty wine glass. I'd already had a few glasses.

Dearest Protector

Me: *Katie and I already had some. Maybe it would be a good idea if we rode together. Or I could just stay home, Ben. I really don't want to intrude.*

"Please tell me that you want me to go," I whispered breathlessly as I waited anxiously for his reply.

Ben: *I'm only going because you are. Text me your address. I'll be there as soon as I get home and change.*

My heart skittered inside my chest as I answered.

Me: *No hurry. Dinner isn't until seven. See you whenever you get here.*

I sent him my new address, and then I plopped my phone onto the wireless charger and stood up.

I was wearing a bright red, off the shoulders top and a pair of jeans that hugged the crap out of my backside. The outfit would work fine for a casual gathering.

I went into my bedroom to grab a pair of sandals and a tote bag. I put my pool stuff into the bag and slid my sandals onto my feet.

I chastised myself for pausing to put on some makeup, change my earrings, and spritz on some light fragrance, but it had been a while since I'd seen Ben, so maybe I was slightly nervous.

Since I had time, I also tamed my wayward curls and slipped on a colorful bracelet that matched my outfit.

"Ready," I said as I nodded to my reflection in the mirror like I was giving myself a pep talk.

I hesitated as I really took in my image in the mirror, realizing that I no longer disliked the woman I saw there anymore.

I actually liked being me.

I put a finger to the place at my hairline that would forever be scarred from my accident.

It was barely visible anymore, especially when I had on makeup, but I hardly noticed it, even when I wasn't wearing foundation.

I really was okay with the woman looking back at me, even if she wasn't perfect.

I was smiling as I left the bedroom.

I forced myself to sit on the couch and get distracted with a project on the computer until the doorbell rang.

"That was fast," I said under my breath as I went to the door.

My heart was racing at about a million beats per minute as I pulled the door open.

It was stupid.

It wasn't like I didn't know Ben...intimately.

Still, when I pulled the door open, I felt like I was seeing him for the first time in a very long time.

And God, he looked good.

I swallowed hard as I took in his hard body and his gloriously handsome face. He was dressed in tan chinos and a casual navy shirt.

"Hi," I said breathlessly as I waved him inside. "Let me grab my stuff and we can go."

His heated gaze was almost predatory as it roamed over my entire body.

"No hurry," he said in that fuck-me baritone I loved. "We have plenty of time. You look absolutely stunning, Ariel. How have you been?"

"I'm good," I told him as he entered and I closed the door behind him. "I've been busy. I have more work offers than I can handle at the moment."

God, I'd forgotten how Ben towered over me in height, and just how much space he seemed to consume in a smallish apartment.

"Are you going to show me around your new place?" he asked, his eyes glued to my face like he was trying to figure out what I was thinking.

I laughed nervously. "There's not much to show. It's just a tiny one bedroom, but it has a nice balcony."

"I like it," he commented as he finally stopped checking me out and looked around the space. "It looks like you."

It did, which was why I liked it.

I showed Ben around the inside, which took all of two minutes.

The tour ended on the outdoor balcony I'd liked so much that I'd jumped at the chance to rent the apartment.

Dearest Protector

It was warm outside, and humid, but I normally spent my time out here later at night.

Just like Ben and I did so often at his place.

I turned and leaned against the railing, the breeze ruffling my curly hair.

Ben moved closer, so close that I couldn't have escaped inside if I wanted to, and I wasn't sure that I wanted to move away.

He reached into his pocket and pulled out what looked like a piece of paper.

I only realized that it was the check I'd sent him when he held it out for me to take.

"You know I'm never going to cash this," he said, his expression troubled. "Take it back."

I shook my head adamantly. "I never meant to hurt you by sending that. I guess I wanted you to know that I didn't need to lean on you anymore financially. That I could stand on my own two feet. Maybe what I really wanted was a clean slate. I don't want you for your money, Ben. I never have."

He put the check back in his pocket, his eyes much warmer. "I never thought, not even once, that you wanted my money, Ariel. Anything I ever did for you was done strictly because I wanted to make your life easier. I'll still never cash this, but I'll hang onto it for now if that's what you need from me. Hell, if this is what it takes for the two of us to be together, I'll frame it and hang it on my goddamn wall."

My heart ached as I realized just how much Ben was willing to do to make me happy. It wasn't really in his nature to take no for an answer, but he didn't try to cajole me to get his way.

I sighed. "I'm trying to leave that old life behind me, Ben. The accident is over. The pain of my injuries is done now that the hardware is out of my foot. My struggles are part of my past, and instead of waiting for the other shoe to drop, I want to live my life without regrets. I've lived most of my life being told exactly what to do, which was essentially nothing unless it involved dancing. What I could eat. What time to sleep. What I could wear. What I should do with any free time I had, which always involved dance obligations. Now that my life doesn't revolve around dancing, I've been trying to figure out what I want and who I really am. Maybe that sounds a little crazy—"

"It doesn't," Ben said as he placed his hands gently on my bare shoulders. "I get it. All I've really wanted was for you to feel like you're free of that prison, Ariel. To figure out that you're still just as amazing as you've always been, even if dancing *isn't* in that equation."

Tears welled up in my eyes as I looked up at him and nodded. "I'm figuring out that I really am enough, no matter what I do and who I choose to be. I've never felt this way before, but it's kind of… powerful."

He nodded like he'd known that I'd find myself all along. "You're not just powerful. You're extraordinary. You always have been. You just never saw it."

I lifted my hand and stroked his jawline. "So are you. The most extraordinary man I've ever met. I overreacted when you told me the truth, Ben. I realize that now. I should have appreciated the fact that you struggled with that decision because you gave a damn about *me*. Maybe it wasn't right to lie or hold back the truth about something that important, and it probably wasn't the best decision you've ever made, but you have so much integrity that in the end, you *had* to tell me. You could have said nothing, and I never would have known. Everything had just happened so fast for us that I was confused. I think expecting perfection from someone you care about is totally unfair. I wouldn't be where I am right now if it wasn't for you. Please, just don't ever lie to me again or hold back on something important that I should know. You don't have to. I can handle the truth about anything now."

"I won't," he vowed huskily. "Nothing about us was ever a lie, Ariel."

My hand was shaking as I rested it on his chest. "I know."

He stepped even closer and threaded his hand through my curls. "I can't go back and do things all over again, but I like the idea of

Dearest Protector

that clean slate. I'm not going to press for more right now, but if we do end up together, I'm always going to be protective, and probably possessive. I just want to put that out there right now. And you will never, ever, be able to pay or pay me back for anything I give you. Those are things you should probably know upfront. If you can't live with that, you better say so right now. Otherwise, we move forward and figure this out as we go along."

A tremulous smile formed on my lips.

Ben was always going to be...Ben.

I wouldn't love him so much it hurt if he wasn't a protector by nature. I adored that man.

It was lies that I couldn't handle, and I totally believed that he'd never do something like that again.

He'd been backed into a corner, and everything that had happened between us was because he...cared.

I could live with his protectiveness and his possessiveness. I knew him well enough to know that he'd try to compromise if I thought he was being completely overbearing.

Could I deal with the fact that he'd never let me pay for anything? *Maybe.*

He'd never said I couldn't buy *him* anything.

"There's not a single thing I'd change about you, Ben Blackwood," I murmured, drowning in the heat of his gaze.

And *that* was the truth.

The man was almost perfect, and he needed a few imperfections to make him human.

"Maybe it does kill me just a little that you don't *need me* anymore," he said in an ungodly sexy voice. "But I want to be *your choice* if and when you decide that you want to be stuck with me. Not because you need me financially, but because you know I'm the only guy on the planet that you want. You can let me know when you've finally made that decision. But I think I should warn you that I plan to do everything in my power to try to be the guy that you choose, Ariel."

Before I could respond, he lowered his head and kissed me.

- 203 -

The embrace took my breath away.

Dear God, could there be any other choice for me?

Maybe I didn't need him financially, but every cell in my body needed and wanted this man.

I wrapped my arms around his neck, savoring the sensuous feeling of his mouth on mine.

He held the back of my head, holding it in place while he devoured my lips.

I was swept away, and my knees were weak by the time he let me come up for air.

"Ben," I breathed out, my head spinning from the ferocity of that kiss.

"I swore I wasn't going to touch you," he said as he held me tightly against his body. "But it's almost fucking impossible for me *not* to touch you. My dick is hard the second I see you or when I even think about you when you're not around. But that's not *all* I want from you, Ariel."

Still dizzy from that kiss, I asked, "Then exactly where do we go from here?"

"We…date," he said firmly. "I treat you like an incredible woman deserves to be treated, and you decide when you're ready for something more. We skipped the whole dating part of this relationship, and you fucking deserve that."

Honestly, I was ready to haul him into my bedroom and strip him naked, but I was wary of going too fast, too.

I loved Ben, and that was never going to change.

I was always going to need him, and I was always going to want him.

Maybe I was independent now, and I valued that independence. But Ben was essential to my happiness.

But maybe we both needed to heal from this bump in our relationship before we really moved forward.

We'd jumped from friends to lovers quickly last time, and it had screwed with both of our heads.

Dearest Protector

"I won't try to get you naked. Just don't expect me not to touch you, because I think I just proved that isn't going to happen," he added belatedly in an unhappy tone.

I laughed delightedly as he took my hand and led me into the apartment.

I locked the sliding door behind us, my heart a thousand times lighter and more hopeful as I went to gather my things so we could go have dinner with the people we both cared about.

Chapter 24

Ben

"So," Ian said expectantly a few hours later as he handed me a beer. "How did it go? You picked her up to come here. You must have talked."

"We did," I answered briefly.

I watched as Ariel, my mother, and Katie had a discussion near the pool, their chairs close enough so they could chat comfortably.

Ian and I were still seated at the table where we'd eaten earlier.

I couldn't take my eyes off Ariel.

I couldn't hear what the women were talking about, but it didn't matter. All I wanted was to feast my eyes on the woman I thought I'd lost because of my own stupidity.

It felt like it had been years, not weeks, since I'd seen her.

"Earth to Ben," Ian said drily as he waved a hand in front of my face. "Are you going to fill me in on what happened? What's the status on your relationship?"

I reluctantly pulled my eyes away to focus on my brother. "We're dating. It's probably best if I just sit back, wait, and be patient. I'm not going to get impatient and screw this up, Ian."

Dearest Protector

I felt better now that we'd at least be seeing each other on a regular basis.

I'd been completely honest when I'd told her that I wanted her to chose me.

Hell, I knew what I wanted. I'd probably known since the first time I saw her.

Maybe it would kill me, but I was willing to suck it up if I got what I wanted in the end.

We were committed to moving forward with our relationship at a more cautious pace. For now, I was happy with that, considering the possible alternative.

"Is the dating thing with or without sex?" Ian asked before he took a slug of his beer.

It wasn't like I discussed my sex life with Ian, but he obviously knew that Ariel drove me completely insane.

"Without. For now," I confessed. "It was my idea. She's going through a lot of changes, Ian. She's got her confidence back, and she's becoming her own person. Her business is flourishing. She doesn't need a lot of other bullshit to get in her way right now."

If I took Ariel to bed right now, I'd lose it completely.

I'd do whatever it took to make her mine for the rest of our lives, and she didn't need to be pressured to make that decision.

"You're going to hate yourself for that suggestion," Ian warned me.

"I already do," I scoffed. "But I'm playing the long game because I want Ariel for the rest of my life, Ian. There's no one else for me but her. If I screw this up, I lose for the rest of my goddamn life."

"So you'd rather have blue balls for a short time instead of forever?" he asked with humor in his tone.

"Basically, yes," I said shortly.

Ian shot me a sympathetic look. "I can tell you from experience that it's hell trying to keep your hands off a woman you love."

"I don't care," I shot back. "And I never said that I wouldn't touch her. I just said no sex."

I wasn't even going to try to deny that I loved Ariel. Ian had been in my shoes. He knew the truth.

- *207* -

Ian chuckled. "Christ! That makes it even worse."

I glared at him. "Go ahead and laugh, asshole. I'm not the one waiting to marry a woman I love until she finishes her master's degree."

He grinned. "At least she has my ring on her finger now. It's not quite as painful. You realize we're both pathetic, right? We like to think we're in charge, but in reality, those two women have us wrapped around their little fingers, and neither one of us really gives a shit."

I grinned back at him because I knew it was true. "It's not easy to hand a woman your heart and your balls and let her do with them what she will."

"It's not so bad," Ian mused. "As long as you know she doesn't plan on stomping on either one of them, it's tolerable. I trust Kate completely because she's basically done the same for me. She trusts me not to ever hurt her again. You might just try telling Ariel that you love her."

Hell, it wasn't that I didn't *want* to say it. I just didn't want to tell her something she wasn't ready to hear yet. "I trust her, but she hasn't said those words, either. I'm not sure she's ready for that."

"Just remember that one of you has to be the one who says it first," Ian informed me.

I swallowed a mouthful of beer before I answered, "I just convinced her to date me. I need to give it a little time. She deserves to find out what it's like to live in the moment for a while before I ask for her entire life. She has some kind of eco tour near the Everglades tomorrow so she can take some photos. After that, I'd like to take her to wherever she wants to go. I just want to spend time with her right now, Ian. I honestly thought I'd lost her."

Ian lifted a brow. "Sounds like you could use some time off without thinking about work."

"It would definitely help," I admitted.

"Are you sure you can handle being away from Blackwood long enough to woo your woman?" Ian joked.

"Do you think that's possible?" I asked. "I'd really like to focus on Ariel and our relationship for a while."

Dearest Protector

Ian shot me an exasperated glance. "Ben, you've been working nonstop for years and you practically lived at the Blackwood headquarters. You've told me yourself that Blackwood is perfectly capable of continuing on without us now for an extended amount of time if necessary. But it won't have to. *I'll* be there. I still work in the lab in the morning, but I'm in the executive offices all afternoon. I can handle the meetings next week. You don't even need to check in. It's not like you're not needed at Blackwood to help me make the important decisions, but you really need to take time out to handle your personal life. I know you sacrificed almost everything to be at Blackwood. It's time, little brother. Take a fucking vacation. Blackwood Technologies is still going to be there when you get back. You managed to handle everything for years at the office without me. I think I can deal with it for a few weeks."

I inclined my head. "Thanks."

"No problem," he replied. "And just so you know, I am not planning on checking in when I go on my honeymoon."

I smirked. "Understood."

Ian and I were still trying to figure out exactly how to run Blackwood together, and that meant I needed to learn to let go of some of my responsibilities as CEO.

The opportunity to lighten my workload wasn't unwelcome because I was exhausted, but it wasn't all that easy after years of handling everything at headquarters myself.

I nodded toward Ariel, Katie, and my mother. "What do you think they're talking about?"

"I have no idea," Ian answered drily. "But I'm sure Mom's ecstatic because she may get to help plan more than one wedding in the next year or two."

"Fucking hell," I cursed. "Do you think I need to go rescue Ariel?"

Ian shook his head. "Nah. She doesn't look the least bit uncomfortable. Whatever they're saying, Ariel seems to have plenty of input of her own."

"Mom gets a little carried away sometimes," I reminded him.

"It looks to me like both Kate and Ariel can hold their own with her," Ian observed.

I looked at Ariel, her head thrown back, her laughter ringing through the backyard because of something my mother had just said.

"Obviously," I agreed.

She didn't look like she needed rescue.

She looked...happy.

Relaxed.

Carefree.

And incredibly sexy and gorgeous.

My already hard cock twitched as I looked at her.

"I'll give that no sex thing less than forty-eight hours," Ian said as he scrutinized my face. "You look like you're ready to pick her up and haul her out of here right now."

I shook my head. "Earlier today, I wasn't sure if we'd ever talk again. My dick can wait. She's changing. She's comfortable in her own skin. She's happy, Ian."

He lifted a brow. "And you don't think that you're a big part of that happiness, little brother?"

I shrugged. "Not really."

"Maybe she is changing and figuring out who she is, but you *are* a big part of that, Ben," he told me. "You helped her get here, and you'll be there to support her as her career grows. Just like she'll be there to help you learn how to let go of work sometimes, and to remind you that there's more to life than Blackwood. She'll be a true partner. Best damn feeling in the world if you ask me."

I looked at Ian closely. "You're really happy," I stated.

"Yep," he agreed. "I really am."

That in itself was a miracle to me.

Not very long ago, my older brother hadn't really cared if he lived or died.

Katie had changed everything for Ian.

She'd somehow managed to reach Ian when nobody else could.

Now, he'd not only rejoined life, but he was happier than I'd ever seen him before.

Dearest Protector

All because one intrepid woman had dared to love him and accept him exactly the way he was.

"I'm glad you're happy," I said soberly. "I wasn't sure you ever would be again."

Ian let out a long breath before he answered, "It was never that you and Mom weren't enough for me to want to straighten my shit out. I was just too selfish to realize what I was doing to both of you until Kate came along and kicked my ass to get my head straight."

Months ago, I might not have understood what he was saying.

Now, I did.

I shook my head and answered, "It doesn't matter why or how it happened, I'm just glad it did."

Ian inclined his head in acknowledgement as he stood. He slapped me on the back before he went to join the women. "Then maybe you can understand why I want to see you happy, too, little brother."

I swallowed hard as I rose to follow him.

I couldn't predict the future, but he had no idea what it meant just to know that Ian gave a shit about me again.

Chapter 25

Ariel

I stepped onto Marilyn Blackwood's patio for a breath of fresh air. The charity event she'd invited me to attend a few days ago was lovely, but it was crowded.

Not that it was any cooler on the patio because summer was here in South Florida, but at least there was a breeze, and there wasn't another soul around.

I took a deep breath and braced my hands on the railing, staring out at the lawn, knowing the water was just beyond the grass.

It had been a busy few days.

Ben had gone to the Everglades with me on Saturday.

He'd been incredibly patient as I'd shot photos of seashells, birds, dolphins, alligators, and whatever else I could find that would make great images later.

On Sunday, we'd started to play.

We'd hit the beach on Sunday. I hadn't taken a single photo, but we'd laughed more times than I could count.

Ben had chartered a boat to take us out snorkeling yesterday. Okay, maybe it had been more like a super yacht than just a boat, but I

Dearest Protector

wasn't about to complain about the comfort level of the watercraft. He had tried to help me improve my technique because I was a novice, but I'd ended up with a mouthful of water several times anyway. Even though I'd ingested a little seawater, I'd had an amazing time, and the fact that Ben had been so relaxed was a major bonus.

We'd met for an early dinner tonight, and now, we were here at Marilyn's charity event.

Just seeing Ben in a tuxedo again had been worth the slight discomfort of the crowded ballroom.

I'd gone out earlier in the day to buy myself the quintessential little black dress with a halter top that left my back almost bare and a hem that ended above my knees.

Ben had stated that he had a love/hate relationship with the dress. In other words, he loved seeing me in the dress, but he hated the other men who looked at me while I was wearing it.

Personally, I thought he was a little bit crazy, but I loved the heated looks he'd been sending me all night long.

Okay, maybe he was *somewhat* possessive and protective, and I'd seen that in action a lot during the last few days, but I wasn't complaining. I loved it when he acted like I was the only woman who existed for him.

Although I wasn't sure if I could take much more of him looking and hardly touching.

Yeah, he'd kissed me, and he never missed an opportunity to lay those dangerous lips on mine, but he hadn't tried to take it any further than that.

Maybe we'd wanted to slow it down, but Ben and I had obviously come too far to go back now. It wasn't like we were trying to get to know each other like we'd been strangers just a few days ago.

Maybe we'd never really dated, but we'd spent a lot of time together as friends.

I'd been rethinking this whole idea of dating with no sex.

It was almost impossible for me not to want to tell Ben exactly how I felt, and then get him naked.

In fact, I'd started making a real effort to seduce him.

~ 213 ~

Obviously, *that* wasn't working.

Probably because I had absolutely no idea how to seduce a guy.

I was lifting the hair off my neck to try to cool off when a male voice suddenly sounded behind me.

"Hello, Ariel. I see that you're still dressing like a whore."

The hair stood up on the back of my neck.

I let go of my curly locks and turned around, even though I already knew exactly who I'd see.

"Leland," I said in a calm tone. "Who let you in?"

I took another calming breath as I stared at my old boss. Ben was having Leland investigated because he suspected that his business practices were shady, but there wasn't enough evidence to put the man in jail...yet.

Leland moved forward until he was standing right in front of me.

Strangely, the dirtbag didn't scare me anymore.

His face was red from exertion in the heat of summer, and I could hear him wheezing.

He wasn't nearly as frightening as he used to be, but he was just as repulsive.

My lack of fear was probably because I wasn't the same woman I was when I worked for him, and I definitely wasn't dependent on him to put food on my table.

Right now, he was nothing more than a creepy bully to me.

He clamped a hand around my wrist, and nothing but fury rose up inside me.

Same patio.

Same place.

The same asshole boss who had manhandled me for months.

But a way different situation, and with a whole different woman.

I wasn't afraid to make a scene anymore if it was warranted, thanks to Ben.

The man I was currently dating had also taught me a few moves to defend myself, and I was grateful right now for his obsessive need to keep me safe.

Dearest Protector

"How many men have imagined what you look like underneath that slutty dress," Leland asked nastily as he tightened his grip on my wrist. "When are you going to learn?"

Katie's right. He doesn't just hate me. He obviously hates all women. He's just using me as his target.

I took a deep breath. "I asked who let you in, Leland," I reminded him. "This is a private event."

"None of your goddamn business," he hissed. "I have a right to be here. I'm a donor to this charity. Do you think you're better than me just because you're Blackwood's whore now? I know what you've been up to Ariel."

I had to force myself not to shudder because he'd apparently been checking up on me.

I snorted, shrugging off his disparaging comments. "You actually gave up a few bucks so you could attend?"

"Bitch!" he snarled.

"Ariel?" Ben's voice sounded from the entrance to the patio.

I held up my free hand so he didn't interfere. I knew if he laid a hand on Leland, this wouldn't end well. "Don't," I said to Ben as our gazes locked. "I've. Got. This."

"Bastard!" I countered as my gaze fell back on Leland. "Don't you ever touch me again."

My rage guided me as I broke his grip on my wrist and let my hand fly with every bit of anger I'd stored up inside me for months. I slapped him so hard that his ears were probably ringing.

While he was still off-balance, I stomped and ground my heel into his instep until he whined and fell over onto his ass.

"You broke my foot," he howled as he tried to grip his foot, his face even redder than it had been earlier.

"Is there something I can do to help, Mr. Blackwood?" one of the big, burly staff guys asked as he stepped outside next to Ben.

"Yeah," Ben snarled, his turbulent gaze locking on mine. "Get this asshole off my mother's patio and make sure he doesn't come back. He just assaulted my girlfriend."

~ 215 ~

The burly staff member hurried to assist. He took Leland by the jacket, easily hefted him up, and hustled him toward the parking lot.

"You broke my foot," Leland screamed again as he was led away limping. "This isn't over. You'll pay for this."

I moved to Ben and put a hand on his chest, urging him not to follow and beat the crap out of the man who had just grabbed me and tossed insults my way. "Don't, Ben. He's not worth it. I'm not terrified by him anymore. He's a bully. He's not worth going to jail. That would upset me, and it would definitely upset your mom. Let the investigator finish his work."

I could feel Ben's body shake with anger as he glared at the man who was being forcibly removed from the gathering.

I could tell he was in a struggle between his urge to hurt Leland and his want to respect what I asked him to do.

I lifted my hand and turned his head until he was facing me instead of looking at Leland. "Look at me. He's not worth it."

His eyes locked with mine. I had to wait until the venom in that hazel-eyed gaze started to dissipate.

"He. Fucking. Touched. You," Ben said gutturally. "Did he hurt you, Ariel?"

I snorted. "Nope. But I think I hurt him. Thanks for the self-defense lessons, big guy. Jesus! That felt good. I don't think I realized how much rage I had locked inside me."

Ben wasn't amused. "He. Threatened. You."

"Bullies threaten a lot of things," I told him gently. "They're just threats, Ben. I took care of him well enough. I really needed to stand up to him myself this time."

He wrapped his arms around my body and pulled me close to him. "You did deal with him," he acknowledged. "But you'll never know how difficult it was to stand by while he had his hand on you. Don't ever ask me to do that again."

Oh, I definitely knew how hard it was for him to wait when he perceived that I was in danger. It wasn't in his DNA, but he'd done it because I'd asked him to wait.

Dearest Protector

I wasn't about to let Ben get arrested for defending me, and judging by his level of anger a moment ago, Leland would have been in bad shape.

Besides, it *was* something I'd really needed to do myself. I'd put up with Leland's abuse for months, and I needed the release of the anger that had been buried inside me.

I put my arms around his neck. "I'm sorry. I just really wanted to see how those moves you showed me worked in real life on someone I despise."

I could feel his muscles relax as he pulled back and skewered me with a doubtful expression. "I think you also wanted to make sure I didn't kill the bastard," he said unhappily.

I sighed. "If you did, I'd have to live without you because you'd be in jail. Not happening, handsome."

"Smartass," he said gruffly before he lowered his mouth to mine.

The kiss was filled with passion and leftover adrenaline, but I savored the protective embrace.

I was panting by the time he released my lips.

"Dance with me," I said in what I hoped was a persuasive tone.

His eyes ran lovingly over my face as he replied, "I thought you didn't dance anymore."

I didn't.

Not really.

But...

"Your mother said you're a great dancer. I have yet to see you prove that. I think I can probably keep up with you," I teased.

He shot me a questioning glance. "Your foot—"

"Is just fine," I interrupted. "Definitely well enough for a slow dance."

Two seconds later, he was pulling me through the crowd until we got to the dance floor.

I noted that it was much easier to navigate through the people with Ben acting as a bulldozer in front of me.

Once we were on the dance floor, Ben wrapped a strong arm around my waist and took my hand. He entwined our fingers and started to move.

I put my other hand on his shoulder with a sigh.

Ben's mother had been right.

This man was smooth, and easy to follow.

"Anything that allows me to keep my hands on you for an extended period of time right now works for me," Ben grumbled next to my ear.

I giggled. "So you're only dancing with me so you can feel me up, Mr. Blackwood?" I asked teasingly.

It felt good to be dancing again, especially with my current partner.

"Pretty much."

Ben moved me effortlessly around the dance floor as I answered, "Then this basically works for me, too."

Chapter 26

Ben

I woke up the next night fighting with my own fucking pillow. I sat up and rubbed my hands down my face, exhausted, but knowing I wouldn't go back to sleep immediately.

I wasn't sleeping much these days, and now, instead of having nightmares about Ariel's accident, I was dreaming about her being assaulted by Leland Brock.

"Bastard," I said out loud, pissed off because the asshole still hadn't been arrested.

Soon after Ariel had come to work for me, I'd put a private investigator on a case to find out all of Leland Brock's business practices.

Ariel had shared that she'd very rarely seen any of Leland's business paperwork, and that he had a lot of things locked up.

What legit small business needed to be that anal?

And why had he hired Ariel if he never had her in his office?

It hadn't been difficult to put two and two together and find out that his so-called business was little more than a shell company for illegal activities, and it wasn't the only one he had.

He didn't work.

He frauded and laundered money that was obtained illegally.

Which was why Ariel was little more than a go-to woman for him to run ragged on personal errands.

He hadn't wanted a real assistant.

He'd been trolling for a woman to torment when he'd found her.

We'd uncovered a lot more than we'd expected, which had been turned over to the authorities.

I'd told Ariel about it soon after she'd come to work for me, but I hadn't been able to give her any kind of real update until after she'd kicked Brock's ass last night.

Shortly, Leland Brock would be serving so much time that he'd probably never get out of prison.

That's probably the only thing that had kept me from disabling the asshole the night before so he would never be a threat to Ariel again.

Well, that and the fact that she'd kicked his ass *herself*.

I grinned as I thought about how Ariel had, once again, gone after what she wanted, and what she'd wanted at that moment was Leland Brock on the ground howling with pain.

Obviously, she *had* harbored a lot of suppressed anger.

It had taken everything I had to pause for even a few seconds when I'd seen him trying to hurt Ariel. But in the end, it had been worth the brief hesitation to see my girl demolish her previous tormentor.

I can wait a few more days until the piece of shit is in jail.

The problem was, in the meantime, it was driving me insane that Ariel was alone at night.

I wouldn't put it past Brock to retaliate because Ariel had humiliated him.

Yeah, she lived in a second story apartment, which she reminded me about every time I told her to be careful.

I also had my own security outside her apartment, which she'd told me was unnecessary. The only reason she'd finally relented was because she knew it would make me feel better.

Nevertheless, I dreamed about Brock taking revenge, and it was definitely not pleasant.

Dearest Protector

I wanted her here, in my bed, draped over my body naked and completely sated as she slept.

It was about the only thing that was going to give me any peace.

"Shit!" I cursed as I looked at the clock and realized I'd only been asleep for an hour.

It was a little after one.

I'd crashed as soon as I'd gotten home from dinner with Ariel earlier.

I glanced at my phone and snatched it when I realized I had a few text messages from Ariel.

Ariel: *Are you awake?*

Ariel: *Never mind. You must be asleep and you need to get some rest. It's nothing. You don't need to text me back.*

Something definitely wasn't right.

Ariel never texted me late at night, and those messages had just been sent twenty minutes ago.

I didn't bother texting her back.

I hit the button to call her.

"What's wrong?" I asked the second she answered.

"Nothing. Honestly," she answered, sounding like she hadn't been to bed yet. "I shouldn't have texted. I just felt like…talking."

"You could have called me," I pointed out. "Tell me what's wrong."

There would never be a time that I wouldn't wake my ass up if she needed to talk.

"Were you sleeping?"

"Yeah. I woke up. Now tell me what you want to talk about?" I cajoled.

"I got the information on my DNA sample," she said, her voice troubled. "It's not a big deal. For some reason, my father put his information into that service, too, and I got a direct match to him. He was alive until two years ago, Ben. He was from *New York City*. We were actually in the same city at the same time."

And…he'd died in that city while she lived there.

She didn't say that, but I was certain it was on her mind.

Ariel had told me that she'd submitted a sample of her DNA so she could see if she could find out who her father was, and I'd really hoped it wouldn't be bad news.

"I couldn't find out much about him," she added. "All I could find was his obituary. But I guess at least I know who he is."

Nah. Fuck that. All this had done was to bring up more questions for her.

Like…why had her mother lied to her?

And…had her father known that he'd fathered a child?

Plus…was her father really so horrible that she was better off without him?

"We can find out more," I told her. "I know a good private investigator who isn't busy trying to put Leland Brock in jail anymore."

She paused before she asked hesitantly, "Would you mind asking him to find out more information? It probably shouldn't matter, but I'd like to know a little more about my father. I know he's gone now, and there's nothing I can do about that, but I still have…questions."

Would I mind?

Hell no, I wouldn't mind.

If I were her, I'd want to know more, too.

"You know I don't mind," I said. "Text me what you have, and I'll call the investigator first thing in the morning."

"Thank you. Go back to sleep, Ben. We'll talk tomorrow. I could have waited to contact you," she murmured.

"Wait!" I demanded before she disconnected. "Are you really okay?"

For her, this wasn't a small thing, even though she acted like it was nothing that important.

She'd just found out that her father had been alive for most her life, and she'd never met him.

"Yeah. I guess all this has just thrown me for a loop. I don't understand why Mom never told me," she said, sounding confused and a little brokenhearted.

Shit! I hated that.

"We'll find out, sweetheart," I promised. "You couldn't sleep?"

Dearest Protector

"No. I miss you, Ben," she told me in a barely audible voice.

Someone could probably have stabbed me in the heart and it wouldn't have hurt more than her words.

Ariel wasn't exactly clingy or needy, which made that statement all the more painful.

I swallowed hard.

Ariel continued, "I know we spent most of the day together and it's really silly—"

"It's not," I interrupted. "I miss you, too. Every. Fucking. Night."

"I think..." she started hesitantly.

She coughed and started over again. "I really think we need to rethink this whole dating-but-no-sex thing. I've tried getting myself off every night, but it's kind of empty once it's over and you're not here."

I closed my eyes, and my grip tightened on the phone.

"Also," she added. "I really suck at this whole seduction thing. I could use a little help here. I'm not a virgin anymore, but I'm also not sure what I need to do to get you...interested. I feel like I'm dangling the bait, but you're not biting."

I flopped backward until my head hit the pillow, trying like hell not to groan out loud.

She had absolutely no clue that she didn't need to do a damn thing to get me *interested*.

My dick was hard from the second I saw her until way after we'd parted ways at night.

"Are you still there?" Ariel asked softly.

"Listening, babe," I replied, barely able to get the words out of my mouth.

"Well, good," she said awkwardly. "At least I was able to get that off my chest."

"Ariel?"

"Yes?"

Christ! She might not be a virgin anymore, but she was still so damn innocent.

I took a deep breath. "You will never, ever have to worry about seducing me. For you, I'm always going to be a sure thing. If you're in the same room, my dick is hard. All you have to do is tell me you're ready. I told you that the ball was in your court. Your decision. I didn't want to move too fast for you."

"Um…okay," she said nervously. "Then I'll tell you that I'm ready tomorrow. I'm getting really frustrated, and there's something else I want to tell you tomorrow, too."

I smiled into the darkness.

Fuck! She was adorable, and I wanted to kick myself in the ass for not noticing that she was actively trying to seduce me.

Hell, I'd been so busy trying *not* to get her naked that I hadn't recognized her subtle hints.

The physical part of our relationship was so damn new to her that she was still uncertain.

I'd make damn sure that never happened again.

"You can tell me now," I persuaded, not wanting her to hold anything back with me anymore.

"No. It's something I really need to tell you in person."

"I do live about three minutes from you. Do you want me to come over?"

Christ! Please say *yes.*

"I-it's late," she stammered. "Go to sleep. I'll see you tomorrow. Night, Ben."

"Sleep tight, sweetheart," I drawled. "We'll talk tomorrow. Don't be afraid to tell me anything. The ball is in your court. It has been since the day you decided to forgive me for holding back on the truth."

I was disappointed when she disconnected without another word, but I was relieved that she was apparently willing to take another step forward in our relationship.

Maybe I'd managed to wait beyond Ian's predicted forty-eight hours without the sexual portion of my relationship with Ariel, but my patience was razor thin.

Dearest Protector

The only reason I hadn't broken yet was because Ariel was way too important to me to lose my shit now.

I was willing to go through hell if that meant that I'd get all of *her* when the torture was finally over.

Wide awake and with a dick hard enough to cut diamonds, I got up, pulled on a pair of sweatpants, and went to the kitchen for something to drink.

Chapter 27

Ariel

"The ball is in my court. The ball is in my court," I chanted as I walked up to Ben's door.

The moment I'd disconnected from that call with Ben, I'd decided that I couldn't wait anymore.

I wasn't that frightened woman I used to be who was afraid of speaking her mind.

So here I was, sweltering in the bathrobe I'd yanked on over my sleep shorts and tank, standing in front of Ben's front door.

God, he's probably going to think I'm a lunatic.

Wasn't I the one who had just told him that he needed to get some sleep?

Don't chicken out. Don't chicken out.

I'd probably known exactly what I wanted since the day he'd picked me up to go to Ian and Katie's house for dinner, but now, there wasn't a doubt in my mind about Ben and me.

The man would die before he'd ever hurt me again.

Hadn't he already proved that in a million different ways?

Dearest Protector

I had gotten my shit together, and my life almost perfect except for one very big element of it.

There was one gigantic, gaping hole in that almost perfect life right now, and that missing piece was Ben Blackwood.

Maybe I didn't need him to survive anymore, but I needed him to feel like a whole person.

I hadn't recognized that connection at the very first instant I'd seen him in person like Ben had, but I'd sensed it.

I'd just been way too screwed up to even imagine that I could end up with a man like him someday.

I'd texted Ben's security guys and asked them to bring me over to his place within minutes of ending our call.

It had taken me all of five minutes to get here, but during that brief period of time, I'd had a few second thoughts about this whole idea.

"I'll just tell him and leave. At least I can get that off my chest, too," I said under my breath as I finally pushed the doorbell.

Certainly, he was still awake, right?

I mean, it had only been a matter of minutes since I talked to him.

The door swung open, and my mouth went dry.

Oh, dear God.

I blinked, taking in his muscular body once he'd opened the door. He was wearing nothing but a pair of sweatpants.

His upper body was completely bare, and I salivated as I took in every muscle and dip beneath that huge expanse of bare skin.

Ben was breathtakingly gorgeous. Always.

He looked like he'd just rolled out of bed, which I personally thought was a really hot look on him. Then again, when did this man *not* look smoking hot?

"Ariel?" Ben questioned with a frown. "What in the hell are you doing here? What's wrong?"

"I decided I needed to tell you that thing that I told you I wanted to tell you in person," I babbled, still dazed by all of that bare skin as I stayed glued to his doormat. "I'm not going to stay long."

He reached out and pulled me gently into the house, closing the door behind us. "Please tell me you didn't walk here," he said gruffly.

- *227* -

I shook my head. "I didn't. Your security guys brought me. They're waiting out front."

"Thank fuck!" he cursed as he stared at me. "Are you wearing your pajamas?"

"Yes. I wanted to cover them up. I wasn't all that comfortable hopping into the car without a bathrobe," I explained.

"It's not that I'm not happy to see you," Ben said carefully. "But—"

"I love you," I blurted out, finally freely saying the words I'd wanted to say for a long time.

Ben's expression changed to something broodier. "What?"

"I choose you, Ben, because I love you. Not because I need you to survive, but because you're the only man on the planet I want."

Pure relief spread over his handsome face as he replied huskily, "I'll spend the rest of my damn life making sure you never regret your choice. But would you mind repeating that first part again?"

"I love you," I said again, clearer this time. "That's the thing I needed to tell you in person. That's it. I love you. I just decided you needed to know, and it's not something I should really say on the phone the first time. Now that I've told you, I feel better, so I'll just go—"

"Oh, hell no, you won't," Ben growled as he put his hand on the door to keep me from opening it again. "Did you honestly think you were going to say that to me and waltz your gorgeous ass back out this door again?"

My breath caught as he trapped me against the door, his big body in front of me, and a hand planted beside each of my shoulders.

"Are you upset?" I asked as I looked up at him, his eyes stormier than I'd ever seen them.

My always rational, always patient Ben looked like he was about to completely break.

He shook his head. "No. I'm fucking humbled. And now I really wish I had said it first because I'm pretty sure I felt it before you did. I love you, too, Ariel. Probably have since the first time I saw you, and I definitely did the first time I saw you again here. You're probably the bravest woman I've ever met."

Dearest Protector

I let out a sigh of relief, my heart about to soar out of my chest because he'd said it, too.

"Not so brave," I argued. "I probably could have mentioned it before it was almost two am on a sleepless night. I'm not sure why, but I couldn't let another moment pass without you knowing how I felt. You did say the ball was in my court."

"I didn't want to rush you or pressure you by telling you that I loved you too soon," Ben said regretfully. "I fucked up once. I didn't plan on doing it again. I need you in my life for the rest of my life, and I was willing to wait as long as necessary to get that commitment."

I could see it now, how worried he was about scaring me away.

Like that was ever going to happen?

Ben Blackwood was my soulmate.

I'd forgiven him a long time ago for lying about our previous encounter.

Other than that, he was nearly perfect.

We were nearly perfect together, and I didn't even want to think about what my life would be like without him in it.

Did he really think I'd ever toss that away?

"Please don't wait any longer," I entreated. "You have me, heart, body, and soul."

"Be sure of what you want, sweetheart," he said in a low voice that was hoarse with emotion. "Because after this, I don't know how in the hell I'd ever let you go."

"I don't want you to let me go. I just want…you," I said softly.

"You've got me," he informed me right before his lips came down on mine.

Passion exploded from my body the moment his tongue invaded my mouth.

I wrapped my arms around his body, and touched every bit of his bare skin that I could find.

I was ravenous, and we'd both waited for so damn long.

"Fuck me, Ben," I pleaded as his mouth roughly explored the sensitive skin at my neck.

~ 229 ~

Jesus! I needed him inside me before I lost my mind.

If I couldn't get closer to him, I felt like I was going to die.

"Ariel," he groaned as he moved to push the robe off my shoulders. He immediately lowered his head again and started nipping at the skin on my shoulders.

I shrugged out of the robe impatiently, letting it drop to the floor.

I reached down and ran my hand over the crotch of his sweatpants, finding what I so desperately wanted there.

His cock was extremely hard and ready, and I was so hot I was ready to combust.

I wrapped my arms around his neck and hopped so I could wrap my legs around his hips, needing that connection.

He palmed my ass to keep me supported.

"Not like this," Ben said, his voice tense as his lips rested on my clavicle.

"Just like this," I insisted as I fisted his hair. "I need you inside me right now. It's been way too long."

"Fucking hell," he rasped as he lowered my legs just long enough to divest me of my sleep shorts. "Do you really want it hot and hard against the front door?"

"Oh, hell yes," I moaned.

"Then you're going to get your wish because I can't wait any longer, either," he said harshly as he pulled me up again with both hands on my ass. "Christ! You make me crazy, Ariel."

I shivered as I wrapped my legs around him again, loving the fact that he was losing his iron control completely.

I tangled my hands into the hair at the back of his neck and kissed him, so wound up that my core clenched violently in anticipation.

Ben thrust a hand between our bodies. His fingers invaded my pussy, and he groaned into my mouth as he found out just how wet and ready I was to take his cock.

A heartbeat later, he was buried to his balls inside me.

I lifted my lips from his and let out a hiss of satisfaction. "Yesssss. Fuck. Me."

There was zero pain involved in his dominant possession. Just a bone-deep feeling of connection that sated some primal need that I didn't understand.

He'd promised me hot and hard, and that was exactly what I got.

He shifted me until my clit was stimulated with every hard thrust.

It was rough.

It was primitive.

And it was satisfying my elemental need to be taken and claimed by this man that I loved.

Ben was giving me everything he had, no holds barred and with zero hesitation.

We were both way too lost to care, too needy to worry about anything except this moment of wild freedom that we both desperately craved.

I reveled in his unbridled passion, and the way he could play my body without even trying.

"You feel so good," I whimpered as he squeezed my ass, holding me exactly where he wanted me so he could bury himself inside my body as deeply as possible.

"I need you to come. I'm not going to last very long," he said roughly as he pummeled inside me over and over again.

Harder and harder.

Faster and faster.

My head fell back against the door, my body screaming to climax.

He reached between us again and moved his thumb over my engorged clit.

I went off almost instantly, and so violently that I thought I was going to pass out.

"That's it, babe," he encouraged as he stroked my clit harder. "Let. Go."

I did, and I felt the ferocity of my orgasm in every nerve ending in my body.

"Ben!" I screamed, my neck arching against the door because my release was so intense. "I love you!"

"Fuck!" he cursed as his entire body jerked. "I love you, too."

The intense internal spasms that never seemed to end for me milked Ben's cock, and he found his own release with a strangled groan.

The room suddenly went silent.

The only sound was our harsh breathing as we recovered.

I couldn't speak.

I couldn't move.

All I wanted to do was stay like this forever in this intimate position, wrapped up and entangled with Ben.

"Next time, we're using the damn bed," he growled, shifting so his cock would finally disconnect from my body.

I laughed as he pulled away from the door. He lowered my feet to the floor and then picked me up and carried me upstairs without another word.

Chapter 28

Ben

"What in the hell possessed you to come over here at this time of night just to tell me that you loved me?" I asked as I buried my face in her silky hair.

Not that I was complaining that she'd finally put me out of my fucking misery.

I'd gotten both of us naked and had collapsed onto the bed with her in my arms, pulling her closer so I could spoon her body into mine.

She sighed as she stroked one of my forearms that was resting around her waist. "I couldn't wait any longer. Maybe I don't remember exactly what happened after that taxi hit me, but I know how close I came to dying that day, Ben. I don't ever want to be that close to dying again and know that I never told you how I felt. I'll always choose you, and I had to let you know that."

My arms tightened protectively around her body, and I closed my eyes, grateful as fuck that she was here with me now.

Not only was she here the way she was always meant to be, but she fucking loved me, too.

I felt like the luckiest asshole in the world.

I couldn't even think about seeing Ariel like that again, so damn close to death that I was afraid her next breath could be her last.

It had nearly killed me the first time.

A second time would totally destroy me.

"Not. Happening," I growled against her hair. "I do remember what happened, and it scared the shit out of me. I knew from the moment I saw you on stage that night that you were supposed to be mine, Ariel. I don't think I'll ever understand how I knew that, but I should have been more careful. I shouldn't have let that happen to you the first time. I should have never jumped that curb, and I sure as hell should have done more to help you get through your injuries after the accident. I can't change what happened, but I'll do everything in my power to make sure you never get hurt like that again."

She turned in my arms until we were face-to-face before she said, "None of the accident was ever your fault, nor were you responsible for my welfare. We'd never even officially met in person, Ben."

"Didn't matter," I said bluntly. "I knew I needed you, Ariel. Why in the hell do you think I was so damn eager to get to that afterparty to meet you, even though I thought you were already involved with Chris? I wasn't a guy who believed in fate or love at first sight. Hell, I'm not sure I believed in romantic love at all. I was totally blindsided, but I couldn't ignore that instinct to find you once I'd seen the woman who I just somehow knew would make me the happiest guy on Earth. Unfortunately, I never even got the chance to try to steal you away from Chris."

She brushed a lock of hair from my forehead as she asked softly, "Was that your plan? To try to steal me away?"

I nodded. "Hell, yes, I was going to try if I thought you weren't deliriously happy or completely serious about that relationship. I had to know. Unfortunately, I never got that chance. I ended up being the asshole responsible for your accident, and I thought you were in much better hands being with someone you cared about after it happened. Had I known that you and Chris weren't a couple, and that no one would be there for you, do you think I wouldn't have been there beside you through every step of your recovery?"

Dearest Protector

A small smile formed on her lips. "Honestly, you're so stubborn that I'm sure you would have been," she murmured. "Not knowing me well certainly didn't stop you from stepping in that night on your mother's patio with Leland. It didn't stop you from giving me everything as a friend, either, or trying to protect me from everything bad that could have happened because I lost my job."

"There wasn't a single day after we met here in Florida that I didn't want to be more than your friend, Ariel," I confessed. "But I didn't think you were ready for anything more, and as much as I wished I could tell you what I really wanted, I didn't know how that would work out. How was I going to explain something I didn't understand myself back then? All I wanted was to be close to you, and if friendship was the only way to accomplish that, I was willing to wait."

"You were that certain I was going to fall in love with you?" she asked teasingly.

"Hopeful, maybe," I admitted. "But I was never sure of how things would turn out. I fell harder for you every single day, sweetheart, but I knew I was digging myself into a hole by not telling you the truth about what happened the night of your accident. Have you really forgiven me for that?"

It killed me when I saw a tear leak from her beautiful blue eyes.

She nodded firmly. "It was one omission out of a sea of truths we'd told each other. I was confused, but I realized that you'd never do anything to intentionally hurt me. How could I not know that after everything you'd done for me? You made me believe in myself again, Ben. You made me believe I could still take my life back and be happy after I'd lost myself because I couldn't dance anymore."

I swiped the tear from the side of her face before I took her hand and rested our conjoined hands against my heart. "Are you happy now, Ariel?"

"More than I ever thought possible," she replied immediately. "I found myself, and I found you. Maybe sometimes it's still hard to believe that someone like you fell in love with me. I mean, you are Ben Blackwood, the hottest and the most eligible billionaire on the planet."

I grinned. She didn't give a shit about my billionaire status. She never had, which had only made me adore her more.

She saw me, and I saw her.

I couldn't explain that connection if I tried, but I *felt* it every single day.

She continued, "I knew you probably had gorgeous women hitting on you all the time."

"I haven't noticed another female since the day I saw you over a year ago, Ariel. I was too busy being obsessed over the one I'd lost, over the opportunity I'd lost. Every time I closed my eyes, all I could see was that taxi hitting you, over and over again, and how fucking brave you were right after the accident."

She took a deep breath and let it out slowly. "I was probably brave because you were there with me," she said earnestly. "If everything I dreamed about that night is true, I connected with you in some way *that night*, too, Ben. I can't really explain that, either. You were a stranger to me, yet you…weren't. In my dream, I trusted you instinctively. Even when we met here and became friends, there was always something familiar about you. Something drew me to you. That attraction was there for me almost immediately, and it wasn't just your hot body and your gorgeous face that sucked me in."

I lifted a brow, interested in everything she'd felt back then. "But you still wanted me?"

She took her free hand and smacked me on the shoulder. "Don't be silly. Every woman who is single and not completely blind wants you."

"You do realize that very few people would dare to tell me I'm being silly. And I don't give a shit what anyone else thinks," I growled. "I only care what one woman thinks."

Her.

Just…her.

She sent me a sultry smile that made me completely insane as she wrapped her arms around my neck. "If you're trying to scare me with that powerful billionaire thing, give it up. I see you, Ben Blackwood. I always have. You're kind. You're considerate. You always try to do the right thing, even when it's difficult. You're a good brother to Ian, a caring son to your mother, the best friend a person could ask for, and the man of my dreams. Maybe I don't need you to exist, but I'll always need you to be happy. I don't think I could ever stop wanting you or loving you."

"That's good, sweetheart, because you're stuck with me now," I told her, my heart in my throat.

I felt like I'd wanted this woman forever, and now that I finally had her, all I could feel was fucking gratitude.

"I think I can handle that," she said, her tone happy and amused as she tugged my head forward. "Kiss me."

I leaned forward and took her lips until my dick was so hard it was painful and my heart was pounding so hard that I could hardly think.

Slow down, asshole.

Fuck! I'd already mauled her the second she'd walked in the door and told me that she loved me.

Only Ariel could make me this crazy in seconds, but she didn't really need a repeat of my earlier, very short performance.

I wanted to take my time with her.

I wanted her to feel how much I loved and cherished her.

I wanted to explore every inch of her body until she was begging me to make her come.

Truthfully, I wanted her to need me bone deep, because I needed her exactly the same way.

Even though we'd had sex in almost every conceivable position, she still wasn't experienced.

She deserved better than to have a guy who couldn't control himself every damn time he touched her. I wasn't sure how long it would take before I could get a grip on my emotions when she was this close to me.

Right now, I didn't see that day arriving anytime soon, but I could try to do a little better than what had happened against the fucking door downstairs.

I was the one with the sexual experience, but I'd certainly performed without an ounce of finesse earlier.

If I felt less, I'd probably perform better, but I knew that was never going to happen.

While I'd always thought that I was the calm, fixer kind of guy in my family, the word *control* wasn't even in my vocabulary when it came to the woman I was holding right now.

Ariel was everything.

She was my entire life, and I really didn't give a shit who knew that.

She wiggled against my hold and put her palms on my chest.

I grinned and let her push me until I was on my back, bemused, and wanting to see what she'd do next.

I stopped smiling as soon as she started kissing her way down my body.

I groaned as she explored with her mouth on her way down, lovingly tracing her tongue over my abs.

Oh, fuck no!

If she was planning on going *there,* my plan of taking things slower was going to be shot all to hell.

"Ariel," I said in what I hoped was a stern, warning voice.

"If I'm yours, are you mine, Ben?" she purred as she wrapped her fingers around my cock.

"Yes," I answered, my voice strained.

"Then I want to claim *you,*" she said insistently.

Jesus! The woman was going for exactly what she wanted without a second of hesitation, and it was hotter than hell.

Every muscle in my body seized up as she wrapped her lips around my cock.

"Fucking hell!" I rasped as she sucked like my dick was the best thing she'd ever tasted.

What she lacked in experience she made up for in enthusiasm.

I fisted a handful of her hair and guided her.

Control, Blackwood! Find your damn control!

Then, I made the mistake of propping myself on one elbow and watching her as she devoured my cock.

I nearly lost it.

Dearest Protector

I had to force myself not to explode instantly because the sight was so damn erotic and she was so into what she was doing.

She moaned as she took me deeper into her hot, greedy mouth, lost in her desire to please me.

Christ! It was good.

So. Fucking. Good.

But I wasn't about to end the night this way.

Not when every instinct I had was screaming at me to make *her* come.

I wanted to watch her come apart more than I wanted release right now.

I'd gotten exactly what I'd wanted when I'd nailed her against the door downstairs, out of control, and with a complete lack of finesse.

That shit *was not* happening again.

Chapter 29

Ariel

"Ben!" I squealed as he abruptly sat up and pulled me up his body until I was straddling him.

My hands landed on his shoulders, and I was suddenly staring down into a very fierce pair of hazel eyes.

"Did I do something wrong?" I asked him hesitantly.

God, I'd really wanted to make him lose it again, but obviously, what I'd done hadn't worked.

"You did nothing wrong," he said tersely. "But a few more seconds of having those gorgeous lips wrapped around my cock would have wrecked me, Ariel."

"I wanted to wreck you," I confessed. "You've driven me crazy before. I wanted you to come in my mouth this time. I wanted to taste you."

A strangled groan left his lips before he pulled my head down and kissed me.

I leaned forward into the powerful embrace.

Ben kissed me like he wanted to possess me, and I reveled in the possessiveness, the total greediness as his tongue dueled with mine.

Dearest Protector

I was breathless when we finally came up for air.

"It was so good that you almost got your wish. Another time, babe," Ben said gruffly. "You wrecked me downstairs earlier. Right now all I want is to watch *you* come apart for me."

My disappointment completely dissolved, and I hissed as Ben's fingers caressed my wet pussy.

Obviously, what he needed right now was non-negotiable.

Ben's bossy, inflexible side was in full force, and I was totally okay with that.

I loved every facet of him, and when we were in bed, this side of him was overwhelmingly hot.

God, I wanted him, too, and I ached to have him inside me.

I panted as his finger stroked boldly over my clit, forcing a moan of pleasure from my lips.

"Ben," I panted, throwing my head back as he stoked the flames that were already burning out of control. "I need you."

"Ride me, beautiful," he demanded as he grasped my hip with his free hand.

"Show me how to please you," I begged, not completely sure what to do to soothe the enormous ache inside me.

We'd done this before, but I wasn't really that good at being in this position because I was still inexperienced.

The pressure he was putting on my clit already had me in a frenzy.

I needed…

I wanted…

I craved…

Him.

Just him.

I had to get closer. As intimate as the two of us could get.

Our gazes locked and held as Ben stopped tormenting my clit so he could lower me down on his hard cock.

An electric sensation slithered down my spine as I continued my descent until Ben was fully seated inside me.

"I've noticed that you need very little tutoring when it comes to driving me crazy," he drawled. "It seems to come naturally for you."

I raised up and sank back down.

My breath hitched as I savored the feeling of him stretching me. Consuming me.

"It only comes naturally with you," I confessed breathlessly.

Ben was the only man I'd ever wanted this way, and he'd be the only one I ever needed.

I felt like he'd always been inside my soul, waiting for me to recognize him.

And now that I did realize what he was to me, the two of us *had* to be fused together.

"I'm yours, Ariel. Probably always have been and always will be. Take whatever you need," he said, his voice roughened with desire.

My heart stuttered as I realized that he was giving me complete control, which wasn't easy for a man like him.

Ben was almost always willing to compromise, but blind and total trust wasn't easy for a guy who was used to getting what he wanted most of the time.

I rose and fell, relishing every stroke as I rode him, glorying in every touch as his hands moved from my hips to stroke down my bare back.

I lost myself to the rhythm and the heat in Ben's eyes.

He showed me everything in his molten gaze, no holding back, making himself completely vulnerable.

And it made the dam of emotions I'd held back for so long completely explode.

He loved me.

He trusted me.

He adored me.

He was willing to show me every emotion he was feeling right now.

And that broke me like nothing else ever could.

This big, strong, powerful man would do anything I asked, give me anything I needed, just to make me happy.

"I love you," I choked out, holding back a sob of pure bliss.

"I love you, too, baby," he answered like it was a vow as he ran a finger from my shoulder to my breast.

Dearest Protector

He fingered one nipple, and then the other, increasing my pleasure until my body started to shake.

I wanted to climb inside Ben Blackwood, but even that probably wouldn't be enough.

Tears started to pour down my cheeks as I finally broke eye contact and threw my head back.

It was too much.

Everything was too intense.

In an instant, Ben rolled me until I was under him, our bodies still connected.

"What's wrong?" he asked as he loomed over me. "Look at me, Ariel."

I shook my head as I wrapped my legs around his hips. "Nothing. Sometimes I just love you so much it's overwhelming for me."

"Look at me," he commanded.

I complied, and almost started to sob as I saw the look of understanding in his gaze.

"Do you think I don't feel the same way?" he asked.

He brushed the hair from my face and gently wiped the tears from my cheeks.

"I don't know," I answered tearfully, joy expanding in my soul until my heart ached.

"I do," he confessed as he stroked my curls. "You're the only woman who will ever make me feel like this, Ariel, but I don't give a shit if I lose my mind. I've waited a long time for you."

I urged him into motion, and he surged inside me again, burying himself to his balls.

Over and over again.

Soothing my need to be closer to him.

I reached up and stroked my palm over his stubbled jaw. "I don't ever want to be without you again, Ben."

When he started to pummel into me with the fast, deep rhythm that I desperately craved, I began to raise my hips to meet the power of every thrust.

I could feel my climax start to build.

"More," I pleaded, my eyes never leaving his.

Our bodies were damp with perspiration, and our skin slid together with every movement.

"I'm going to come," I whimpered.

"Let go, baby," Ben demanded.

I knew that he wanted me to trust that he'd be there when I came apart, and I did.

He watched my face as my powerful orgasm rushed over me.

I finally closed my eyes as my body shook, and the agony and ecstasy of my climax rushed through my body so intensely that it stunned me.

"Ben! I love you so much!" I cried out, feeling like I died just a little, even though I'd never felt more alive than I did right at this moment.

"Christ! Ariel!" Ben groaned as I milked him of his own release while I spasmed hard around his cock.

He kissed me, and then rolled, our bodies still connected as I sprawled out on top of him, completely spent.

Every sensation, both emotional and physical, had been wrung from my body, but I'd never been more content.

Ben would always be the man who demanded everything from me, but I knew he'd always give the same thing back to me.

We were silent as we caught our breath.

God, how this man rocked my entire world every time he touched me.

I could feel his pounding heart slowly returning to normal as my palm rested on his chest.

Would there ever be a day when Ben didn't try to shield me from even a tiny bit of pain, emotional or physical?

Probably not.

Ben was a protector by nature, and I wouldn't change that about him. *Ever.*

"I think you ended up wrecking me anyway," he said in a sexy baritone next to my ear.

I smiled and stroked a hand down his damp chest. "Are you complaining?"

Dearest Protector

"Hell, no," he denied. "Feel free to wreck me any time you want, beautiful."

I let out a sigh of complete bliss as he stroked his hand over my hair.

I had absolutely no idea how Ben and I had ended up together like this.

If someone had told me months ago that I'd end up being the woman Ben Blackwood would fall in love with, I would have laughed my ass off.

But this was no joke.

He was real.

He was here with me.

And most importantly, he was mine.

"I want to make you happy, Ben," I murmured.

"Sweetheart, all you have to do is stay with me to accomplish that," he said, amused.

I swatted him on the shoulder playfully. "I mean it. You've seen me at my worst. You've taken care of me. Now I want to take care of you."

"I think you just did," he teased.

I raised my head to look at him and saw nothing but contentment and love in his gorgeous hazel eyes.

"Thank you for loving me," I said, my emotions raw. "And thank you for believing in me when I didn't have faith in myself. You changed my entire life. Now I have more than one passion, and I don't regret the fact that I can't dance anymore. Well, not professionally anyway."

I'd always feel the music, and that irresistible pull to move to that beat, but dancing with Ben as my partner was more satisfying than performing on stage.

Since all of the pieces had fallen together for me, I knew in my heart that I was exactly where I was supposed to be.

I was driven to create my artwork, and that compulsion was even stronger than dancing for me now.

He grinned. "I hope I'm listed as one of those passions."

I stretched up and gave him a tender kiss before I said, "You're not just my passion, Ben. You're my everything."

He was my soul and my heart.

"You're my everything, too, Ariel," he said like it was a pledge to me. "You always will be."

I sighed.

Ben was a guy I'd never expected, but I knew he was the gift I'd cherish for the rest of my life.

Chapter 30

Ben

"Where exactly did you say we were going?" Ariel asked as she smiled at me from the seat next to mine. She knew damn well that I'd never mentioned where we were going.

It was a surprise, but I was starting to rethink that idea right now.

What if this wasn't what she wanted?

What if it wasn't such a great surprise?

What if she was actually crushed by this particular trip?

Maybe I should have asked her first.

It wasn't the first time she'd flown on my private jet in the last month, but it was the first time I was second-guessing our destination.

"Are we going back to your private island resort in the Bahamas again?" she questioned, her tone hopeful. "That place was amazing. I still can't believe you'd never been there before. Who owns a private island in paradise and never goes there?"

I shrugged. "I never had a reason to go there before. I didn't have you to share it with."

Honestly, I'd been too busy working to see the island I'd bought on a whim because I'd gotten a deal on it. Mostly, it was a very high-end rental.

I never would have enjoyed it as much if Ariel hadn't been with me.

Now, I'd never rent out the place again. We'd had way too many intimate and carnal moments in that place in almost every room of that home. It would forever be our escape when we needed to get away together.

I'd taken plenty of time off work in the last month, and I hadn't thought about work even once during our private time together.

It had taken me a while to find some kind of work/life balance, but having a woman like Ariel had made it pretty easy to remember what was really important to me.

She smiled wider. "Then I'm glad that we got to see it for the first time together."

Hell, me too, sweetheart. Me, too.

I'd probably never forget the look on her face when we'd flown into that secluded location in the Bahamas or her expression of pure joy as we'd explored. She'd shot pictures of the entire island and the beaches.

Yeah, we'd spent a lot of time naked there, too, but I'd managed to get dressed several times to explore with Ariel and to take her off the island for a few more adventures.

It was probably the best week of my entire life.

However, there weren't really any moments that I spent with Ariel that weren't special in some way.

She still technically lived in her apartment, but there were very few nights that we didn't end up in the same bed.

Thankfully, Leland Brock's ass was in jail where he belonged, so I didn't have to worry on the rare nights that she wasn't in my bed.

I wanted her to come live with me, but things had been so good that I hadn't wanted to push my luck.

"We're landing," I told her. "Put your seatbelt on."

She looked surprised. "Already. That was really fast."

Yep. It was a short plane flight. We hadn't even had time to make use of the bedroom, which was unfortunate for me.

"We're landing in New York," I informed her. "I have something I want to show you and someone I want you to meet."

"Do I need to be nervous? Is this someone important to you?" she asked hesitantly.

I shook my head. "You never need to be nervous, even if we were meeting someone I know, because no one will ever be as important to me as you are. But in this case, we'll both be meeting this person for the first time."

She frowned. "Maybe I should have dressed a little better for this."

"You look gorgeous," I told her simply as I took her hand.

She was wearing a pair of jeans that hugged her beautiful ass lovingly and a colorful blouse that made her blue eyes darker than usual.

Ariel was stunning, no matter what she wore.

Again, I wondered if I was doing the right thing by springing this on her without some warning, but it was a little late to worry about that now.

We didn't say much until we were in the limo headed for Chelsea on the West Side.

"Okay, Ben, you're killing me right now," Ariel said anxiously. "You're way too quiet, and I don't have a clue where we're going. I mean, I trust you, but are you okay?"

Fuck! I should have known that her first thought would be about me because I was more silent than normal.

"I'm fine," I assured her as I finally realized I needed to give her some kind of warning. A surprise was one thing, but the thought of possibly blindsiding her emotionally was completely different. "I'm just concerned that this might not be a pleasant surprise for you. I know you wanted to know more about your father, but I'm not sure how much you want to know."

"If this is about my father, then I definitely want to know," she said wistfully. "Really, all I know is that his name was Julian Hayden, he grew up in the Bronx, and that he worked most of his life as a janitor here in New York. That may be how he and my mother met since he worked at the same theater where my mother performed when she was a ballerina here. My mother said very little about my father except for the fact that he had died before I was born. I'm assuming that he wasn't well off financially, so she took on the burden of supporting me herself, and moved back to Florida when she got pregnant. I have so many questions, Ben, but I might never have those answers."

I let out a sigh of relief. I'd learned some additional things about her father after having my private investigator dig a little more. I wasn't sure I could give her a lot of answers to some of her important questions, but I could give her…something.

"The PI got me some info," I told her.

She squeezed my hand. "Then I'm excited to find out what I can. Nothing factual is going to upset me, Ben. Okay, maybe I won't be excited if it turns out that he was a serial killer or something, but I didn't know him, and he wasn't part of my life. I'm just…curious. I'd love to have some closure, but it won't make or break me either way. I'm happy now, and nothing is going to change that or the way I feel about myself. I shared DNA with my bio dad, but that's about it."

I was going to do my best to give her the closure she sought.

She deserved it.

My mother had practically adopted her, and I knew Ariel was grateful for that because she'd never known unconditional love from her own mother.

We'd talked a lot about her childhood.

Ariel had come to the conclusion that her mother had loved her as much as she was capable of loving another person, but she was also realistic about her upbringing. She knew it was dysfunctional, and that she had deserved better than that conditional love her mother had given her.

Still, she had loved her mother, and she accepted the way she'd been, even though she was well aware that it wasn't normal.

Her attitude didn't surprise me since I knew Ariel, and I knew just how forgiving she could be.

Personally, I wasn't sure I could ever forgive her mother for not loving Ariel without the conditions, but my woman's view about her parent was probably healthier than mine.

Dearest Protector

I took her hand and led her inside the smaller art museum until we got to our destination.

"It turns out that you got your talent and passion for ballet from your mother," I explained as we stopped in front of a collection. "But you may have gotten your artistic talent from a completely different source. Your father wasn't just a janitor. He was an artist, too. But his talent wasn't recognized until the tail end of his life. His passion was watercolors. This is his collection, sweetheart. I thought you might want to see them."

I watched Ariel's face as her jaw dropped.

It took a few minutes for my words to sink in, but when they did, she wandered around the room in fascination, taking in every piece of art her father had ever created.

I had to admit that Julian Hayden was good. Really good. It was obvious to me exactly where Ariel had gotten her passion for creating emotionally expressive pieces of art.

Most of his pictures were of the city of New York. In particular, a lot of the gardens in the city and Central Park.

"He really liked doing landscapes," Ariel said in a hushed voice. "God, these are amazing. Now I really wished we would have met before he passed away."

"I think he would have loved that, too," a solemn male voice said as he approached Ariel. "Had he known that you existed, he would have sought you out, Ariel."

She turned to look at the source of that voice.

I recognized the older man from a photo that the investigator had included in his file and put my hand out, "You're Ernest Hayden, I presume. Ben Blackwood. Thank you for coming."

I put my arm around Ariel as I told her, "Sweetheart, this is your father's brother, Ernest. He graciously agreed to come and answer all of the questions he can for you."

She looked stunned as she held out her hand and Ernest shook it. "Then you're my..."

Her voice trailed off as tears formed in her eyes.

~ *251* ~

So much for her being unemotional and pragmatic about her father.

But I'd already known that wasn't going to happen.

"I'm your uncle," Ernest said as he shot her a charming smile. "The fact that I had a niece surprised me, too, young lady. Your father never married, and he had no idea that you even existed. I know my brother. He never would have ignored you if he would have known. You have his eyes."

He motioned to Ariel and then to her father's photo that was hanging on the wall in between two of his larger paintings.

I looked more closely at her father's image and realized that Ariel did, in fact, have her father's eyes. She actually had several of his features.

She shook her head slowly, like she was trying to shake off her surprise. "I didn't know he had any family left. I didn't know I had an uncle."

She didn't sound upset in a bad way, which made the tense muscles in my body start to relax.

Ernest smiled. "I have a daughter. So you have a cousin, too. Her name is Olivia. She wanted to meet you, but I thought that might be a little too overwhelming for you today. Sadly, your grandparents are gone now, but I know they would have wanted to know you had that been possible. I have to say that I'm absolutely delighted to get this opportunity myself."

I'd talked to Ernest several times on the phone, and he'd never shown anything except eagerness to meet his niece.

That was the *only* reason I'd agreed to this meeting.

Ariel's uncle was successful in his own right. Ernest Hayden was a renowned architect, and had been responsible for designing many iconic buildings in the city over the years.

Ariel's eyes stayed glued on her uncle. "I-I didn't know," she stammered.

"Ah, but you're here now, and I'll tell you everything I can about your father," Ernest said in a quiet, kind tone. "He was a good man who would have been proud to have you as a daughter."

Dearest Protector

Much as Ariel had protested that she hadn't known her father, and that no information about him was going to make her or break her, she was definitely touched that she had family who wanted to know her.

I swallowed the lump in my throat when her lower lip trembled, and tears started to roll down her cheeks.

Ernest held out his arms.

Obviously, the older man was as moved by her tears as I was, because his eyes were a little moist as well.

I wasn't surprised when she threw herself into the older man's arms without hesitation.

Generally, I wouldn't have been able to tolerate seeing her toss herself into another man's arms, but in this case, I could definitely make an exception.

I grinned as she hugged the older man enthusiastically, and started to ask questions so fast that Ernest couldn't answer them quickly enough.

I hadn't been exactly sure where this meeting would go, but maybe my girl would get her closure after all.

Chapter 31

Ariel

"God, this is all so incredible," I told Ben as we sat in his gorgeous penthouse later that evening. "I'll probably never really understand why my mother didn't tell me the truth about my father, but I don't think it was because he was a horrible person. I'm thinking it was a brief affair that she didn't want to extend, so she never said anything to him."

I took a sip of my wine and sighed as I took in the gorgeous view of the city at night. The city lights were breathtaking from the wall of windows in the penthouse.

Of course Ben owned an amazing penthouse in New York, just like he owned fabulous homes in many other cities around the globe.

I was slowly getting used to being the significant other to a man who had an enormous amount of money, power, and influence.

We'd gone to several of Ben's obligatory swanky events together, and I'd gotten the chance to see that powerful billionaire side of my boyfriend.

Yes, people bowed down to him, and treated him like some kind of American royalty.

Women who were almost green with envy stared daggers at me sometimes, but I wasn't intimidated by a single one of them.

I was way too secure in the fact that even though I gave others some of Ben's time at those functions, inevitably, he was *always* going to go home with *me*.

There was always a part of Ben that was connected to me, even when his attention was turned toward another conversation at those functions, and he never let me forget that.

It was pretty easy to be gracious to other women when he made it so evident that the only woman he wanted was me.

"Most likely, the relationship between your mother and your father was pretty brief. That's the only thing that really makes sense," Ben agreed as he toyed with my hair while we sat on a comfy sofa in the living room. "But it sounds like you got the rest of your answers."

I had.

I'd spent the day getting to know my father through my uncle.

I now believed that my father *hadn't* known about me, and that if he had, he would have *wanted* to be in my life.

Really, that might be the reason that my mother had never wanted me to know the truth.

She had apparently wanted to be back in Florida after her career in ballet was over.

My father had obviously belonged in New York.

Having parents in two different cities that weren't close geographically would have jeopardized my ability to focus on ballet, which had been my mom's only goal for me.

Much as I wanted to hate her for taking away my chance to know my father, I couldn't.

She'd raised me.

She'd provided shelter and food for me.

She'd provided for me as a single parent.

She'd worked hard to help me achieve goals.

There was no way I could know exactly what was in her head while I was growing up or why she'd done what she'd done.

Ultimately, all of her choices had led me to this current life that I loved, the people I loved, and the man that I loved and could never live without now.

I knew in my heart of hearts that things had worked out exactly as they were supposed to be.

Life was filled with pain and joy. One didn't exist without the other. If I had to go through all the pain of my earlier life all over again to end up where I was right now, I'd opt to do it all over again the same way.

Nevertheless, I *was* grateful to have answers about my father and to discover a biological family that I wanted to get to know.

"Yes, I got my answers and my closure about my father," I finally answered Ben happily. "He was incredibly talented, and maybe it's weird, but his art actually tells me a lot of things about him as a person, too. I can almost sense what he was like by looking at his images. It was generous of Ernest to offer me one of my father's paintings that he owns. I think I'm going to enjoy having dinner with him and Olivia before we leave on Sunday."

Ben and I planned on exploring the city for the next few days.

Yeah, I'd lived in New York for years, but I'd had so little time to really *see* the city.

I'd taken pictures of things I'd passed by on my way to career obligations.

Mostly, I'd danced here, but I'd never really investigated most of the sights and amazing things this city had to offer.

Monday, we'd both go back to work, but until then, I'd enjoy every moment I could get soaking in the atmosphere of New York City with Ben.

"So, this was a good surprise?" he asked as he took my empty wine glass, put it on the end table, and then lifted me onto his lap.

"A very good surprise," I told him as I snuggled up to him. "Thank you for this. Thank you for this entire month. You've taken a lot of time off just to be with me."

We hadn't taken the entire month off, but we had blown off work a lot to spend time together.

Dearest Protector

"And don't you dare say that I don't need to thank you," I warned.

He smirked. "I think I did tell you that I might let you thank me in other ways someday."

The mischievous expression on his face made my heart flip inside my chest.

Ben smiled much more often these days, and he appeared to be more relaxed than he'd ever been since I'd known him.

I knew he and Ian had gotten a lot closer, too, and their relationship was more lighthearted and tighter than it had been for years.

Blackwood Technologies was important to both of the brothers, but it wasn't Ben's entire life anymore.

He knew when to stop working, thank God.

Ben Blackwood was finally happy, his life was balanced, and occasionally, he did something he wanted just for himself instead of other people or his business. I'd do almost anything to see him stay like this for the rest of his life.

After all that he'd been through, he deserved it.

The man jumped through hoops to make sure I was happy, and I wanted to be certain that I was always doing the same for him.

He'd arranged this entire trip to New York just to give me peace of mind and to get my questions answered.

I leaned forward and locked my lips with his, trying to show him just how appreciative I was of everything he did for me.

He put his hand on the back of my head and kept me in place while he explored my mouth thoroughly.

"Like that?" I questioned breathlessly when he finally released my mouth. "Do you want me to thank you like that?"

He grinned. "Just like that," he agreed. "I'll never argue if you want to kiss me like that to say thank you."

God, I adored this man and the way that he loved me.

He accepted everything about me that *wasn't* attractive; he actually loved every flaw I had.

The crazy man thought I was the most beautiful woman on the planet, which made me *feel* beautiful.

He didn't want to change me.

And most importantly, his love was unconditional and seemingly endless.

He could be stubborn sometimes, especially when it came to my security, but I really didn't mind because even that concern was coming from a place of love and concern for my well-being.

I'd happily put up with his security guys tailing me when he wasn't around if that's what it took to ease his mind. *His* peace of mind was important to me, too.

"Have I told you lately what an incredible man you are, Ben?" I asked softly as I ran a loving hand along his rugged jawline.

"Yes," he replied. "But it never hurts to hear it again, especially today."

I tilted my head as I looked at him. "Just today?"

He shook his head. "Not *just* today, but those words make me feel a little better about the question I want to ask you."

He gently lifted me and sat me back into my seat on the couch.

I watched as he pulled something from the pocket of his jeans and turned toward me.

Our gazes locked, and the look in his eyes took my breath away.

My heart began to skitter as I realized exactly what question he was going to ask.

"Maybe this is much too soon, and if it is, you can just tell me," Ben said huskily. "But I can't wait another fucking moment to ask you if you'll marry me, Ariel. Maybe I shouldn't be so damn impatient. Believe me, I'm happy with the way things are now, but I want you to live with me permanently, and I want you to know that you're my future. The wedding doesn't have to happen soon, but I want my damn ring on your finger so that every man who sees you knows that you're already mine."

I gasped as he opened the box he was holding.

The diamond winking at me was almost spellbinding.

There was a gorgeous and somewhat large solitaire in the middle flanked by multiple smaller diamonds resting on what I assumed was a platinum band.

It wasn't so large that it was gaudy.

Dearest Protector

It was elegant and obviously quality.

Ben had pressed me on my jewelry preferences before, and he'd given me some beautiful gifts, but none that were nearly as important as this one.

"Oh, God, Ben. It's beautiful," I said as I reached out to carefully touch the stones that were offered with so much love and devotion that it brought tears to my eyes.

Yes, I knew that he loved me, but I hadn't been expecting *this*.

My eyes left the beautiful ring and locked with his again.

I fell into those gorgeous hazel eyes filled with promise and a vow that left me speechless.

I knew this man.

I knew what he was offering.

Ben never did anything with me halfheartedly.

He was promising me everything he had.

And if *that* wasn't enough, he'd keep trying.

I shook my head, still in shock. "I-I wasn't expecting t-this," I stammered, my heart so full of love that I suddenly couldn't breathe.

Ben Blackwood was offering to love me for the rest of our lives.

Yes, please.

Maybe I was learning to live in the moment, but I wasn't going to argue with forever.

Not with *him*.

My heart ached with longing at the thought of sharing everything, good and bad, that happened in our future.

"So, is that a *no* for now?" he asked hoarsely.

The disappointment in his tone broke me and yanked me out of my own thoughts.

Here he was, asking me to love him for the rest of our lives, and I could hardly speak because I was so happy.

Was there even an inkling in his brain that I'd actually turn him down?

If there was any apprehension about my answer, then I wasn't making myself clear enough to him.

"No!" I squeaked. "You crazy man. How could it even enter your mind that I might refuse? I love you, Ben. Yes! I want to marry you. I want to have our children at some point in the future. There isn't any man for me *but you*. I thought you already knew that. Yes, you surprised me, but you had to know that I'd never say no to you. Put that stunning ring on my finger right now."

My hand shook just a little as I held it out for him.

He took the ring from the box and gently slipped it onto my finger as he grumbled, "You made me a little nervous for a minute, sweetheart. You looked like you were going to say no. I was a little worried that I'd jumped the gun, but I had to ask, Ariel. This is one of those selfish things that you want me to do, but I knew it was probably a little soon. I don't think I know how to take it slow when it comes to us."

"I was shocked," I replied. "But you once told me I'd always be a sure thing for you. Well, I'll always be a sure thing for you, too. I'll gladly dump my apartment in a heartbeat if you want me to live with you. But I didn't want to just assume that was what you wanted."

He kissed the ring he'd put on my finger and pulled me into his lap again as he informed me, "Hell, it's what I've wanted since the day I asked you to take the job I was offering. I love you, Ariel. Your smiling face is the last thing I want to see at night, and the first thing I want to see every single morning for the rest of my fucking life. You're still young. I'm not going to push you to get married anytime soon. I'm happy to just to get that ring on your finger so I know that will definitely happen someday. Would I love to have kids with you in the future? Yes, it would make me fucking ecstatic, but I could live without them if that's not what you want. All I really want is you."

His heartfelt words brought more tears to my eyes.

God, what had I ever done to deserve a man like this one?

I wasn't *that* young, and I'd felt like an adult for most of my life.

Committing to Ben for the rest of our lives didn't feel like a burden.

It felt like…freedom.

Dearest Protector

The two of us belonged together, no matter how peculiar and unbelievable that fact might seem to me sometimes. I wasn't completely myself without *him*.

"You don't need to wait until I'm ready this time," I murmured as I stroked the hair at the nape of his neck. "I want to marry you, Ben. I want to be your wife. I might want to wait a while to have children until my career is better established, but nothing is going to change about the way that I love you."

"Christ! Don't tell me that," he said, his voice gravelly and rough. "I just might start planning a wedding. You know you can't just throw out that kind of opportunity and not expect me to take advantage of it."

"I'll help you," I promised as I buried my face in his neck and breathed in his masculine, unique scent that always made me crazy.

"Don't tell me that, either, woman. I'm trying to be patient," he growled.

I nipped his ear before I teased, "I actually love it when you lose your patience once in a while. I saw a very comfortable and very large bed that I'd love to get you into naked as soon as possible."

My body was aching for this man, and I couldn't wait for him to throw caution to the wind between the sheets.

He got to his feet almost instantly, with me still in his arms.

I had no idea how he'd managed to swing the both of us up and off the couch at the same time, so I was a little startled.

"What are you doing?" I squeaked as he repositioned my body while I clung to him, my arms still around his neck.

"I've never been a stupid man, and I just told you that I never miss an opportunity," he said in that fuck-me baritone that I'd always love. "You don't have to ask me twice, sweetheart."

I actually giggled before I said, "I love you, Ben Blackwood. Take me to bed so I can thank you the way you really like for this gorgeous ring on my finger."

He grinned. "Definitely no need to thank me for that. You just put me out of my misery."

I threaded my fingers into his hair and put my forehead against his as I whispered, "Then just take me to bed and love me, Ben. I need you."

"I can absolutely do that," he replied as he carried me into the bedroom.

And he did.

He showed me exactly how much he loved me.

All. Night. Long.

Epilogue

Ariel

Three Years Later...

I sighed as I watched my husband sleep peacefully in our bed beside me at our home in the Bahamas.

I'd just woken a few moments ago, and watching Ben sleep when I woke up first had become one of my favorite habits over the last few years.

Our lives were busy, and it gave me a chance to remember how damn grateful I was that I was married to the most amazing guy on the planet.

Ben and I had gotten married a little over a year after the date of his proposal in New York.

Ian and Katie had married a few months later, shortly after she'd finished her master's degree.

The last three years had been the happiest years of my life.

"All because of you," I whispered softly as I reached out a hand to smooth an errant lock of hair from Ben's forehead.

My life was full of people I loved, and who loved me back, but none as much as this man did.

My wedding day had been like a dream come true, and my life after that was even better.

My career had reached heights I could only dream about a few years ago.

Despite the distance, my relationship with my uncle Ernest and Olivia was extremely close. It was almost like we'd known each other our entire lives.

Ben's mother had become just like the mom I'd never had.

Katie was still like a sister to me, and Ian, no matter how overwhelming he could be at times, was like a protective older brother.

My family circle was beyond complete.

I had exactly what I'd yearned for a few years ago: a lot of people who loved me unconditionally that I could love back without reservations.

I stroked Ben's jaw lightly, not wanting to wake him up.

And Ben? Well, there really weren't words to explain how connected the two of us had become over the last few years.

I couldn't even imagine my life without this incredible man anymore.

He was my best friend.

He'd been my biggest fan when it came to my career.

He was a hotter lover than I could even fantasize about.

He supported me in everything I wanted or did.

We were tightly bound in body, heart, and soul, and I wouldn't have it any other way.

I couldn't say things were *always* perfect.

We butted heads, occasionally, especially on matters of my safety, but we always managed to compromise.

"I love you so much," I said in an almost inaudible voice as I let my hand rest lightly on his bare shoulder.

"I love you, too, sweetheart," he said in a sleep-roughened voice, his eyes still closed.

"Crap!" I said remorsefully. "Did I wake you up?"

Dearest Protector

He opened his eyes and our gazes locked.

We'd been married for two years now, but my heart skipped a beat, just like it always did when our eyes met.

The man was so breathtakingly gorgeous and so dear to me that I couldn't stop my heart from reacting when I looked into his eyes.

He grinned. "If you're already awake, it's probably about time I woke my lazy ass up."

I shrugged. "We are on island time. We don't have to get out of bed early."

It wasn't the first time Ben and I had escaped our busy lives to concentrate on each other and what really mattered.

We'd spent an idyllic honeymoon at this private island retreat, which was probably why we loved to return here so much when our lives got too chaotic.

This particular vacation had been planned because both Ben and I had experienced some busy months at work.

But we'd also escaped to our quiet place a few times on short notice when we realized that our lives had gotten a little too chaotic.

Neither one of us hesitated to slow life down so we could concentrate on each other when we needed a break.

I had a few things I wanted to talk to Ben about, but I'd waited until we could be alone here to spill my news.

He reached out, snagged me around the waist, and pulled my body flush with his. "I'm not going anywhere," he told me gruffly. "You told me on the jet that you had a few things to tell me. Shoot."

I took a deep breath. "A few days ago, I started remembering what happened the night of my accident. I'm not sure why it's happening several years later, but I'm pretty clear on how things went until I lost consciousness in the ambulance."

His body tensed, just like I knew it would.

I knew there was a part of Ben that never really wanted me to remember what had happened that night.

He didn't want me to relive that tragedy.

And I was pretty sure he also feared me remembering that it was his fault that I'd stepped in front of traffic that day.

~ *265* ~

"It wasn't your fault," I said to him for about the millionth time since I'd known him.

Maybe he'd accepted that rationally, but I wasn't sure he'd ever really settled it with his subconscious.

There was a part of him that still blamed himself for what had happened, and that needed to end right now.

"I was stressed out and in a hurry, and I couldn't wait to get to that party so I could go home and relax. I remember all of it with crystal clarity, Ben. Yes, I caught your movement out of the corner of my eye, but I rushed ahead because of my own stupidity. Please stop blaming yourself. The fact that you do and that you always have blamed yourself hurts me more than that stupid accident," I ended in a rush.

His arms tightened around me reflexively, and I wrapped my arms around his neck and rested my head against his shoulder.

"It was an accident, Ben," I said, trying to reassure him. "Almost everything I dreamed about was actually the reality. You being there saved my life. I probably would have given up if it wasn't for you and your pigheaded determination to keep me conscious and breathing."

"I've tried to get over it," Ben said hoarsely against my ear. "Fuck! I've really tried, Ariel. There are long periods of time that I don't think about it now, but it still pops up sometimes out of the blue. A guy doesn't just forget something like that, especially when it's a man who loves you as much as I do."

"Try harder," I insisted. "I hardly think about it anymore, Ben. I'm not sure why I got those memories back, but I can't stand the fact that there are moments when you still feel like it's your fault. I'm exactly where I'm supposed to be. I'm doing what I was meant to do. Maybe I'm not a huge believer in fate, either, but I do believe that we were meant to be together just like this. Losing my ballet career is the only thing that brought me to art. Everything that happened was meant to be."

"Do you have any idea how fucking hard it is to believe that?" Ben rasped into my ear and he held me tightly.

Dearest Protector

"Says the man who knew that I was the woman for you the moment you saw me?" I cajoled.

"That's…different," he argued.

"It's not," I said adamantly. "Maybe I remembered because it's time for both of us to completely let go of the past. Now I know exactly what happened. I know it wasn't your fault. I also know that you saved my life. I wanted to let go that night, Ben. You were the *only* thing that made me fight for my life. Your voice. Your presence there. The weird connection that I felt with you. Tell me that you know that you saved my life that night. Say it right now."

His body relaxed a little as he said, "I don't think I'm ready to say that, but now that you remember, maybe I can slowly forget."

"Were you really afraid that I'd blame you if I did get my memories back?" I asked gently.

"Maybe," he said noncommittally. "You've always gone on assumptions. It's a little different from having real memories of what happened."

"I do remember," I assured him. "And I was a twit. Just about anything probably would have set me off that night. I was high on adrenaline from dancing my first lead role, and more impatient and twitchy than I'd ever been in my life. I made a mistake. I don't want to beat myself up anymore over that one stupid mistake. That part of my life is over, and I'm so happy now that I don't want to think about it anymore."

"Then don't," Ben said in a deep, guttural tone. "I'll do my best to let it go so that you can, too. Now that you know what really happened, and you still don't blame me, it might be a lot easier to let go. You make me so fucking happy that I can't keep hanging onto that forever. You know me so damn well now that you probably sense it every time I think about it."

"I do," I admitted as I cuddled up as close to his body as I could get. "I want you to talk to me about it when you feel that way. I'll remind you in every way possible that you saved my life whenever you feel guilty. Eventually, you'll let it go completely."

"Why didn't you say something before now if you knew I was thinking about it sometimes?" he asked as he tenderly kissed my forehead.

I shrugged. "What could I say to make you feel better? It wasn't like I haven't tried in the past to make that clear before, but you're so damn stubborn. You're a rational guy. I was hoping you'd realize that it wasn't your fault, consciously and subconsciously."

"I tried," he confessed as he stroked a hand down the naked skin of my back. "But somehow it stayed stuck in the back of my mind that you really didn't remember."

"It didn't make a damn bit of difference when I did remember," I informed him. "Everything happened exactly the way I dreamed that it did."

Ben rolled me onto my back and hovered over me, his eyes burning with intensity as he growled, "Do you have any idea how much I love you?"

"I do," I said calmly as I wound my arms around his neck again. "Just as much as I love you. And I don't want you to hurt anymore, even occasionally. You should know that feeling since you feel the same way about me."

"Fuck! I do," he said in a raspy voice. "I promise we'll talk if I ever feel guilty again."

I smiled up at him, anxious to wipe that semi frown off his gorgeous face. "Then this discussion is over. I'd much rather concentrate on you at the moment now that we're in our own little paradise for a week."

"What exactly do you have planned?" he asked in a more sensual tone. "And didn't you have something else you wanted to tell me?"

I put the past in the past where it belonged as I gazed at him lovingly.

Maybe we'd have a few bumps along the way, and maybe Ben would have an occasional stumble to chuck away his guilt entirely, but we'd figure it out together if and when it happened.

We always did.

Dearest Protector

"I think I'd really like to try to have a child now," I blurted out without any preamble. "I'd really like to go off the pill and try if you're willing."

The look on Ben's face was stunning.

There was some apprehension, but the hope and happiness in his expression far outweighed the negative.

"Are you sure?" he asked.

I nodded. "I know we've talked about it recently, but I'm ready. I want to have a child. *Our child.* I know nothing is guaranteed, and if it doesn't happen, I guess it wasn't meant to be. But I'd like to try. My career is flourishing, and I'll be able to work my own hours now. I can easily manipulate my hours in the future. I don't have to take commissioned pieces anymore. I don't need the name recognition. I can sell as many images as I want, whenever I want."

He grinned. "The less pieces you produce, the more expensive they'll become."

I rolled my eyes. "We certainly don't need the money. I'll never out earn the ridiculous billions that you make from Blackwood, but I make a stupid amount of money for every piece I sell now. And I kind of like being particular about what I create. I'm at the point where I can just focus on the things that really matter in my career and in my life."

"And a baby is a priority?" he questioned.

I shook my head. "*You* are always going to be my priority, but a baby would be amazing, too. I'm ready to take that leap if you are. There's no guarantees that it will happen, but it's something I want if it does."

Ben nodded slowly. "I want that, too. I think you already know that. But Christ! I really don't want to get as flipped out as Ian is right now."

A laugh escaped my lips as I thought about how badly Ben's brother had reacted to the news that Katie was pregnant a few weeks ago.

Ben frowned as he added, "Ian is already worrying about the whole birthing thing, and Katie is barely eight weeks pregnant. You probably already know that I'll probably be the same way if you get

~ *269* ~

pregnant, right? Don't get me wrong. I'd be ecstatic, but I don't like anything that causes you any pain, and you hate the hospital."

I smiled at him brightly, my heart aching. It wasn't unlike Ben to worry about me, but it always touched my heart. "I think I can handle childbirth in a hospital. We'd be there for something happy. The thought of having a baby there doesn't make me panic."

Ben scowled. "Are you bullshitting me?"

I smiled wider. "Nope. No panic at all."

Relief spread over his handsome features as he grumbled, "Maybe you won't panic, but I might. Christ! I want this, but it's going to be hell every day for me until you deliver. I don't like anything that causes you any discomfort or puts you at risk."

He probably would panic, and then he'd calm down and *try* to be rational for my sake.

Because that was who Ben was.

He cared too much, and loved too deeply. At times, those traits didn't mix with a rational mind.

But he wouldn't be the husband I loved so damn much if he didn't have those characteristics that I completely adored.

I lifted a brow. "Aren't we jumping the gun a little, handsome? You haven't even tried to knock me up yet, and even when you do, it could take a while."

He lowered his head and gave me a toe-curling kiss before he answered huskily, "Maybe not, but we've practiced plenty of times, sweetheart."

I pulled him closer and wrapped my legs around his waist. "You can practice right now or we could wait until I'm fertile," I teased, knowing Ben wasn't about to wait.

He gave me a heated look as he replied, "You know damn well that I don't need much encouragement. Fertile or not. I love you, Ariel Blackwood. Baby or no baby, that's never going to change. I'll always want you. But when you do go off the pill, I'll do my damndest to get you pregnant as soon as possible if that's what you want, too."

"That *is* what I want," I murmured. "But at the moment, I think I'd really like it if you started practicing more."

"Like I've said before, you don't have to ask me twice. I'm a smart man. The most intelligent thing I've ever done was marrying you."

His grin was wicked before he lowered his head and locked those sensual lips with mine.

Maybe there would be a baby in our future, but at the moment, the only thing that mattered was this man, our love, and the things I knew he was going to do to my body within the next few minutes.

Right now, living in the moment with my unbearably sexy husband and not worrying about the future was more than enough.

~The End~

Please visit me at:
http://www.authorjsscott.com
http://www.facebook.com/authorjsscott

You can write to me at
jsscott_author@hotmail.com

You can also tweet
@AuthorJSScott

Please sign up for my Newsletter for updates,
new releases and exclusive excerpts.

Books by J. S. Scott:

Billionaire Obsession Series
The Billionaire's Obsession~Simon
Heart of the Billionaire
The Billionaire's Salvation
The Billionaire's Game
Billionaire Undone~Travis
Billionaire Unmasked~Jason
Billionaire Untamed~Tate
Billionaire Unbound~Chloe
Billionaire Undaunted~Zane
Billionaire Unknown~Blake
Billionaire Unveiled~Marcus
Billionaire Unloved~Jett
Billionaire Unwed~Zeke
Billionaire Unchallenged~Carter

Billionaire Unattainable~Mason
Billionaire Undercover~Hudson
Billionaire Unexpected~Jax
Billionaire Unnoticed~Cooper
Billionaire Unclaimed~Chase

British Billionaires Series

Tell Me You're Mine
Tell Me I'm Yours
Tell Me This Is Forever

Sinclair Series

The Billionaire's Christmas
No Ordinary Billionaire
The Forbidden Billionaire
The Billionaire's Touch
The Billionaire's Voice
The Billionaire Takes All
The Billionaire's Secret
Only A Millionaire

Accidental Billionaires

Ensnared
Entangled
Enamored
Enchanted
Endeared

Walker Brothers Series

Release
Player
Damaged

Dearest Protector

The Sentinel Demons

The Sentinel Demons: The Complete Collection
A Dangerous Bargain
A Dangerous Hunger
A Dangerous Fury
A Dangerous Demon King

The Vampire Coalition Series

The Vampire Coalition: The Complete Collection
The Rough Mating of a Vampire (Prelude)
Ethan's Mate
Rory's Mate
Nathan's Mate
Liam's Mate
Daric's Mate

Changeling Encounters Series

Changeling Encounters: The Complete Collection
Mate Of The Werewolf
The Dangers Of Adopting A Werewolf
All I Want For Christmas Is A Werewolf

The Pleasures of His Punishment

The Pleasures of His Punishment: The Complete Collection
The Billionaire Next Door
The Millionaire and the Librarian
Riding with the Cop
Secret Desires of the Counselor
In Trouble with the Boss
Rough Ride with a Cowboy
Rough Day for the Teacher
A Forfeit for a Cowboy

Just what the Doctor Ordered
Wicked Romance of a Vampire

The Curve Collection: Big Girls and Bad Boys Series
The Curve Collection: The Complete Collection
The Curve Ball
The Beast Loves Curves
Curves by Design

Writing as Lane Parker
Dearest Stalker: Part 1
Dearest Stalker: A Complete Collection
A Christmas Dream
A Valentine's Dream
Lost: A Mountain Man Rescue Romance

A Dark Horse Novel w/ Cali MacKay
Bound
Hacked

Taken By A Trillionaire Series
Virgin for the Trillionaire by Ruth Cardello
Virgin for the Prince by J.S. Scott
Virgin to Conquer by Melody Anne
Prince Bryan: Taken By A Trillionaire

Other Titles
Well Played w/Ruth Cardello

Printed in Great Britain
by Amazon